STORM'S RITE

AMELIA STORM SERIES: BOOK SIX

MARY STONE
AMY WILSON

Copyright © 2021 by Mary Stone

All rights reserved.

No part of this book may be reproduced in any form or by any electronic or mechanical means, including information storage and retrieval systems, without written permission from the author, except for the use of brief quotations in a book review.

❦ Created with Vellum

Mary Stone
To my readers, who are the best ever. You mean the world to me. Thank you from the bottom of my grateful heart.

Amy Wilson
To my one and only, my husband and best friend, and the best boys a mother could dream of, who all worked with me to make this all possible.

DESCRIPTION

Last chance or last rites?

When the corpse of a drug dealer turned federal informant is fished out of Lake Michigan, Special Agent Amelia Storm knows it's more than just a drug deal gone bad. Not only is the body hideously mutilated and the blood drained, but a number has been carved into the victim's chest.

And he isn't the only one.

Is a hitman responsible for the gruesome murders, or could a larger organized crime enterprise be involved? Or is something—or someone—far more sinister behind the killings?

As Amelia and her partner spiral down yet another deadly rabbit hole, every second counts as the two agents hunt a killer with a mystifying motive before he strikes again. But when demons from Zane's past surface, it threatens not only his blossoming relationship with Amelia, but the investigation . . . and their lives.

From the wickedly dark minds of Mary Stone and Amy Wilson comes Storm's Rite, book six of the Amelia Storm Series. Pray for mercy. You'll need it.

1

Celebrating the Life of Viola Poteracki.

Massaging his temples, Lars Poteracki dropped to sit on the center cushion of his micro-suede couch and stared at the black and white funeral pamphlet on the coffee table.

"Celebration, my ass." The words were filled with so much bitterness and pain, they tore at Lars's throat as he whispered them.

Somehow, Lars's heart managed to thud in his chest, though he didn't know how it was possible. As far as he was concerned, his heart had been buried tonight, right alongside the body of his twin sister.

He *wished* he'd been buried beside her.

His stomach lurched as the taste on his tongue turned bitter. With a trembling hand, he loosened the black tie around his neck. Funerals had always made him queasy, but the weariness from this one ran deeper than just nausea. It had cored him out. His bones felt like beams of an old house hollowed out by termites and years of rot.

For the past few days, every morning had been a battle

just to get out of bed. All he had left of Viola were memories, and though he cherished each remembrance, he wished his mind would go blank.

Even the damn furniture reminded him of Viola. The sofa and accompanying loveseat, along with a bookshelf housing a respectable collection of battered paperbacks, had all been given to him by her. She'd furnished more than half his apartment after he'd finished rehab and gotten clean.

Viola had been so excited to share her love of reading with her brother. Once he'd obtained his own apartment, she'd shown up twice a week to dump a heap of books in his arms.

Lars had never taken to studious activities like his sister. Just like the idiot he was, he'd chosen a more self-destructive path. While working as an industrial contractor, he'd blown his respectable wages on the mounting addiction that eventually swallowed him whole.

Viola was the only one who'd ever believed in him. Teachers, family members, so-called friends. They'd all been adamant that Lars would never amount to anything.

They were right. He was troubled, and wherever he went, despair followed.

But Viola never lost faith in him. She'd known who he was before the world had sunk its claws into his heart and mind. And unlike the others, she'd believed that person was still there.

Older by six minutes, Viola had always asserted herself as the protective big sister, even when Lars had surpassed her in height during their final years of high school.

When their mother's alcohol addiction had left them in the care of their abusive grandfather for more than three years, Viola had looked out for him and he for her. She supported him the best as she could after learning that the vile man had made a habit of slipping into Lars's room late at night after he'd downed three-fourths of a bottle of whiskey. He'd…

No!

Lars ripped off his tie, tossing it into the corner, refusing to let his grandfather's nocturnal visits penetrate his mind.

In addition to the years Lars had spent in the throes of a vicious heroin addiction, that had been the worst period of his life. But in the seemingly impenetrable darkness, he'd always had a light. He'd always had Viola.

And now she was gone. Dead, just like their mother. Just like anyone else who'd been an important part of his life.

Maybe I'm cursed.

Tears stinging the corners of his eyes, Lars lowered his face into his hands. The ache in his chest—the feeling that a part of him had been ripped away—hadn't lessened since he'd lost his twin.

A few days earlier, Viola had been on her way home from work when she was killed in a head-on collision near the outskirts of Chicago. A drunk driver had drifted into her lane, and the crash had claimed both their lives. Viola's death was instant, and the man who'd hit her had passed a couple hours later in the intensive care unit.

Lars had been at work stocking groceries when the accident occurred. A surge of nausea had struck him seemingly out of the blue, and he'd assumed his dinner was to blame. The subsequent ache above his ribs had puzzled him even more, but then he'd gotten the call.

The following day, his desire to use, to feel the familiar weightlessness as dopamine flooded his brain, had driven him back to Washington Park—the part of Chicago he'd frequented during the height of his involvement in the drug scene. He'd spotted a couple familiar faces, but he'd slunk back to the elevated train system known in Chicago as the L before any of them had noticed his presence.

Viola wouldn't want this. She wouldn't want me to relapse. She'd want me to...to...

To what? Live out a full and productive life?

The thought was almost funny...if it hadn't been so sad.

He was already thirty-six, and he'd been effectively blacklisted from obtaining work as an industrial contractor. The felony conviction that had landed him in prison for two years was a guarantee he'd never rise above his current status.

Sure, he didn't mind his work at the grocery store. The mindless hours of stocking shelves gave him plenty of opportunity to come up with guitar melodies and song lyrics. Most of his coworkers were younger by a decade or more, but there were a handful who'd tripped, fallen, and pulled themselves out of the mire.

They had kids, spouses, family members who believed in them. They had a reason to keep going.

But for Lars, the dark curtains of despair had begun to fall closed, blocking out the dim light of hope that had guided his way for the past two years. This time, he wasn't so sure he had the strength to open them again.

Throat clenched by an invisible hand of despondency, Lars slumped forward and picked up a framed eight-by-ten of him and his sister. Tears blurred his vision, but his mind's eye recalled each detail of the image with vivid clarity.

Resting one arm on Lars's shoulder, Viola wore a wide grin revealing bright white, slightly crooked teeth. She leaned on him in the same manner she'd lean against a doorway, showcasing the seven-inch gap in height between them. Sunglasses held the stray strands of sandy blonde hair from her bright blue eyes, and her Hawaiian shirt was just as tacky as his.

"I'm sorry, Viola. I'm trying. I swear I am. But I don't know how much longer I can keep doing this. I just feel like the world's trying to squeeze every drop of happiness out of me before it throws me aside. With you gone, I'm just an imposter. A junkie pretending he's something more."

Lars blinked away the tears and turned his focus to the image of himself. With his shoulder-length, dark blond hair pulled back in a low ponytail, eyes the same bright shade as Viola's, and the handful of tattoos on his arms, he could have passed for a normal, functional member of society. A mechanic, maybe, or a bartender.

He'd been thirteen months clean at the time, though most of his income was still earned by slinging dope in Chicago's shadier neighborhoods. Between his lack of relevant work experience and the felony that marred his criminal record, he hadn't even tried to obtain a legal job when he was released from prison.

Only his run-in with the FBI had changed that mindset. If the Feds had sent him back to prison instead of utilizing him as an informant, he'd have undoubtedly relapsed.

Not that it mattered anymore.

Melancholy tightened its grasp on his throat. He returned the photo to the coffee table, facedown. He didn't want his sister to see what he'd become.

Fuck it.

Jaw clenched, he pushed to his feet. He couldn't stay here. Not in this apartment where even the furnishings called to him from the grave.

He needed this ache to stop. The pain was worse than opiate withdrawals, worse than the handful of beatings he'd received during his days in Washington Park.

There was one way to make the hurt subside. He'd used it to numb himself for years and to avoid confronting the demons that had haunted him since childhood.

"Screw it."

Swallowing the sting of bile in the back of his throat, Lars set about changing into a pair of worn jeans, a zip-up hooded sweatshirt, and an olive drab jacket. He considered changing his dress shirt too, but the thought of working all those buttons just seemed like too much to deal with.

He was so very, very tired...but he had one last thing to do.

Each step toward the door added weight to the sinking stone in his stomach.

Hand resting above the light switch beside the doorway, he glanced over his shoulder to take in the sight of the tidy living room.

"I'm sorry, Viola." The apology was barely a whisper. "I don't know what else to do."

Guilt sawed at his heart. Maybe he could fight his way past the agonizing loss, attain some semblance of normalcy, but his entire life had been one battle after another. It was like a boxing match that never ended, where the opponent never tired, never showed so much as a shred of weakness. Deep within his gut, Lars knew the rounds would never stop, and he was tired of fighting.

Fighting the memories...the pain.

Though the past year was a slight improvement, making ends meet by working for a hair above minimum wage and taking occasional handouts from his sister wasn't much better than slinging heroin in Washington Park.

If the good Lord wanted to take him, then here he was. Hell couldn't be much worse than fighting the demons on this side of the grave.

He just wanted to rest. It seemed fitting that his end came about with the same substance that had driven him under in the first place.

Switching off the lights, he stepped into the hall, locked the door, and headed toward the stairwell. Crisp December air greeted him when he stepped out into the night. The cold, coupled with the colorful, twinkling lights wound around the rails of a handful of balconies, reminded him that Christmas was only a few weeks away.

He ignored the onslaught of memories and increased his pace to a brisk walk. He was more eager to get this over with now. He certainly didn't need to be around for the holidays and the profound loneliness that was his new reality.

I really don't need to see the start of another miserable year.

Side streets in Chicago could be treacherous at this time of night. Typically, Lars kept a keen watch on his surroundings, especially after the work he'd done with the FBI at the beginning of the year.

The agent with whom he'd interacted had assured him his name and likeness would be kept out of publicly accessible records, but Lars had never fully trusted the government. He'd heard about far too many cyber-security breaches to remain confident in his supposed anonymity.

However, he was almost a year removed from his stint as an informant. If anyone in the scene was going to kill him, they'd have already done it.

At least, that's what he told himself. Tonight, he didn't care.

The walk to the L, as well as the train ride itself, was uneventful. He and a handful of others departed the car at the same stop in Washington Park. After only a couple blocks, Lars was on his own. None of the men and women who lived above board wanted to follow him. They didn't want to cross into *this* part of the city.

Shadows closed in around him as he drew farther and farther from the main street. His footsteps echoed off the tall, derelict buildings as he cut through a narrow alley. After a few more blocks and another alley, he emerged on the same street he'd visited earlier in the week.

A handful of working girls mingled around the

condemned building on the corner, and he turned to make his way in the opposite direction. The man for whom he was searching was nearby. Lars knew this because the dealers never strayed too far from where the prostitutes set up shop.

Sure enough, Lars spotted the figure of a man leaning casually against a metal railing in front of a vacant duplex.

He and the dealer were familiar with one another, but they didn't exchange pleasantries. Buying heroin wasn't quite the same as running into an old friend at the grocery store. Lars simply slapped the cash in the man's palm and accepted the little baggie of powder.

As he began the return journey, the heroin was like a pool of molten lava in the pocket of his jeans. He was relieved to be done with the deed, but a shroud of doubt weighed on his shoulders.

You can still turn back. Throw it away. Toss it in the dumpster when you get to the alley. Go home and sleep. It's what Viola would want. She'd want you to try.

His heart clenched. Viola had always believed in him, and he was about to let her down.

Again.

Strides growing slower, Lars reached into his pocket to touch the baggie.

Before the forlorn introspection could swallow him whole, he caught movement—the shape of a person on the other side of the street as they ducked around the corner of an apartment building.

A resident? Or was someone following him?

Holding his breath, Lars stood still as the seconds ticked away.

Traffic hummed in the distance, and a dog barked somewhere farther down the block. Otherwise, there was nothing.

Blood pounded in Lars's ears as he resumed his trek, albeit at a faster pace. Perhaps this was his punishment.

Another addict had spotted him, and they'd determined he was a newcomer to Washington Park. With his clean clothes, neatly brushed hair, and healthy complexion, he didn't quite blend in with the neighborhood's usual occupants.

He scowled at the thought. If a scrappy user assumed he'd be easy pickings because he didn't *belong*, then they were in for an unpleasant surprise.

No one was going to take his one-way ticket from this miserable life.

He patted his pocket to make sure his drug of choice was still there.

Twice more before the alley, he could have sworn he spotted someone lurking in the shadows. He couldn't decide if his overactive imagination was taunting his poor decision, but he wasn't keen on taking an unnecessary risk with his stash. In the end, the alley only shaved a few blocks off the walk anyway. When he came upon the shortcut, he ignored it and kept going.

By the time he made it to the next street, he was sure he was jumping at shadows. Greystone houses, almost all of which had been converted into cheap apartments during the nineties, loomed to either side. The sickly white glow of the streetlights caressed the sides of the crumbling buildings, revealing pockmarks, gouges, and crude graffiti. Over the years, the neighborhood had changed hands from one gang to another, and the city only occasionally bothered to fund crews to paint over the tags.

Just past a condemned, three-story apartment building was the entrance to the alley. The exit from the shortcut he'd been too chickenshit to take.

Glancing toward the shape of a rusted dumpster, he sighed. "There's nothing here. I'm losing my mind."

There wasn't a single strung-out person in the damn city who'd have been able to maintain enough stealth to catch

Lars unaware. Some users were dangerous, sure, but their motivations made them predictable. And if an enigmatic figure was out for vengeance, they'd already had plenty of opportunities to put a bullet in Lars's skull.

No one was waiting to ambush him.

He had enough on his mind. The last thing he needed was to manufacture more problems for himself.

Swallowing a resigned groan, he started to make his way past the alley.

His mind began to drift back to the baggie in his pocket and the peace it would provide, but the quiet scuffle of a shoe stopped his thoughts in their tracks.

A rush of adrenaline jerked him from the cloud of melancholy. As he spun around on one heel, Lars clenched one hand into a tight fist, preparing to take a swing at his newest opponent in the endless boxing match that was his life.

All he caught was a sideways view of a man clad in jeans and a dark jacket as he followed Lars's sudden movement, like a prizefighter anticipating his opponent's jabs. Like he'd *wanted* Lars to whip around with his fist leading the way.

Before Lars could throw a punch, a gloved hand slammed a sweet-smelling cloth over his mouth and nose. The stranger's arm circled around Lars's chest and clamped him in place with vicelike strength. Lars tried to throw himself forward to at least loosen the grip, but the arm didn't budge.

As best as Lars could tell, the man stood almost as tall as his six-two. He'd find no height advantage against this adversary.

At first, Lars resisted the urge to breathe as the true-crime documentaries he'd watched flashed through his mind. Within those shows, he'd learned that chloroform—if that's even what *this* was—wasn't an immediate knockout like popular media tended to portray. Four to five minutes of constant inhalation was needed to render a person unconscious, depending on their size and the chemical's potency.

He could fight his way out of the man's grip in that amount of time, surely.

Of course, the surge in availability of drugs like fentanyl made it possible for would-be kidnappers to create their own chemical concoctions to render a victim helpless, quickly and efficiently. As he thrashed against the iron grip that held him in place, his lungs burned, and his eyes watered from whatever mystery drug coated the cloth.

He was fighting a losing battle. Sooner or later, he'd have to take a breath. Unless he wrested himself away from the stranger's grasp, he *would* inhale the noxious chemical.

He needed air. He needed to breathe.

Lars jerked his head to the side, hoping he'd free part of his face from the cloth. Like the arm clamped around his chest, however, the man's hand didn't budge.

Clawing helplessly at the sleeve of the man's jacket, Lars's lungs took over, forcing him to drag in a frantic breath. But instead of fresh, life-preserving air, he sucked in more of the foul chemical.

Darkness shimmered at the edge of his vision, and the world around him was little more than a blur. Weren't they on the street? Why couldn't anyone see them? How had no one called for help or stopped to intervene?

Because he was in a crime-ridden part of Washington Park. That was why. Even if anyone *had* spotted his struggle with the man from the alley, they'd be just as likely to hurry on their way than they would be to call for help.

Though his muscles were rubbery and seemingly weighted down with lead, Lars half pulled, half flung himself forward in a last-ditch attempt to wrest out of the man's hold. His boxing-match life had been turned into an MMA fight for which he was unprepared.

Have I been fighting the wrong battle all this time?

After another reluctant breath, his vision dimmed. Each movement was weaker than the last, but he knew if he gave up now, he was as good as dead.

Wasn't that what you wanted?

The question took him by surprise, and his answer was even more surprising.

No. It wasn't what he wanted at all. Not like this, at least.

There was no way for him to tell how long he was locked in the struggle against the stranger. A minute? An hour? The concept of time eluded him.

Lars's eyelids grew unbearably heavy, and the little remaining strength evaporated from his tired body. Knees buckling, he gave in and let the darkness claim him as the bell clanged, signaling the end of the round.

As Lars drifted back toward consciousness, each beat of his heart sent shockwaves from his throbbing head down to his toes. The inside of his eyelids felt as if they'd been swapped for sandpaper, and his mouth was crammed full of invisible sawdust.

Where am I? What the hell happened?

Based on the faint musty scent and the cool, rough concrete floor beneath Lars's cheek, he was in a basement. And based on the details he could discern, it was a residential space, not the underground level of a warehouse. He'd spent more than enough time in industrial settings to tell the difference between the two.

He tried to move his arms to assuage the ache in his shoulder, but he was greeted with a sharp sting as hard plastic dug into his wrists.

His hands were bound in front of his body, and his mouth was taped shut.

The night's events rushed back to him. A sweet-smelling cloth. Hands covered with black leather gloves. A dark jacket. Those were the only details about the assailant he could recall. He hadn't caught the man's face, but he'd spotted enough of his figure to be certain he was indeed a man. One more thing he was certain of...

He was still alive!

When he'd finally given in and inhaled that drug, he'd been certain he'd never awaken. But here he was. Not only glad to be breathing in and out but happy about this realization.

Now, he just needed to make sure he stayed that way.

His mind raced as he thought through his options. He was alive, yes, but if the stranger from the alley had kept him alive, he wanted something.

Swallowing the grit in his mouth, Lars cracked open one eye, just a slit at first. He fought to keep his breathing even as he searched for movement or any other sign that would indicate the presence of another person.

Golden light shone from the lamp perched atop a shelf at the other end of the room. No, not a lamp. Candles. The glow illuminated the uneven divots and crags in the cinderblock walls, and ominous shadows surrounded a high-set window.

The candles weren't quite sufficient to chase the darkness from the far reaches of the open room, but as Lars held still and waited, he didn't spot even a hint of movement.

So, he was in the basement of a house.

Why?

He blinked to clear the film from his vision and peered around the space. Other than the shelf, a laundry sink, and a set of stairs that led up into the gloom, the basement was empty. With no other item to give him an inkling of his captor's identity, Lars turned his focus to the shelf.

Light glittered off an ornate, golden cross situated in the center of the top shelf. Two jar candles were spaced evenly to either side of the religious symbol.

As Lars's gaze settled on the red paint scrawled on the wall above the cross, his blood froze in his veins.

1 John 2:17.

And the world passeth away, and the lust thereof: but he that doeth the will of God abideth for ever.

Were the words actually written in paint, or was it blood?

He blinked again and studied the wall even harder. Paint. It had to be paint.

Please let it be paint.

Though Lars had never been an especially religious person, religion was often at the core of drug and alcohol recovery. During his stint in rehab, he'd picked up on a handful of bible verses. He'd found many of the texts inspiring at the time, but down in this veritable dungeon, the passage was ominous.

Was the kidnapper part of a religious cult? Had he taken Lars to forcibly convert him? To use him as a sacrifice?

Terror prickled the base of his scalp.

He needed to get the fuck out of here.

Pulling in a deep breath of cool but musty air, Lars glanced down to his bound wrists. His time as an informant for the FBI had been fraught with risks, and one of the tricks he'd researched on YouTube was a method to break free of zip ties. There were techniques to loop the ties and make them virtually impossible to escape, but Lars's captor must not have known about them.

As Lars propped himself up with an elbow, he flexed his fingers to encourage blood circulation. He didn't have the first clue how long he'd been unconscious, and his captor could return at any second.

Weak as he was, he needed to hurry.

Once he'd managed to sit up, he looked over his shoulder in hopes he'd find a door. All that greeted him was more dusty concrete and another high windowsill. The only ways out were either through one of the windows—though there was no guarantee Lars would even be capable of pulling himself through the narrow opening—or up the stairs. Again, ascending the dilapidated wooden steps was no guarantee of success. More than likely, each creaking step would call out to his jailer. The door leading to the main level of the house could be locked, or worse, barred.

Only one way to find out.

Gritting his teeth, he staggered first to his knees and then to his feet. His muscles ached with the effort, but to his relief, he had full control over his extremities. The pounding in his head was the only apparent side-effect of the substance used to knock him out.

He started toward the base of the stairs, but a faint *scuff* overhead froze him in place. Ice-cold dread crept in to take hold of his heart.

Shit.

The faint drum of footsteps followed. They were headed for the stairs.

Stomach churning, Lars tightened both hands into fists, raised his arms, and brought his bound wrists down against his hip bone with as much force as he could manage. He nearly shouted in victory at the light *snap* of the plastic breaking but managed to remain silent.

Hurry. Hurry.

From the stairwell came the metallic click of a lock and the squeal of rusted hinges.

Jaw clenched to brace himself, Lars slowly peeled back

the silver duct tape from his mouth, careful to conceal the sound of his flesh fighting to break free. A hundred little pinpricks of pain followed the motion, but thankfully, he'd shaved his face that morning.

I'll be damned if I'm going to die like this. Prepare for a fight, you son of a bitch.

Determination settled in alongside the adrenaline, and Lars searched desperately for a weapon. Aside from the typical basement dust, however, the cement floor was clean. There were no tools, no small appliances he could use to bludgeon his attacker. Nothing.

When his gaze reached the shelf—the *shrine*—against the wall, his attention quickly fell on the polished, golden cross. The length was close to that of Lars's forearm, and it *looked* solid.

As quiet as a ghost, he hurried across the room. Wood creaked beneath booted feet, and from Lars's periphery, he spotted the black-clad man as he descended into the twinkling candlelight.

He was out of time.

Lars closed his hand around the base of the cross just as the man reached the bottom step. As he lifted it from where it had leaned against the cinderblock wall, his heart fell to the floor along with his momentary optimism.

What he'd thought was metal was light as a feather. Nothing more than cheap plastic coated with a layer of gold paint.

Disappointment was like a physical assault as Lars ran through his options.

He could try to reason with the man, could promise to keep his mouth shut if he let him go. Or, if he was affiliated with the traffickers that Lars had helped the FBI put away almost a year earlier, he could try to explain himself.

Or he could fight.

Based on the physical strength the man had displayed during the one-sided brawl in the Washington Park alley, Lars would be facing an uphill battle. Though his captor was clad in black cargo pants and a matching sweatshirt, Lars could tell his shoulders were broad, and his arms filled out the sleeves.

Whatever in the hell he was going to do, he needed to do it *now*.

"What do you want?" Lars's voice was hoarse and weak, his tone more akin to a dying bird than a man. "Do you want money? Revenge? Who are you?"

A glimmer of anticipation sparked to life in the man's eyes. "I don't want anything from you, Mr. Poteracki. In fact, I'm here to help *you*."

Alarm bells clanged in Lars's head. "What? What the hell are you talking about?"

As the captor took the final step onto the basement floor, Lars knew he was cornered. His only route to the stairs, and to escape, was *through* the musclebound kidnapper.

He didn't waste any time.

Just as the man started to speak, Lars threw the cross at him, then rushed forward, hoping to catch him unaware. Using his momentum, Lars slammed both hands into the man's broad chest.

As the guy stumbled backward a couple feet, eyes wide with shock, Lars clambered up the first few stairs. For a beat, he thought he might actually make it to the freedom that loomed above. If he could get out that damn door, he only had to make his way to the street. He'd rush to the first house he could find, bang on the door, and tell them about the madman who'd kidnapped him.

Maybe they'd believe his story, maybe not. He didn't care. He'd let the cops sort through the situation, or maybe even the Feds.

His optimism came to a crashing halt as a gruff hand clamped around his ankle. The man jerked Lars's leg out from under him, and he barely managed to throw an arm in front of himself to prevent his face from smashing into the sharp edge of a step.

Flipping over to face the kidnapper, Lars brought his free leg up in a haphazard kick. The man leaned away from part of the blow, but the toe of Lars's boot still connected with his chin, snapping his head to the side. Lars jerked his other leg out of the man's grasp before he could regroup.

As Lars balanced one hand on the stairs to steady himself, a thick splinter pierced his palm. Ignoring the sting, he shoved to his feet.

The abductor grunted, and wood creaked as he lunged toward Lars. A shoulder collided with Lars's knee, shattering his precarious balance. He pitched to the side, and his upper arm crashed into the wooden handrail. The railing groaned loudly beneath his weight.

Flailing his other arm, Lars made a desperate attempt to right himself as he caught the first crackle of splintering wood. If he fell to the ground below, he'd have to fight his way past the madman all over again.

Like a viper coiled and waiting to strike, the man's other hand snapped out to take hold of Lars's forearm. Rather than immediately jerking away, Lars used the powerful grip to pull himself the rest of the way upright. Once his feet were steady, he tightened his free hand into a fist, dug his heel into the stair, and swung with all his might.

At the awkward angle, the left hook didn't connect with as much force as he'd wanted. The captor didn't loosen his hold on Lars's right arm, even when Lars's knuckles grazed his chin. Lars had dropped men with a well-placed blow in the past, but now, when he most needed to land a solid hit, he'd failed.

Story of my life.

With one swift yank, the kidnapper pulled Lars down the handful of stairs he'd worked so hard to scale. The man finally relinquished his iron grasp on Lars's arm, but Lars didn't have a chance to take advantage of the momentary freedom to put distance between them.

He was a split-second too late to spot the dark shape of the man's fist. Though Lars lurched backward to dodge the punch, he only managed to avoid a fraction of the forceful blow.

Stars exploded in the side of Lars's vision as his teeth slammed together. Like a spiderweb of lightning, sharp pain lanced through his already aching head. His vision swam, and he struggled to keep himself from slumping to the dusty ground.

As Lars staggered to the side, the man flung one arm around his neck, securing the other beneath Lars's armpit to hold him upright. Desperate to clear his swimming vision, Lars blinked repeatedly as the man's grip constricted. He tried to take in a much-needed breath, but his airway was closing, and he managed only a weak gasp.

Seemingly spurred on by the choked sound, the man squeezed tighter.

Dread in the pit of Lars's stomach became a living thing.

Keep fighting. Don't let it end like this. Don't give this bastard what he wants.

Lars raked his eyes over the basement room again, hoping he'd simply missed an item he could use to turn the tide. Nothing.

His flailing arm touched the wall, but like the rest of the space, it was unadorned. No glass frame or decorative item was there for Lars to smash over the man's head.

Lungs on fire, Lars dug the fingers of both hands into the

man's forearm. He pulled and pulled, searching for even the slightest leeway.

"Stop fighting," the man grunted. "This is what you were destined for. You've spent your life in sin, but this is your chance to make the world a better place. You give your life so that others might live in freedom from your missteps."

Lars barely heard the ominous statement. He couldn't breathe, and he didn't give a shit what this lunatic had to say.

He sank his fingernails into the exposed skin of the man's wrist and dragged, pushing up the sleeve of his sweatshirt.

Grim consummation crept to Lars's mind as the captor hissed in pain, and for a beat, the pressure on Lars's throat lessened.

Sucking in a feeble breath, Lars dug his nails deeper into the man's skin. He didn't give the guy a chance to reposition himself before he sank his teeth into the exposed flesh like he was taking a bite of an oversized drumstick. The iron tang of blood filled his mouth, and the hiss escalated to a howl.

As the bastard tried to yank his arm away, Lars clamped his jaw down even tighter. A chunk of muscle and skin came away, as did the crushing pressure on Lars's throat. Blood dribbled down Lars's chin as he spat out the flesh and gulped a lungful of precious oxygen.

Before Lars could lunge out of the lunatic's range, a hand closed around the back of his neck. Strands ripped away from Lars's scalp as the seemingly possessed man took a handful of his hair. The devil smashed Lars's head into the cement wall.

Pain exploded from his temple, but he barely registered the crippling sensation. The world changed all around him in an instant. Instead of the insidious basement, he stood in the small foyer of his apartment.

I'm here.

As if she'd heard his unspoken words, the door swung

open to reveal his sister's blue eyes. At the sight, his heart grew lighter.

"Welcome." Her voice was even more beautiful than the angel she was.

A wide grin brightened her face, and she held up the armful of paperbacks she'd brought for him.

He took them gladly.

2

As Special Agent Amelia Storm ducked beneath the yellow crime scene tape behind her partner, Special Agent Zane Palmer, she swept her gaze over the marina. In the dark of night, red and blue lights glinted off the shifting waters of Lake Michigan like sparkling sapphires and rubies. A white boat bobbed to one side of the boardwalk, but other than a second, larger vessel in the distance, the small marina was empty.

Due to the nature of the FBI's jurisdiction, instances where Amelia was called directly to the site of a body retrieval were unusual, at least compared to the number of murder scenes a homicide detective might see. But a little more than a half hour ago, a Chicago Police detective had reached out to Zane to advise him that the corpse of a federal informant had just been fished out of Lake Michigan.

That put the case firmly in their jurisdiction.

The drive to the small, private marina hadn't taken long, but Amelia had used the opportunity to conduct a cursory check of the scant information they'd received from the CPD.

Fiona Donahue, a special agent who had been part of the Organized Crime Division that specialized in drug trafficking, had worked with the victim at the beginning of the year. Since Fiona had taken a position at the FBI's Portland office four months earlier, Zane and Amelia had been summoned to the scene of her informant's murder.

Amelia's cheeks heated as she recalled the precise moment Zane had received the call. He'd pulled her close, and she'd gladly melted into his lean, muscular frame as their lips met for the first time.

Though they'd been friends since their first case together more than half a year ago—roughly three months after they'd each arrived in Chicago—the past couple months had seen a shift from platonic to something more. As much as the prospect of a romantic relationship made Amelia nervous, the idea of being with *Zane* brought on the stomach full of butterflies she never thought she'd experience again.

Cold wind buffeted the side of Amelia's face, reminding her she'd have plenty of time to mull over Zane Palmer when she *wasn't* at a crime scene. She'd only been with the FBI for two years, but the ten years she'd spent in the military beforehand had taught her the art of self-discipline.

Especially since, for most of the decade in the armed forces, she'd been a sniper. Her dream had always been to land a spot in the Army's elite Green Beret forces, but until a few years ago, specialized warfare factions of the military didn't even permit women to enlist.

The stagnancy of her military career had come to a head with the combined stress of her older brother's death a little more than two years ago. Trevor Storm had been shot to death in the line of duty as a Chicago homicide detective. The crime had been investigated and the case closed, but recently, Amelia had begun to suspect there might be more to the story than what the CPD had uncovered at the time.

Rather than remain where she was stationed on the East Coast, Amelia had elected not to renew her contract with the U.S. military. She'd had her eye on investigative work ever since her brother had made detective, and she'd followed in his footsteps. After training at Quantico, she'd worked in the Bureau's Boston field office for close to a year before an open position allowed her to transfer to her hometown of Chicago.

She was good at her work in the FBI, and though the job was stressful, the work was gratifying. To be sure, the Bureau was still a boys' club, but she knew damn good and well that she'd have more luck advancing a career with the FBI than she would in the military.

Amelia pulled up the collar of her knee-length trench coat as a gust of wind swept past her and Zane. A cold front moving in from the north was predicted to pick up energy over Lake Michigan and dump a truckload of snow on the city. Lake-effect snow wasn't particularly common in Chicago, but it seemed to have become more frequent in recent years.

A man drew her attention away from the orange-tinted sky. As a piece of dark hair blew in front of Amelia's eyes, she mentally cursed herself for neglecting to pull the strands back in a ponytail. When the temperature dropped like it had over the last few hours, she preferred to leave her hair down to keep her neck warm. Not that it mattered when the wind was blowing at twenty-five miles per hour.

Clenching her teeth to keep them from chattering, Amelia followed Zane over to a man with a silver badge draped around his neck.

He pocketed a small notepad as he met them halfway. "Agents, I'm Detective Clark. Thanks for getting here so quickly."

Though a normal person's first inclination might have

been annoyance at being pulled away from the warmth of their homes at nine o'clock on a weeknight, her job as a special agent for the FBI's Organized Crime Division wasn't the typical nine-to-five grind.

She was here for a damn good reason. A man—a federal informant, someone who'd put his life in harm's way to help law enforcement—had been murdered, and his body had just been pulled from Lake Michigan.

Whoever he was, he was someone's son, someone's brother, uncle, or friend.

As Amelia glanced to Zane, she noted the same determination on his unshaven face. He'd pulled up the collar of his black frock coat, and the wind rustled his sandy hair. His gray eyes shifted between Amelia and the detective. Since he'd received the call, Amelia decided to let him lead the conversation.

"It's no problem, Detective. Could you tell us where we're at so far?" Zane had been in Chicago for nine months at this point, but a trace of his native Jersey accent still tinged his words.

Detective Clark beckoned her and Zane to follow him toward a gurney. "The vic is Lars Poteracki. The body was found by a civilian who was at the marina to work on their boat. They saw the vic and called us around sundown, but it took a little while to get to him. There's a cold front coming in, so currents are a bitch right now. Vic's wallet was in his back pocket. There were a few credit cards, a hundred, and a couple twenties still inside, so it doesn't look like robbery."

Not that the CPD would have called the FBI in for an apparent robbery turned homicide. Amelia kept the thought to herself. "How'd you know that he was a federal informant?"

The detective jammed both hands in the pockets of his coat. "I recognized him. The wallet confirmed his identity.

Back at the beginning of the year, I worked a triple homicide. The vics had rap sheets, but they'd mostly just been popped for petty shit like possession and shoplifting. Two males, one female." He tightened his jaw, his expression darkening. "They were dealing in Washington Park, but they were just kids. Ballistics confirmed all three were killed by the same weapon, a Beretta nine-mil that was used to execute two other small-time dealers the week before. Long story short, Poteracki helped us put the guy away."

And now he was dead.

"Joint task force between the CPD and the Bureau, right?" Amelia hadn't needed to ask the question, but she wanted the confirmation anyway.

"Right. The killer was Kevin Ersfeld, a dealer with a violent rap sheet that read like a horror movie. Domestic abuse, rape, assault and battery, attempted murder. You name it, he'd been charged with it. Ersfeld was terrorizing Washington Park. All the small-time dealers and the working girls out there were scared shitless. All of 'em except Poteracki, anyway."

A bright light shone on their backs, and Amelia reflexively shot a venomous glare to the group of bystanders clustered behind the crime scene tape. A small news crew powered on their camera lights, illuminating the onlookers in the otherwise dark marina.

Zane ignored the lookie-loos. "You knew Poteracki and Ersfeld?"

As Zane took over the dialogue, Amelia scanned the handful of civilians who'd clustered away from the reporter and her crew in an effort to catch a glimpse of the CPD and the body they'd just pulled from Lake Michigan. The old adage about killers returning to the scene of their crime was cliché, but it had become routine for a reason. Murderers loved to revel in the fallout of their actions. It was part of what got them off.

Clark rubbed his hands together to combat the frigid air. "I wouldn't say I *knew* either of them. I met Poteracki a few times. Enough to know that he was a decent guy who'd been dealt a shitty hand. From what I could tell, he was trying to make things right. Trying to stay on the straight and narrow."

"Poteracki had a rap sheet too, didn't he?" Zane asked. "A lot of informants do."

"Yeah. He did time for possession with intent to distribute, and he got clean while he was on the inside. He went back to dealing when he got out, and one of yours popped him for it while she was undercover. That was around the same time that Ersfeld was starting to terrorize Washington Park, and as luck would have it, Poteracki was familiar with the guy."

Zane pulled a pack of gum from his coat. "Agent Fiona Donahue. She did a lot of undercover work before she moved out to Portland a few months ago. Poteracki was her informant for about six months, give or take. He helped her and the CPD take down Ersfeld, and then all his accomplices." He offered a piece of gum to Detective Clark, who declined, and then to Amelia.

As she popped the gum into her mouth, she was surprised at the rush of cinnamon where she'd expected mint. If she hadn't been fully awake before, she was now.

Prisoners successfully completing rehab while in prison didn't happen often, Amelia knew. The hostile environment filled with repeat offenders, plenty of whom were violent, wasn't conducive to sobriety. Drugs and other contraband were readily available, no matter the strict policies and searches conducted by prison staff.

For Lars Poteracki to break free from a heroin addiction

while behind bars was no small feat. The man had to have been driven.

The trio came to a halt by a broad-shouldered man standing behind the metal gurney. The lettering on the man's dark blue jacket proclaimed him as a forensic pathologist—part of a small group of licensed professionals who worked under the umbrella of the Cook County Medical Examiner's Office.

Clark made the introductions. "Agents, this is Dr. Adam Francis. Dr. Francis, this is Special Agent Palmer and Special Agent Storm."

"Evening, Agents." The forensic pathologist gestured to the body bag atop the gurney. "We're about to load him up. Did you want to have a look before we take off?"

Amelia stepped closer. "If you don't mind. Detective, you said that there was a message carved in his skin. Any idea what it says?"

Clark dropped both hands to his hips as he peered at the black bag. "Couldn't quite tell, no. It's on his chest, and we could only see a little of it without removing the clothing. But we didn't want to disturb anything we didn't need to."

A sense of foreboding wriggled into the back of Amelia's mind. "Let's see it."

Snapping on a fresh pair of nylon gloves, Dr. Francis slowly tugged on the zipper of the body bag, pulling down to the middle of the victim's torso.

Lars Poteracki's skin was the same shade as pale moonlight, though a short, neatly trimmed beard shadowed his face. A series of scratches ran from his forehead to his angular cheekbone, either the result of whatever scuffle had killed him or drag marks from his time at the bottom of Lake Michigan. Sandy brown hair hung in ropy strands beneath his head, dotted with the occasional speck of debris from the water.

When her gaze reached the vicious gash on his neck, Amelia's stomach clenched. Though faint, a hint of white was visible amidst the mutilated flesh. The man's spine.

The wound was so garish, Amelia almost didn't notice the neat line that had been carved just under Poteracki's collarbone. Beneath an olive drab jacket and a black, hooded sweatshirt, the first few buttons of his white dress shirt were undone.

Amelia leaned a little closer to study the cut on Lars's chest. It was a straight line, but whoever had carved it had taken care to add a slight tail at the top as well as another at the bottom. "It's a number."

Detective Clark crossed both arms over his chest. "That's what I thought. It looks like a one."

Who the hell carved a number into the flesh of their victim? Was the mark a hitman's calling card, or was the killer trying to send them a message?

With a gloved finger, Dr. Francis pushed aside a piece of hair at the victim's temple. "There's a nasty contusion on this side of his head. I thought at first that the slit throat was likely the cause of death, but these blows look like they were sustained antemortem."

To Amelia's side, Zane rubbed a hand over his unshaven cheek. "So, the killer smashed his head in and then slit his throat for good measure?"

Dr. Francis lifted a shoulder. "Possibly. I'll know more when I have him on my table."

Peering down at the victim's lifeless face, Amelia noticed the physical resemblance between Lars Poteracki and Zane Palmer. Hell, the two of them could have been brothers.

Her stomach constricted even tighter, and she pushed aside the sudden urge to wrap Zane in a protective bear hug.

She gave herself a mental shake. "There's not a lot of

visible decomposition yet. How long do you think he's been in the water?"

The forensic pathologist glanced over his shoulder at the shifting waters of the lake. "Depends on the water temperature. Cold temperatures can delay almost all signs of decomposition." Dr. Francis pulled the zipper down and reached for Lars's arm. Gingerly, he took hold of the man's wrist and tugged. The limb hardly moved.

"Rigor mortis." Zane tapped an index finger against his side, a common tic Amelia had noticed when he was thinking. "Rigor usually dissipates after about forty-eight hours. But like you said, Dr. Francis, that all depends on temperature."

"It does." Dr. Francis weighed his empty hands. "The fact that rigor is still present is a good indicator that he hasn't been dead long. The temperature of the lake, depending on how long he's been underwater, would have prolonged the rigor. But chances are still good he's been dead fewer than two days, three at the most."

Zane pressed his lips together. "Bodies don't usually float to the surface until they've been dead longer than that, though. What's different about this one?"

"Currents," the pathologist replied. "The cold front that's been bearing down on the city today. High winds can impact the speed of the water."

Amelia's gaze drifted back to Lars's pale face. When a shadow shifted beneath one of the man's nostrils, she assumed at first the movement was the result of the odd lighting. A combination of harsh white streetlamps, strobing red and blue police lights, and blazing lights from the news crew gave the entire area an otherworldly feel.

As the supposed shadow under the victim's nose grew longer, Amelia froze. Zane asked Dr. Adam Francis another question, but she didn't even hear him.

Was the victim's nose bleeding? How was that even possible?

This was certainly not the first dead body Amelia had seen, but admittedly, her experiences with corpses who'd been submerged in water for days or weeks before discovery was limited. Back in Boston, she'd stood by as divers had recovered the decomposing remains of a teenaged male.

The kid had spent almost two weeks in the Atlantic in the middle of August, and the recovery of his body was still one of the most disgusting sights Amelia had ever witnessed.

Skin had slogged off his bones like melting wax, and his eyelids, lips, and cheeks had been mostly consumed by marine scavengers. His abdomen had swelled to more than twice its usual size, and a putrid mixture of water and liquified tissue had oozed onto the gurney beneath him. Then, of course, there were the bottom-feeders that had burrowed into the corpse to feed.

Amelia was still impressed she'd managed to keep herself from vomiting. Even the twenty-year veteran agent working the case with her had stepped away for a breath of fresh air.

This was different.

The shadow beneath Lars Poteracki's nose kept growing until Amelia finally realized what was happening. As a dark, wormlike creature slid out of the dead man's left nostril, she spat out a series of four-letter words.

Zane's stunned expression must have mirrored her own. "What the hell is that?"

If the macabre sight fazed Adam Francis, the man gave no indication as the creature wormed its way into the corpse's mouth. "Looks like a parasitic lamprey. Probably a sea lamprey, which are an invasive species to the Great Lakes. Ever since the government and NOAA took note of the havoc they were wreaking on native fish populations, their numbers have declined. But we still see plenty of them when we pull bodies out of the water."

Detective Clark tucked both hands into his pockets. Like Dr. Francis, his expression had changed little. "I thought those damn things fed on fish, though?"

"They do. At least, they're supposed to. But lampreys have been around for millions of years. If they're hungry enough, they'll go for other sources of nutrients." He waved a hand at the body. "Like a corpse on the bottom of Lake Michigan. They're opportunistic little bastards."

Scratching his temple, Zane faced the doctor. "All right. When will you be conducting the autopsy?"

Dr. Francis zipped up the body bag, peeled off the gloves, and checked his watch. "Within a couple hours, I hope. I called in my assistant, so she ought to be in the office soon, if she's not there already. With bodies we pull from the water, even if they don't *look* all that decomposed, we want to get to them as quickly as possible. Being out of the water can sometimes accelerate the decomp process after a body's been submerged for a time."

"We'll be there. We'll head that way as soon as we finish up here."

Amelia blinked in surprise, flashing Zane a quizzical *we will?* glance. She wasn't sure what good their presence would do in an autopsy room, but she kept the skepticism to herself.

"I'll see you there, then." Adam Francis beckoned to a uniformed officer, and the pair disappeared with the gurney and Lars Poteracki.

The case had barely begun, and already, Amelia had a sinking feeling they were about to spiral down a rabbit hole.

3

Shrugging into the sleeves of a pastel blue medical gown, Zane Palmer glanced at Amelia as she pulled her dark, blonde-tipped hair into a neat ponytail. They'd each stowed their coats and personal effects in lockers located adjacent to the autopsy exam room. Aside from the quiet hum of the harsh fluorescent fixtures overhead, the sterile space was quiet.

Adam Francis and his assistant, Shanti Patel, a woman in her mid-twenties with raven black hair and eyes nearly the same dark hue, were similarly preparing themselves. Though the pathologist had spent the past hour in the same room as Lars Poteracki's body, the upcoming work was far more gruesome to the uninitiated than the medical imaging and trace evidence collection they'd conducted so far.

As eager as Zane was to learn what the killer had carved on Poteracki's chest, the preliminary legwork was just as important. Autopsies were conducted in the same predictable manner every time, and the curiosity of one federal agent didn't supersede procedure.

While Dr. Francis and Shanti Patel had begun the pre-autopsy preparation, Amelia and Zane had been afforded an opportunity to finally delve into the case that Poteracki had helped the CPD and the Bureau close at the start of the year.

The focus of the investigation—Kevin Ersfeld, a brutal drug trafficker who was undoubtedly responsible for as many murders as any given notorious serial killer—had been sentenced to life without the possibility of parole. The U.S. Attorney's office had only brought up charges on three premeditated homicides. Though there was no doubt Ersfeld had killed countless others, the most recent three were the only cases solid enough to garner a conviction.

In fact, the cases had been solid enough to hang the death penalty over Ersfeld's head. The state of Illinois had abolished capital punishment, but the federal government was still able to levy lethal injection against the vilest offenders who crossed their path.

And in the short time Zane had been allotted to research Kevin Ersfeld, he learned the man was indeed one of the worst of the worst.

Rather than contest the three murder charges in a courtroom, Ersfeld had accepted a plea agreement of life in prison without the possibility of parole.

A handful of Ersfeld's accomplices had also been slapped with charges of varying severity, though most of them were more than happy to rat Ersfeld out for leniency. Ersfeld had run his little posse with an iron fist, and in the end, his ruthlessness had resulted in his downfall.

Naturally, the first item on Zane and Amelia's to-do list was to search for a connection between Ersfeld and a larger, more organized criminal enterprise. Such as the León family or the San Luis Cartel. If they could establish a strong link with one of the more influential syndicates, they'd have a possible starting point.

To Zane's relief—and deep chagrin—they'd located no

such relationship. Relieved because it meant that he didn't have to deal with the mafia fuckers in the immediate future. If he never heard the Leóne name again, it would be too soon.

He was chagrined because, dammit, he'd love nothing more than to get that crime family off the street. Sure, Ersfeld and his accomplices had pushed drugs for both the Leóne family and the San Luis Cartel, but neither organization was particularly tight with the man. Certainly not tight enough to risk a federal murder charge to avenge Ersfeld's conviction.

For the next potential connection, they'd turned to Ersfeld himself, thinking perhaps the volatile man had learned of Lars's identity and decided to retaliate.

The theory made logical sense, but there was one major problem. Ersfeld had been stabbed to death in a prison fight more than six months earlier. However, just because Ersfeld clearly wasn't responsible didn't mean they could rule out the potential for organized crime.

And if a new contract killer whose calling card was a message carved into their victim's body had moved into the city, then they needed to find them sooner rather than later. If the information reached the public, civilians would lose their damn minds.

Metal clanged as Amelia shoved her locker closed, and Zane pulled his focus back to the present. Her forest green eyes shifted to his, and he lamented for a split second they'd been called away from her apartment. Had they been left to their own devices, he had little doubt they'd be warm under the blankets on her bed instead of almost shivering in the medical examiner's office.

He pushed aside the mental imagery of stripping off each layer of Amelia's clothes. They were about to sit in on an autopsy of a corpse that had been retrieved from Lake

Michigan. Zane was certain he could ponder for days and still not come up with an activity that was less sexy.

Dr. Francis cleared his throat, drawing Zane and Amelia's attention to him. "All right, Agents. We're about to get started with the autopsy now. We've finished the preliminary imaging, and we've collected what trace evidence we could."

The pathologist's crisp professionalism was yet another reminder to Zane of the grim task ahead of them. "We'll follow the two of you, then."

With a crisp nod, Dr. Francis and his assistant led them back into the hall and then to the exam room. The space was all white tile and stainless steel, each surface so clean that it practically glowed under the harsh fluorescence.

A metal autopsy table stood near the room's center. To one side of the table, a rectangular tray held gleaming metal tools of the trade—scalpels of varying sizes, scissors, forceps that looked more like pliers than a surgical instrument, and of course, the fabled bone saw. A shiver worked its way down Zane's spine, and he turned his attention to the gurney on the other side of the exam table.

Lars Poteracki's complexion was nearly the same shade as the sterile tile that composed the walls. The gaping wound beneath his chin was more a purplish-blue color than the red hue Zane would expect from a person who'd been recently killed. Chances were good that, with such a traumatic injury, Lars had lost most of his blood volume within a few minutes.

The dead man still rested in the black bag as if he were in the midst of emerging from a macabre cocoon. Most forensic pathologists preferred to conduct x-rays *before* they removed the body. That way, if any piece of evidence was left behind in the bag, the x-ray would ensure it wasn't missed.

Turning to Amelia, Zane inclined his chin to an out-of-the-way counter that ran the length of the far wall. They'd be close enough to watch Dr. Francis and Shanti Patel work, but far enough away they wouldn't be underfoot.

Frosted glass cabinets spanned the wall above the counter. The items behind the closed doors were blurred, but Zane quickly spotted a box of barf bags next to a deep sink. He wondered how many seasoned law enforcement officials had abruptly sprinted over to grab one in the middle of an autopsy. Cops had strong stomachs, but even the most gruesome crime scene couldn't quite compare to what a forensic pathologist encountered on a near daily basis.

He hoped *he* wouldn't suffer the embarrassment of losing his lunch in the middle of the post-mortem examination.

As he and Amelia neared the counter, Zane chuckled to himself at the design on the front of the small bags. A barfing emoji.

The levity helped loosen anxiety's hold on his tired muscles. When Amelia arched an eyebrow, he gestured to the bags. His heart grew lighter as she cracked a smile.

"Oh, I hope you like my newest assets," Dr. Francis said. "In a line of work like this, you have to find humor where you can."

Zane flashed the pathologist a grin. "I do, actually. Just hope I won't need to use one." His remark was only partially sarcastic, but he hoped no one in the room noticed.

Dr. Francis snapped on a pair of blue vinyl gloves. "I don't suppose the FBI sits in on post-mortems very often, do they?" He looked between the two agents. "Is this your first?"

Zane hesitated before he answered. As far as his colleagues at the Bureau were concerned, he'd been an FBI special agent for more than a decade.

But that wasn't true. Any paperwork, human resources records, previous addresses, even his case history, all of it was feigned. Drafted by the government to conceal the fact that, from age twenty-one to thirty-one, Zane had acted as a covert operative for the Central Intelligence Agency.

After ten years spent more on Russian soil than American, he'd turned in his resignation with the Agency, though he hadn't quite been ready to leave the entire lifestyle behind. With the experience and the formidable skill set he'd honed as a covert operative, he still had *some*thing to offer.

When he'd been approached by the FBI, he'd been quick to accept a position in the D.C. office's Organized Crime Division.

Three years later—though it looked like ten years on paper—the Special Agent in Charge of the Chicago field office, Jasmine Keaton, had come to Zane's boss with a problem...one of the men or women under her command was in cahoots with the city's criminal underworld. SAC Keaton needed an agent with the expertise to suss out internal corruption.

He'd accepted the Bureau's offer to transfer to Chicago and work with SAC Keaton. Though he'd been in the city for nine months now, he still hadn't located the rat.

Yet.

He had helped eliminate another rodent within the Bureau, though.

More than a month ago, Glenn Kantowski, an agent from the Public Corruption Unit, had murdered City Councilman Ben Storey. Kantowski had planted evidence attempting to frame Amelia for the crime, but in the end, their investigation had proven Amelia's innocence.

Kantowski hadn't been his rat, though.

Kantowski's motive had been simple...she wanted revenge. She and Storey had engaged in a lengthy affair, and like so many other unfaithful men who opted to screw around with a woman more than ten years their junior,

Storey had promised Glenn he'd leave his wife so they could start a life together.

Of course, Storey hadn't followed up on his vow. Instead, he'd returned to his wife, hoping to piece together a marriage that had already been irreparably shattered. Glenn, on the other hand, had already divorced her wealthy husband. A brutal legal battle had resulted in the court awarding Lenny Kantowski full custody of the couple's eleven-year-old son. Never mind that Lenny had quite clearly been the first to have an affair.

The revenge motive made sense. Other than Ben Storey's wife, there were no innocent parties involved in the tangled web of extramarital drama.

Obviously, Ben hadn't deserved to die, but Zane wouldn't have argued against giving the man a swift kick in the ass. He could understand why Glenn had been pissed, but he couldn't quite wrap his head around the reason she'd risk her freedom and her life just to avenge a shitty relationship.

As with most things, though, there had been more to the situation.

Councilman Storey had been a real threat to the incumbent senator, Stan Young. A fierce political contender to an entrenched politician didn't just happen to turn up dead as the result of a separate, coincidental feud.

For now, he'd keep his uncertainties to himself. Because at the end of the day, that's all they were. Suspicions. Paranoia left over from more than a decade of work in a world where nothing was as it seemed.

Webs connected to the wealthy and powerful were like quicksand. Zane would rather observe an autopsy or hunt a small-time hitman any damn day of the week.

Amelia shot him a look that told him he'd been quiet for a little too long.

Right. He asked us if this was our first autopsy.

A ten-year veteran of the FBI would have undoubtedly sat in on post-mortem examinations in the past. Technically, Zane *had* observed an autopsy, though he'd done so in a separate room. A pane of plexiglass and a cement wall had shielded him from the smells of viscera and decay.

Tonight, he wasn't so lucky.

"No, it's not my first. What about you, Storm?"

"It's been a while, but no. Like you said, Dr. Francis, we at the FBI aren't around for very many autopsies. A lot of the time, a case isn't even put in our jurisdiction until afterward."

Dr. Francis pulled on a surgical mask. "That's a good point. I'm used to seeing plenty of homicide detectives, but we don't get a lot of Feds right off the bat." The man gestured to his assistant. "All right, let's get him out of this bag."

Shanti Patel adjusted her own mask and nodded. Though the young woman couldn't have been taller than five-four, she and Dr. Francis hefted Lars Poteracki's body onto the exam table like they were moving a lightweight piece of furniture.

Zane's focus was drawn to the cut along the top of Poteracki's chest. The numeral one.

After Shanti affixed a handful of x-rays to a lightbox above the sink, Dr. Francis selected a pair of scissors from the assortment of tools. "Computer, start audio recording."

From a small, circular device on the shelf beneath the medical instruments, a woman's voice advised that the requested recording had begun.

The pathologist started by listing the date, time, and information about all the occupants in the room. He then moved on to Lars Poteracki, describing the state of the man's body and clothes. As Adam Francis cut and pulled away the victim's jacket and hoodie, bagging each immediately after, Zane's blood pressure gradually increased.

He wanted to know what in the hell was carved on Poteracki's chest. Was it just the number one, or was there more? Beside him, Zane could sense the same sort of grim anticipation rolling off Amelia in waves.

We'll get there. Let the pathologist do his work.

"An incision beneath the victim's clavicle appears to be in the shape of the number one." Dr. Francis pulled a magnifying glass down from the UFO-shaped light above the body. As he situated the glass, he turned on the bright bulb. "No signs of swelling around the wound, and no apparent signs of bleeding. The cut appears to have been made postmortem."

Shanti Patel pointed to Poteracki's white button-down. "No blood stains on the vic's shirt, either. The lake shouldn't have been able to wash away *all* the blood stains if he'd been cut antemortem."

"Very true, Ms. Patel." As the pathologist began to snip away at Poteracki's shirt, his brows knitted together.

Zane focused on the man's hands. If something on Poteracki's body elicited such a quizzical expression from a seasoned forensic pathologist, then Zane wanted to know what in the hell it was.

Adam Francis's dark eyes were a mix of surprise and excitement when he turned his attention to Amelia and Zane. "Agents, come take a look at this."

Curiosity piqued, Zane advanced toward the exam table, Amelia at his side. As Dr. Francis pulled away the fabric of Poteracki's shirt, Zane gritted his teeth. "Holy shit."

"1 Peter 5:10." Amelia's face seemed paler as she read the words that had been carved onto their victim's chest. "It's a bible verse."

The faint *click-click-click* of a camera shutter followed as Shanti photographed the markings.

What kind of contract killer left bible verses carved into the flesh of their victims? What kind of contract killer even *cared* about religion? Their motive for murder was simple. They wanted money.

Having grown up in a nonreligious household, Zane had no idea what the verse on Lars's chest meant. He knew Amelia had gone to Sunday school when she was little, but once her mother passed, her family stopped attending church altogether.

Peering down at the cuts, Dr. Francis began to measure each letter. "Ms. Patel, could you look this verse up for us?"

Shanti snapped off her blue vinyl gloves and tossed them into a biohazard bin. As she strode over to a computer desk nestled in the corner of the room, Zane and Amelia exchanged uneasy glances.

A bible verse carved into a federal informant's chest? What the hell was going on here?

Measuring tool still in hand, Dr. Francis paused in his examination. The room's collective attention was now on Shanti Patel.

The click of the keyboard sounded out above the quiet hum of the building's HVAC system.

Clearing her throat, Shanti straightened. "This is from a bible study website. 'And after you have suffered a little while, the God of all grace, who has called you to his eternal glory in Christ, will himself restore, confirm, strengthen, and establish you.' That's 1 Peter 5:10."

Zane didn't bother to keep the confusion off his face. "Dr. Francis, you said it was postmortem, right? Why the hell would someone carve that on a dead man's chest?"

Amelia appeared no less puzzled than Zane felt. "The killer would've had to unbutton the vic's shirt to make the cuts, and then rebutton it before they dumped his body."

Shit. She was right. "That doesn't sound like something a hitman would do unless they were trying to send a message."

Never mind that the gist of 1 Peter 5:10 is oddly uplifting.

As Amelia and Zane returned to their post in front of the counter along the wall, Dr. Francis went about removing the rest of Lars Poteracki's clothing, documenting each item as he went.

Lifting one of Poteracki's arms, Dr. Francis made a show of bending the limb at the elbow. "Rigor seems to have subsided. When the vic was pulled from Lake Michigan, he must have been in the final stages of rigor. The body is still a little stiff but much more pliable than it was out at the marina."

Shanti took a few more pictures. "I took a look, and the average temperature of Lake Michigan in December is usually around forty-two degrees."

If Poteracki's corpse bobbed along the bottom of Lake Michigan at the beginning of December, there was a good chance the cold water would have slowed down the process of decomposition. How much of an impact, however, was a trickier question. One Zane would leave to the experts.

"Appreciate that, Ms. Patel. We'll double-check lake temperatures with NOAA or the university so we can be as accurate as possible."

Zane stared at the body, thinking back to everything he'd learned about floaters. "With this cut to his neck and the numerous lacerations to his pecs, wouldn't the gases that built up during decomposition escape, keeping him at the bottom of the lake?"

Amelia shot Zane an impressed look. "Then how was he floating?"

Dr. Francis changed into a new pair of gloves. "When a body decomposes, the activity from natural microorganisms creates gases that cause the lungs and various organs to expand, causing even weighted-down bodies to float, at least until decomp progresses and the gasses escape. In addition to that, Mr. Poteracki's clothes appear to have trapped enough air to make him buoyant."

Zane tried to get inside the killer's mind. "Would the killer have done that on purpose…so the corpse was discovered?"

"That I do not know."

Dr. Francis continued the autopsy by gesturing to the scratch marks on Poteracki's face. "There were tiny bits of debris in the injuries on the vic's forehead, indicating to me that these lacerations were the result of currents dragging him along the bottom of the lake. All the trace evidence was collected and will be sent to the FBI's forensic lab."

The mental image of the wormlike creature sliding from Poteracki's nostril popped into Zane's mind, and he barely suppressed a shudder. "What about that lamprey?"

"We've only conducted external evidence collection so far." Dr. Francis shrugged noncommittally as if parasitic fish squirming from one orifice to another was a regular occurrence for him.

It probably is.

Zane had no idea how pathologists kept their sanity. "Any thoughts on cause of death?"

Dr. Francis waved them closer. "I've already explained that the neck wound wasn't the COD, but look at this…" He pointed to a discolored mark on the side of Poteracki's head.

Up close, Zane caught the first scent of rot, a combination of sweet and decay. His stomach curdled, but he ignored the sensation. The wound was even more vicious under the bright lights. "That's a nasty contusion."

"Cracked his skull, if you look at the x-rays."

Zane turned to the light box. Sure enough, a series of fractures spiderwebbed out from the side of Poteracki's skull. "Do you think the blow to the head could be what killed him?"

"It's hard to say." Dr. Francis parted Lars's sandy hair to afford them a better glimpse of the injury. "But take a look. There's the start of scabbing around the edges of the wound. Much of the bleeding would've been washed away by the lake, but some of the clotting blood is still here."

Amelia leaned closer, her gaze fixed on the victim's head. "Then this is an antemortem injury."

Dr. Francis nodded. "Almost without a doubt. The vic would've sustained this blow to the head and been alive for a short period of time afterward. The wound on his neck could've either been inflicted right after he died from the contusions to the head or before. I'll have a better idea of what killed him once I've cracked him open."

Great.

Zane swallowed as he fought to keep from wrinkling his nose at the strengthening odor of rot. Why in the hell had he volunteered for him and Amelia to sit in for the entire postmortem exam? They could have read about all the details in the report that Dr. Francis would compose at the end of the autopsy.

Because if we weren't here, we'd both be wondering what in the hell was carved on Poteracki's chest. Because we want to get a strong start to this case, especially if a hitman is cutting bible verses into Chicago residents.

Grasping Poteracki's shoulder, Dr. Francis lifted the body slightly. "This is interesting."

Amelia stepped closer. "What?"

Dr. Francis rolled the body, frowning at something Zane couldn't see. "The pattern of lividity isn't consistent with what I would expect."

Zane moved to the other side of the table. "How so?"

"In layman's terms, after a person dies, gravity causes blood to pool in the lowest parts of the body, depending on position."

Zane and Amelia both nodded. Livor mortis was one of the ways a victim "told" the story of their death.

"How is our vic different than you expected?" Amelia asked.

Dr. Francis looked up. "Because there is very little blood. It's almost as if our victim here has very little of it at all."

Though he would never admit it in a million years, "vampire" was the first word to pop into Zane's mind. He shook the image of Dracula away and asked the obvious question. "Wouldn't he have lost most of his blood from the near decapitation?"

Dr. Francis pressed his lips together for a long moment. "If the neck wound was the cause of death, then perhaps. But if my theory is true and our victim here succumbed to his head wound prior to the slash, then not likely."

Zane glanced at Amelia, who looked to be as confused as he felt. "You'll call us as soon as you determine cause of death?" Amelia tapped a note into her phone. "If our victim is missing most of his blood in an abnormal way, that could change the course of our investigation."

Dr. Francis smiled at her. "Of course."

The pathologist went through the remainder of the external portion of the exam, documenting Lars's tattoos as well as a handful of bruises, some of which appeared to be new. For good measure, the pathologist even had Shanti turn out the overhead lights so they could view Lars's body under a UV light.

Beneath the ultraviolet rays, the skin of Poteracki's neck was stained a darker color not visible to the naked eye, indicating that the man had been choked before he was killed. A couple other bruises appeared under the purple glow, but they couldn't be certain when the injuries were sustained.

Once the room was returned to its regular fluorescence, Dr. Francis confirmed the strangulation theory by pointing out petechial hemorrhages in Poteracki's eyes. Though Adam Francis was confident Poteracki hadn't been killed by strangulation, the newest observations painted a violent picture of Lars's last few minutes alive.

As Dr. Francis pried open Poteracki's mouth, he paused.

"Did you find the lamprey?" Zane hadn't meant to blurt out the question. He needed more caffeine. Or sleep.

"Not quite." The pathologist scooped up a pair of silver tweezers.

Curiosity piqued, Zane stepped closer to the table, Amelia at his side. "What is it?"

Holding Poteracki's lips open, Dr. Francis tilted the head to the side. "Between his teeth."

Zane held his breath as he leaned in. As he spotted the fleshy substance lodged between Lars's incisor and first molar, he moved aside so Amelia could get a better view. "What is that?"

Rather than answer verbally, Dr. Francis used the slender forceps to pull the substance from Poteracki's mouth. Pressing his lips together, Dr. Francis looked to Amelia and Zane. "It's too early to tell for certain, but this might be a chunk of skin."

Zane's chest tightened with a rush of excitement. "Skin? Human skin?"

"I'm not one-hundred-percent sure. We'll have to run some tests, but it could very well be human."

4

As Alex Passarelli sank into the center of his overstuffed sectional, he gritted his teeth and flipped open a prepaid burner phone. The white glow from the small screen stung his eyes. He'd arrived home to his high-rise condo more than twenty minutes ago, but he hadn't bothered to flick on a light. For reasons he still didn't understand, the darkness often calmed him.

And right now, he could use every ounce of calm he could get.

Acting as a commander for the D'Amato crime family—one of two major Italian crime families who'd called Chicago home since the days of Al Capone—was stressful enough in its own right. But to compound his anxiety, he'd been trying and failing to get ahold of Amelia Storm for the better part of two weeks.

His and Amelia's history together was a complicated one, and their current relationship was no exception.

Then again, considering he was a mafia capo while his ex-girlfriend was a federal agent, complicated was the name of the game.

More than a decade and a half ago, when Alex was seventeen and Amelia fifteen, they'd crossed paths for the first time. Tensions between the D'Amato family and the Leónes were dangerously high, and Alex, as the son of a highly regarded D'Amato capo, had been strongly dissuaded from staying out in public for too long.

Though the D'Amatos adhered to some semblance of morality, the same couldn't be said for their long-term rival. Just because Alex's father, Luca, would have second thoughts about kidnapping or murdering the child of a Leóne commander didn't mean the favor was returned.

There were many inconveniences created by the order to remain behind closed doors. But there was one thing driving Alex to ignore the directive.

A movie.

A film he'd been excited to see for more than a year. He and his friends had watched the trailer over and over until they'd memorized each word, and Alex was determined his veritable quarantine wouldn't interfere with his ability to see that damn film.

And, of course, he'd been a teenager. Mafia royalty or not, what teenage boy heeded his parents' cautionary warnings?

He sure as hell hadn't.

Rather than view the movie in his own neck of the woods —the first area the Leónes might think to search for him— Alex had come up with the idea to sneak off to a theater on the other side of town.

Englewood was a lower income community in Chicago, and even though it churned out some of the city's highest rates of violent crime year after year, that fact hadn't fazed Alex.

He'd been born into a life of violence. Even at seventeen, he'd carried a handgun on his person. And the weapon wasn't just for show. He knew how to use it. The countless hours Alex had spent at a firing range with his uncle Tony had ensured he was adept with a firearm.

So, when opening night came around, he'd grabbed two of his buddies—both young men who, like himself, had been born into the mafia lifestyle. The three of them piled into Alex's friend's car and rode out to Englewood.

Compared to the movie theaters closer to Alex's home in the Near North Side, the Englewood location was basic. There were no leather reclining chairs, no waiters who'd serve him booze during the premier, no adjacent restaurant and bar. Just the typical concession stand with salty popcorn, overpriced candies, and equally expensive soda.

The candy and drinks were nothing to write home about, but Alex's gaze had immediately been drawn to the young woman behind the cash register.

Amelia Storm.

At fifteen, she'd already held herself with the poise of someone years older. In the days that followed, he'd hardly been able to get her dark green eyes and bright smile out of his head. He went back to the theater a couple more times, and on each visit, he had the pleasure of interacting with Amelia.

Until then, he'd never had trouble talking to girls. But *that* girl had been different. No matter how hard he'd tried, he hadn't been able to come up with a conversation starter that would make him seem suave.

On his fourth trip to see the same damn movie, Amelia had finally struck up a conversation with him, one that wasn't related to whether or not he wanted more butter on his popcorn. Spurred on by Amelia's overture, Alex had finally worked up the guts to ask her out before leaving the theater that night. She'd accepted, and for the next three and a half years, the two of them had been inseparable.

Back in those days, Alex had still been under the impression he would live his own life. He was heir to an underworld throne, and though his line of work was set in stone, he'd been certain he had autonomy in his personal life. The D'Amatos had abandoned plenty of outdated mafia customs, so why in the hell wouldn't they abandon those traditions that dictated who he could be with and why?

Alex still couldn't answer the *why*, but now he knew some archaic customs would never dissipate.

His parents, particularly his father, had hated Amelia. Specifically, they'd hated the fact she was an outsider. Moreover, she was an outsider who came from nothing. Had she been the daughter of a Fortune 500 CEO, perhaps Luca Passarelli would have viewed her differently.

When Amelia had ended their relationship and then abandoned Chicago to join the military, Alex truly shouldn't have been surprised. In some respects, he *wasn't* surprised.

He'd never received confirmation, but he strongly suspected his father had played a hand in Amelia's abrupt decision to abandon Chicago in favor of a war zone.

Hell, she was probably safer in Afghanistan than she'd been as his girlfriend.

Despite his ability to sympathize with her decision, Alex had still been heartbroken. He'd kept tabs on Amelia over the years, all while throwing himself into his work and steering the D'Amato family forward into the twenty-first century.

Not too long after losing Amelia, life had dealt Alex another devastating blow. His little sister, Gianna, had been only fourteen when she disappeared on her way home from a friend's house.

As Alex's chest tightened, he gritted his teeth. A decade later, thoughts of Gianna still came with a painful ache unparalleled by any physical injury he'd sustained over the years.

With bright blue eyes the same shade as their mother's

and a sense of humor as sharp as her wit, Gianna was one of a kind. Since neither of Alex's parents had shown a whole lot of interest in raising him and his sister, he and Gianna had grown up much closer than a pair of siblings with an eight-year age gap.

Alex and Gianna, along with their uncle Tony, had been their own little family.

So, when Gianna had vanished, Alex and Tony had taken on the task of searching for her. In those first few days, they'd been so sure they'd find her or that they'd receive a ransom message from a rival. Whatever the sum, Alex would have paid it gladly if it meant he'd see his sister again.

But the days turned into weeks, the weeks into months, and the months into years, all with no kidnappers' demands and not even the slightest hint where Gianna might have gone. Whoever had taken her hadn't done so with the intent to squeeze money from the wealthy Passarelli family.

They'd taken Gianna to send a message. A personal vendetta Alex *still* hadn't uncovered.

Not that he had to stretch his imagination to picture how Luca Passarelli could piss someone off enough to seek retribution against their family. Luca was an ass, even to his own kids. He'd always treated Gianna much better than Alex, but his fatherly ways still left a lot to be desired.

After years of hitting one dead end after another in their search for Gianna, Alex and Tony had decided to seek out the help of a professional investigator. A detective.

Neither of them was under the illusion they'd ever see Gianna alive again, but they wanted, no, they *needed* to know what had happened. To find who was responsible for snuffing out the one bright spot that had remained in Alex's life. They needed closure.

He and Tony had turned to a trusted affiliate of the family, a homicide detective named Trevor Storm. Storm's case closure rate far outpaced that of his peers, and at the time Alex and Tony approached him, he'd been friendly with the family for almost five years.

All unbeknownst to Amelia, who'd been thousands of miles away in a combat zone.

Releasing a breath that was growing stale in his lungs, Alex rubbed his eyes and slumped deeper into the couch. He'd tried to keep the secret from Amelia after she'd returned to the city, but like her brother, she was a keen observer. Even if Alex hadn't told her of his and Tony's affiliation with Trevor, she'd have found out eventually. He maintained it was better she learned the truth from him instead of an outside source.

For the first few months Amelia was back in Chicago, she'd stayed away from him. He'd known she was in the city, but he'd similarly kept his distance.

Out of sight, out of mind, he'd reasoned. His thought was that if he just kept himself off her radar, if he gave her no reason to seek him out, then they could leave the past well enough alone.

He'd been wrong, of course.

Hell, he owed her a *favor* after she'd used her influence to keep one of Alex's lieutenants from going to prison for a murder he hadn't committed.

He shifted in his seat, suddenly uncomfortable. Rising to his feet, he started to pace back and forth next to the coffee table. Despite the fact he hadn't turned on any lights, the glow from the city's skyline was enough illumination to ensure he didn't trip over his own feet.

Jaw clenched, he flipped open the burner phone before closing it with a quiet *snap*. He repeated the motion a few more times, finally forcing himself to hold the damn thing closed for fear his fidgeting would break the cheap device.

"Dammit, Amelia. Why won't you just answer your

phone?" Alex tossed it on the sofa so he wasn't tempted to toss it against the wall. "I'm not trying to get ahold of you because I want to talk about the weather or the Cubs. This is *important.*"

Silence greeted him at the end of his rant.

"Maybe I should get a pet so I won't feel so insane for talking to myself in the dark. Something low-maintenance, like a cat or a fish."

As he paused in his pacing route, he picked up the cheap phone again and flipped it open. He already knew she wouldn't answer, but at this point, all he could do was try. Though he wasn't keen on dialing her personal cell, he couldn't very well call her at the office.

Pressing the green button, Alex raised the phone to his ear. "Answer your phone, Amelia." His request came from between clenched teeth. "You're in danger, and you don't even know it."

The ringtone buzzed once, then a second time. With each subsequent ring, his heart sank a little lower.

When the line clicked over to the operator's voice advising him to leave a message, he flipped the phone closed and spat out a series of four-letter words.

He wouldn't risk reaching out to her if his message wasn't important. Didn't she realize that?

Still cursing under his breath, he made his way to an end table and switched on the light. As he strolled toward the kitchen, a glossy eight-by-ten photo on the dining room table caught his attention. A week earlier, he'd printed the picture. He'd saved the image to the hard drive of his work computer, and he'd made plenty of copies. But this photo was the original.

Pausing in his trek, he peered down at the picture.

Two men leaned on the rail of a mid-sized yacht, sunlight

glinting off the shades they'd each pushed to the tops of their heads.

One man, the fellow with the chestnut brown hair streaked with only the first hints of gray, had become quite familiar to Alex over the past eight months.

Brian Kolthoff, known in more unsavory circles simply as The Shark, had come within a hair's breadth of buying an underaged sex slave from the Leóne family. Amelia had arrested him for the crime with the hope he'd see years behind bars.

Kolthoff hadn't spent a single day in prison. He'd posted bail almost as soon as he'd been tossed in holding, and then his expensive lawyers had gone to work on the sex trafficking charges the U.S. Attorney's office had tried to levy at him.

Tried being the operative word. Kolthoff was a billionaire, an established D.C. lobbyist who spent his weekends with senators and government officials of all shapes and sizes.

The justice system was a joke to men like him.

As Alex's uncle was fond of saying, "Money talks, and bullshit walks."

Judging by the grin Kolthoff wore in Alex's photo, the man next to him on the yacht was a good friend.

The friend was less familiar to Alex, and he'd taken a while to place the guy's likeness. One day, when he'd been in the middle of crunching numbers for the D'Amato family's counterfeit operations, the realization had struck him like a punch to the gut.

Amelia needed to see this, and she needed to see it sooner rather than later.

❄

As the new rush of running water drowned out the quiet hum of the furnace, Cassandra Halcott sat a little straighter. Glancing to the barely ajar door of the master bathroom, Cassandra resisted the urge to bite her nails. A slat of light fell through the opening and onto the plush carpet, and the first traces of a woodsy soap began to drift to where she sat on the king-sized bed.

Her focus on the laptop in front of her had been partly feigned and partly a genuine effort to maximize her time alone. Though she'd become suspicious of her boyfriend of two months, she didn't want him to *know* about her reservations. Faking interest in her computer had been the most sure-fire way to keep from piquing the man's curiosity.

Joseph Larson was a puzzle she wanted to solve.

For the second time that week, Joseph had headed straight to the shower after he'd arrived at her place. Though he was a special agent in the Organized Crime Division of the FBI, Cassandra knew he hadn't been out in the field that day.

What the hell made him exert so much effort that he had to head straight to the shower when he got here? Did he hit the gym?

She snorted aloud at the wishful thinking.

Joseph maintained a muscular physique—the man was built like a Greek god—but Cassandra had picked up on his gym routine.

Midnight on a weekday wasn't Joseph's preferred workout time. Add to that the fact he'd told her earlier in the day he'd be at her apartment before ten, and she was on edge.

Setting aside her laptop, Cassandra swung her legs over the edge of the bed and padded over to the dresser.

Cassandra was an assistant United States Attorney for the Northern District of Illinois, and she hadn't ascended to the position of federal prosecutor without a healthy sense of curiosity.

And an equally formidable mistrust of…well, almost everyone. Just because she was relatively new to the city of Chicago didn't mean she was naïve. Far from, actually. Four years in the foster care system did that to a person.

Before she'd become a ward of the state, Cassandra had been raised by a pair of loving parents. Based on what she'd learned about psychology during her undergraduate, the fact that she'd been nurtured during the critical developmental points in her youth was likely the only reason she hadn't fallen down a spiral of despair when she'd gained her independence.

Resilient. That's what her therapist called her.

Focusing on Joseph's phone, keys, and wallet, Cassandra shoved aside the recollections.

She shouldn't snoop. Such nosiness was a sign of mistrust and going through a partner's things was immature.

What else *could* she do? Sure, she could ask Joseph why he'd made a beeline for the shower when he'd arrived that night, but there was no guarantee he'd give her a straight answer.

As much as she…*enjoyed* Joseph, if that was even the correct word, Cassandra couldn't say she completely trusted him. Her paranoia wasn't any fault of his, at least not that she could tell, but was instead a product of her own development.

Chewing on her bottom lip, she turned away from the dresser and pulled out her phone. An image lit up the screen—a picture she'd taken of her and Joseph—and her stomach twisted. She almost forgot she'd been swiping through her photo gallery before he'd shown up tonight. Cassandra had picked up the habit of taking pictures of everything. As much as she hated to admit it, she was one of *those* people.

While she'd been procrastinating her work by cleaning up her collection, she'd come across a series of photos she'd taken when she and Joseph had spent a weekend up north on the edge of Lake Michigan. Joseph's light brown hair was windblown, and the blue of his eyes was hidden by a pair of aviator sunglasses. He wore an easy smile, his arm draped over her shoulders.

Bright auburn hair framed Cassandra's pale face, but hardly a strand of her neat ponytail was out of place. Her head only came up to Joseph's chin, showcasing the ten-inch difference between her five-four and his six-two. The corners of her pale blue eyes creased from the wide grin that displayed perfectly straight, white teeth she'd worked for years to attain.

As it turned out, foster care wasn't keen on spending money to send its kids to an orthodontist for braces. Cassandra had been forced to take matters into her own hands shortly after law school. Fortunately, the thousands of dollars she'd spent on invisible braces had paid off.

Why had she even unlocked her phone in the first place? As the screen dimmed and then went black, her attention drifted toward Joseph's personal effects.

Don't do it. Don't be that *girl. No one likes a nosy girlfriend.*

Indecision gnawed at her gut like a parasite.

I don't even know the password for his phone. What the hell am I going to find in his wallet?

She wasn't sure. Nothing, probably.

If there's nothing there, then that'll be that. I'll feel like an idiot, and that'll be the end of it.

But would rifling through Joseph's things assuage her trepidation? Doubtful. Deep down, she knew something was off. Her instincts told her as much, and her years as a prosecutor had taught her to trust that sixth sense.

Perhaps that's why she was trying to convince herself she wouldn't find anything in her search. Her mind was turning into a damn courtroom.

Gritting her teeth against the mental discomfort that had begun to manifest as a physical sensation, she glanced to the bathroom door and turned back to the dresser.

One quick look. That's all she wanted. Something to set her mind at ease, one way or another. Either she'd confirm her suspicions, or she'd feel silly after finding nothing.

What would he say if he caught her? Would he be hurt, or would he be mad? Would he break up with her? And did she care if he did?

Shit. She was stalling again.

As she pulled in a steadying breath, she gingerly moved aside Joseph's keys, cringing at the faint metallic jingle that went along with the motion.

He can't hear it. He's in the shower.

Satisfied with the rationalization, she picked up Joseph's wallet. Another pang of doubt singed her mind, but she pushed it aside.

As she flipped open the worn leather, her attention was drawn to a collection of hundreds. Heart in her throat, she quickly counted the cash.

Five-hundred and sixty-seven dollars.

Who the hell carries half a grand in cash?

She knew the answer before her brain even completed the question. Drug users and gamblers. To the best of Cassandra's knowledge, Joseph wasn't much of a betting man, and his job as a special agent at the FBI required routine drug screenings.

He could've just gone to a casino with a friend. People do it all the time. You've done it before, remember?

Chicago was no Las Vegas, but the surrounding areas did sport a handful of land-based and riverboat casinos.

Blood pounded in Cassandra's ears as she pushed aside the cash. Cold dread ran from her neck all the way down to her toes as she spotted the next item.

A condom.

She and Joseph hadn't used a condom since the second time they'd slept together. Her method of birth control, an IUD, was among the most effective at preventing pregnancy, and she'd chosen to believe Joseph when he'd told her he was clean.

So, what was he doing with a condom in his wallet? It sure as hell wasn't for her.

Mouth dry, she pulled on a receipt behind the blue foil wrapper.

Montanelli's Steakhouse. The total bill was just a hair shy of ninety dollars, but the text didn't specify what had been ordered.

From her time as a lawyer, Cassandra was familiar with plenty of pricey restaurants. More often than not, she was able to put such expenses on a work credit card or write the cost off on an expense report. She always suffered a hint of guilt, knowing the price of the entrees was being saddled onto U.S. taxpayers.

To her chagrin, lawyers and judges tended to have expensive taste. Business lunches didn't often occur at a modestly priced diner like Cassandra would have preferred.

There was a distinct possibility Joseph's dinner alone could have set him back a hundred bucks, but the condom hoisted an abundance of skepticism onto the optimistic theory.

He'd only carry a condom in his wallet if he wanted to keep open the option to sleep with another woman. Had he spent a hundred dollars on dinner for himself, or had he been with a woman he was trying to screw? Was *that* why he'd hurried to the shower for the past two nights? Was he sleeping with another woman?

As her frenzied thoughts finally gave way and allowed her

to return her focus to the bedroom, she realized with a start that the place was quiet. The water had stopped.

Shit, shit.

Clenching her teeth together until she thought they might break, Cassandra forced her trembling hand to tuck the cash and receipt back into place around the condom. At the same time, the shower door dragged along its track, followed by Joseph clearing his throat.

She replaced the wallet on the wooden dresser, cringing as she pushed Joseph's keys back to the approximate location they'd rested before she went on her investigative adventure.

Her legs felt as if they'd been replaced with pool noodles. All she wanted to do was curl up in bed and berate her poor life choices until she drifted off to sleep.

But she wanted to do it *alone*.

Calm down, Cassandra. The condom could've been in there for weeks. He could be used to carrying it, and he just hasn't bothered to get rid of it. He might just be going to a casino with a friend and then eating a fancy steak dinner after he wins at one of the tables.

The story made sense, and she desperately wanted to believe it.

Could she, though?

She wasn't so sure.

5

Scooting to the edge of my seat, I turned off the television and pushed open my laptop. Other than the faint glow that seeped through the kitchen doorway, the living and dining rooms were dark. No need to turn on all the lights when I was watching the news. I kept my house tidy and minimalistic, preferring not to be forced to wrangle a truckload of belongings when I inevitably moved.

Well, this wasn't *my* house, but the house I was renting. I relocated often, and I didn't have the ability to set up shop in one location for longer than a year or two.

I scratched my cheek. Maybe this time would be different.

Before Chicago, I'd lived in Detroit for eighteen months and Terre Haute before Michigan. Terre Haute was my hometown, but I had no reason to return. My work in Indiana was done.

For now.

I had to remember that my frequent relocation wasn't for my benefit. It had a higher purpose.

For the past four years, I'd done the work of the divine. My duties affected more people than I even knew, and until the good Lord came to me again, my efforts to cleanse this country would continue.

Modern society was mired in sin, bogged down, and dictated by the faithless.

Those had been my father's exact words, in fact. He'd caught me flipping through a porno magazine when I was eleven, and he'd promptly dragged me to the musty basement by my hair.

My parents had kept an old wardrobe down there, and any time I was caught breaking one of my father's many rules, he'd lock me inside. Sometimes for only a couple hours, and sometimes for days, with only the occasional visit to provide water and food so I didn't die and stink up the place.

Shivering at the remembrance, I powered on my laptop. I'd watched the nightly news earlier in the evening, but there still hadn't been any mention of my…handiwork.

Lars Poteracki. That's who I wanted to see.

A pang of worry struck me as I pulled up a new webpage. I was no oceanic expert, but I was aware that currents in a large body of water could sometimes be volatile. At this point, all I could do was hope that Lake Michigan hadn't pulled Lars's corpse farther out into its depths.

Most killers didn't want the body of their victim to be found, but I wasn't most killers. I didn't consider myself a killer at all.

No, I was a savior, and the people of Chicago needed to know who I'd saved.

More than four years ago, I'd been called to a divine purpose…to cleanse the world of evildoers. I wasn't one of those academic elites who was perched atop an ivory tower with their nose turned up at the world, but I knew a thing or two.

If I'd tried to simply cut a swath through the degenerates of this country, I'd be caught, arrested, and jailed in record time. Though I respected the work done by law enforcement officials around the world, most of them were sandbagged by the same rules they sought to uphold. I couldn't expect them to completely grasp my mission.

So, I had to be creative in order to minimize the body count and maximize the number of souls I reached.

As I pulled the computer onto my lap to shift into a more comfortable position, a flare of pain seared through my arm. Hissing through my teeth, I pushed up the sleeve of my hooded sweatshirt.

A splotch of pink had begun to show through the white gauze. The wound likely needed stitches, but I couldn't go to a doctor's office and show them an injury that was quite clearly a human bite mark.

I'd have a nasty scar once the gash healed, but it wasn't my first. Lars had fought like a man possessed. Maybe he had been.

Rubbing gingerly at the bandage, I made a mental reminder to change the dressing once I was finished with my news search. The human mouth was full of bacteria, and if I didn't keep a close watch on the nasty wound, I risked infection.

As I opened a local news website, a wave of excitement rolled over me.

There it was. Right at the top.

"Body of Unknown Male Pulled from Lake Michigan Late Tuesday Night."

That had to be Lars. I'd driven to an isolated marina north of the city to throw him into the lake early on Monday morning.

Holding my breath in anticipation, I scanned the short article.

Published less than an hour ago, the five paragraphs merely outlined that a dead man had been found floating outside a private marina. No official cause of death was listed, but the report speculated there was foul play involved. For the time being, police were withholding the victim's identity, pending notification of next of kin.

Sandwiched between the second and third paragraphs was a video. I doubted I'd learn anything the text hadn't covered, but I wanted to see for myself.

I pressed play and maximized the window.

Inquisitive, bright green eyes met mine as the camera focused on a petite woman with a microphone in her gloved hand. The hood of her parka was pulled up, and a golden blonde braid spilled over one shoulder.

"This is Angela Jacobs with the WEKV evening news, here at the site where authorities have just pulled the body of an unidentified male from the waters of Lake Michigan. At about nine tonight, the Chicago Police were notified of a possible drowning victim who'd been spotted floating just north of this very marina."

Perfect. Lars had drifted underwater for long enough to remove any lingering trace evidence that could lead the cops back to me.

Angela moved to the side and motioned for a husky woman in her mid-fifties to join her in the shot. *"With us right now is the citizen who notified the CPD, Amanda Wilkins. Ms. Wilkins, could you tell us what you saw earlier tonight?"*

Glancing from Angela to the camera, Wilkins gave a sheepish nod. *"Yeah. Um, I was out here to do a little work on Lady Liberty...that's the name of my boat. I wanted to get some work done before the storm hit. And...that's when I saw him."* Wilkins seemed unsure of herself as she gave the recollection, as if she wasn't clear on how much of the story she was expected to tell or how many details to relay.

Ever the professional, Angela shifted her focus from the camera to Wilkins, appearing thoughtful. *"What was that like, Ms. Wilkins? What were your first thoughts when you saw the man's body floating in the lake?"*

A flush crept to Wilkins's face. *"Well, I...I sure didn't think he was dead. I guess that sounds kinda silly, doesn't it? I honestly thought he was some drunk who'd been out on the lake and fell out of his boat. You know how the holidays are, right?"*

I snorted softly to myself. Ironic that the celebration of the Lord's birth bred so much sin. To me, the month of December was the perfect time to cleanse.

Angela asked a question I didn't catch, and Wilkins rubbed her cheek before responding. *"I threw out a life preserver, and I started yelling to him. This time of year, the water's awfully cold. It doesn't take but a few minutes to kill a full-grown man."*

The reporter continued with her questions for Wilkins, but I tuned out the dialogue to observe the background. Yellow crime scene tape fluttered in the windy night, blocking off the entrance to the boardwalk. A handful of men and women milled about, though in the distance, I couldn't make out many details.

Contained beyond the yellow tape, the news crew's bright lights illuminated two individuals seemingly in a deep discussion with a policeman. I leaned closer and squinted at the screen. Right away, my instincts told me that these two weren't typical city cops. Frowning, I paused the feed.

I'd have much preferred to physically be on the scene, to see for myself the city's response to the discovery of a body in Lake Michigan, but I wasn't that brazen. The old adage of a criminal returning to the scene to observe their handiwork was cliché for a reason.

Despite the longing that tightened around my chest, I wouldn't allow myself to become just another statistic. Another Icarus whose wings had melted when he flew too close to the sun.

Curiosity burned away at the fringes of my mind as I took a screenshot to zoom in on the well-dressed pair. The woman's dark hair had whipped around her head as a gust of wind swept through the marina, mostly obscuring her face. Only the man's profile was visible, albeit somewhat blurred by the enlargement I'd performed. But I could make out his tailored slacks and black frock coat which were better suited for a formal gathering than a crime scene.

I pressed my lips together. The pair conversed with a detective I recognized from an unrelated crime. He had presumably been at the scene since before Angela's cameraman started rolling. I'd noticed him at the start of the video, and other than chat with the overdressed duo, he hadn't moved much. To the side of the gurney stood another fellow, whose jacket marked him as part of the Medical Examiner's office.

Which begged the question, who in the hell were these two? Surely, the homicide detective on the scene hadn't been compelled to call in *two* additional detectives.

What type of cop dressed like that? What cop could even *afford* to dress like that?

Not cops. Feds.

My heart sank to the carpeted floor.

When I'd gone through Lars's wallet, I'd noted his address was local. There was no reason for the FBI to involve themselves in this case, was there? Or was there some fine-print rule about bodies that washed up from Lake Michigan?

No. That's ridiculous. I left his wallet in his back pocket. They'd know he was a local. Even if he was in the water, he was pulled out in Illinois. This is city jurisdiction. It has *to be.*

I set the laptop back on the coffee table.

It didn't matter.

My calling in this city wasn't done yet, and I wasn't going to let the Chicago Police Department or the Feds stand in my way.

6

With her shoulder, Amelia shoved open one of the double doors and strode out of the medical examiner's office, Zane close on her heels. The sky had turned an even more noticeable shade of orange, indicating the dreaded cold front and its promised lake-effect snow were imminent.

Fat, white flakes flew almost horizontally in the night air, their shapes illuminated briefly in the halos of the streetlamps dotting the parking lot. Glancing at the concrete, Amelia noted the snow melted almost as soon as it touched the ground. That wouldn't last for long, though. Within an hour or two, the entire city would be coated in a layer of white.

By then, Amelia hoped to be snug and warm in her bed. Though she'd like nothing more than for Zane to be beside her, witnessing an autopsy had driven almost all the lust-related thoughts from her head. If Zane came home with her, she'd be just as likely to propose a game of cribbage as she would be to come onto him.

As the wind buffeted Amelia's face, she was grateful to be

out in the open for the short trip to Zane's car. Though tinged with the faint scent of car exhaust and wet concrete, the gust was a vast improvement from the decay that had permeated every square inch of the autopsy exam room.

For the past two and a half hours, they'd observed Dr. Adam Francis as he'd cut open Lars Poteracki's body in search of clues that would help them solve the man's violent murder.

Amelia was glad for the infrequency of her visits to live autopsies. She had a strong stomach, but the forensic pathologist dealt with an entirely different level of gore.

Cleansing her lungs with a deep breath, she let herself into the passenger side of Zane's silver Acura. Thanks to remote start, the vehicle was already warm.

Settling into the driver's seat, Zane rubbed his nose. "I don't know how pathologists do it. Even just the smell would make me lose my mind."

The faint odor of decay that had adhered to her hair and skin crept into Amelia's nostrils now that she was out of the wind. "Our vic wasn't even that bad, either. Cold water kept his body from decomposing too much. When I was in Boston, I worked a case where a teenager was pulled out of the harbor in the middle of August. He'd been in the Atlantic for almost two weeks."

As Zane shifted the car into gear, Amelia continued her description of the scene, sparing no gruesome detail. By the time she finished, she could swear Zane's complexion had paled a shade.

He offered her an incredulous glance as they slowed to a stop at a red light. "You sat in on that autopsy and didn't throw up?"

Amelia shrugged off his disbelief. As much as she'd love to puff up her chest and brag about how her stomach was made of cast iron, she admittedly hadn't been present for the postmortem exam. "No. God no. The pathologist actually advised against it. Said she didn't want to have to pause the autopsy to call the cleaning crew in to mop up puke after a couple Feds lost their lunch. Which, to be fair, we probably would have. There's a reason they keep puke bags on hand."

He chuckled. "True. Got to give credit where it's due."

The traffic signal turned green, and as their dialogue ended, the quiet drone of the radio took over. A song had just come to an end, and the station's late-night host rattled off the artist's name and the title of the tune.

"And now, we'll take a quick peek at the weather for the next few days. As we get closer to the holidays, it's looking more and more like Chicago will, in fact, have a white Christmas. We'll be getting plenty of snow over the next couple weeks, and temperatures aren't likely to warm up and melt any of it before the twenty-fifth. A significant low-pressure system is expected to move into the city starting around noon tomorrow. We have a little bit of snow right now as well, but we ought to only get an inch before the morning commute. Think of this as a preview of what's to come."

Curiosity nagged Amelia, and she reached out to turn up the volume. She'd been watching the forecast like a hawk, but somehow, hearing the words out loud made them more real.

"As for tomorrow, we'll start to see some flurries late in the morning, turning to snow showers by around noon. The current forecast says the worst won't hit us until sometime tomorrow night, and it should finish up before the start of Thursday. Now, that doesn't sound that bad, but..." the radio announcer paused to chuckle, *"this is lake-effect snow we're talking about. Predictions right now say we're in for anywhere from eighteen inches to two and a half feet."*

With a groan, Amelia leaned against the headrest. "Are you kidding me?"

Blinking as if he'd just exited a trance, Zane shot her a curious look. "What?"

She hoped he'd spaced out because his focus was on the road and not elsewhere. Gesturing to the center console, she heaved a dramatic sigh. "Earth to Zane. We're about to get dumped on. Two feet of snow by Thursday morning."

"That's…a fair amount of snow."

The man lost his mind any time she mentioned a tornado, but apparently, two feet of the white stuff didn't even warrant a reaction from him. "A fair amount? Were you living in Russia before you moved to Chicago?" Amelia blurted out the question with all the grace of a bull in a china shop.

Zane's jaw visibly clenched, and the blood drained from his knuckles where he tightened his grip on the steering wheel.

Shit.

She hadn't meant for the semi-sarcastic query to come across so haphazardly. Nor had she intended for it to be steeped in any semblance of accuracy.

The image of Zane's shirtless body popped into her mind, and not for any pleasurable reason. While they'd worked their most recent case, they'd stayed at a hotel in Cedarwood—a small town about three hours south of Chicago. Distracted and paying little attention to her surroundings, Amelia had accidentally wandered into Zane's adjoining room while he was in the middle of getting ready for the day.

To her surprise, he'd been clad in nothing but his underwear. No matter how physically attractive Amelia found him to be, she was mortified to have invaded his privacy. Trust was as important to him as it was to her, and she still felt terrible about her mistake.

During the embarrassing incident, she'd noticed a handful of tattoos he'd never mentioned or revealed with his clothing choices. Two blue and black nautical stars, one on each shoulder and an identical star on each knee.

From her time at the FBI, she'd instantly known the significance of the ink. In Russian prisons, and by proxy the Russian mob, a star tattooed on each shoulder signified a position of authority, much like a rank insignia denoted a soldier's status in the military. In a similar vein, the stars on the knees told the world the bearer would bow to no man.

The Russians took the symbolism very seriously. They wouldn't permit an impostor to sport the nautical stars for long.

A man had to *earn* those stars. And in the Russian mob, the only way to earn anything was with bloodshed.

The tattoos had perplexed Amelia at first. She was sure the stars must have been a remnant of undercover work Zane had done while he was on the East Coast, but she didn't understand why he'd have kept such an operation a secret.

Unless the op hadn't been conducted by the FBI, and it hadn't taken place on U.S. soil.

Swallowing against the fuzzy sensation on her tongue, Amelia snuck a glance at Zane. Though his jaw was relaxed, he retained his death grip on the steering wheel, and his posture was rigid.

Guilt sawed at her heart. "I'm sorry. You don't have to answer that. I didn't mean for it to come across so harshly."

His focus remained on the road, but his expression softened. "No, it's okay. I know you've caught on to my…to the fact that there's…more to what I've told you about myself."

Amelia wondered if she should pinch herself to confirm she hadn't dozed off on the trip back to her apartment.

Until now, Zane had never so much as alluded to an irregularity with his past. His secrecy had irked her for a spell, but lately, she'd come to terms with the fact they might never know every single secret about each other's lives.

Amelia had plenty of secrets of her own. She trusted Zane, but sometimes, no good came from revealing the past.

In her case, knowledge of her relationship with the D'Amato family had the potential to put Zane's life in danger. If Luca Passarelli thought she had disclosed their history to another soul...

She pushed aside the notion and turned back to Zane. "It's all right. Seriously."

With a slight shake of his head, he flattened both palms against the wheel. "I know, and I appreciate you saying so. But I can't just pretend you haven't noticed what you noticed. I can't say much, but I did some undercover work internationally."

"For the FBI?" Again, she'd neglected to think through her question.

Zane answered before she could backpedal. She could tell he was fighting the urge to drum his fingers on the steering wheel, one of the few tics he had. "All I can tell you is it was work for the government."

Only one government entity came to mind at the cryptic answer. "The CIA?"

"I can't say."

Amelia merely nodded in reply. Part of her had half-expected to hear the tried and true *"I can neither confirm nor deny this allegation."* She was relieved his tone wasn't defensive, but there was a twinge of melancholy she couldn't quite understand.

All this from the damn weather.

As an uneasy silence blanketed them, she forced herself not to ask any more questions. Though she was curious by nature, she'd taught herself to respect her friends' and family's privacy. If she expected as much from them, then she'd damn well better return the favor.

But here she was, prying into a past Zane was legally prohibited from discussing.

During her tenure in the military, she'd worked alongside

the Army's elite Green Beret forces. Her position on the Cultural Support Team was to help the Green Berets when dealing with locals who'd be controversial for the male soldiers to interact with—women and children, mostly.

Since the Green Berets were a highly trained, highly specialized faction of the military, they were often deployed for sensitive operations. Dealing with classified information eventually became a routine part of Amelia's job, and to this day, there was plenty of her military career she wasn't at liberty to discuss.

This is the last thing I expected to talk about on our ride home from the M.E.'s office. I figured we'd be talking about the case.

Even so, Amelia was glad the subject was out in the open, and she was relieved to know she hadn't been completely off-base about Zane. As much as Zane loved to regale embarrassing stories about his middle school years, he was much less forthcoming about his tenure with the FBI.

A sudden thought blazed through her head like a meteorite.

Was he an FBI agent? Or was he still working for the CIA? And if he was on an assignment for the Agency, how long would he remain in Chicago? Would he be headed back to Russia next week?

Her heart sank through the floorboards. As much as she'd wanted to drop the subject to avoid making Zane feel awkward, they were almost at her apartment, and she had to know.

"Are you still…in the CIA?" Amelia had to force the words from her mouth like she was a champion weightlifter hefting a massive barbell into the air.

Shooting her a look of surprise, Zane shook his head. "No. To be honest, I probably wouldn't have said any of that if I still…well, you know."

Relieved, she slumped down in her seat. "Yeah. That makes sense. Sorry, it was probably a weird question."

"No, not weird at all. Completely fair, if you ask me. You, uh…you probably dealt with the Agency when you were in the military, didn't you?"

As Zane's posture relaxed, so too did Amelia's racing brain. "A little bit, yeah. They were…nice."

He threw back his head and laughed, and warmth crept up Amelia's cheeks. "They were nice? Amelia, that's adorable."

She'd rather utter something that made her sound silly than come across like a nosy jerk. As a smile crept to her lips, she threw a playful jab at his arm. "Stop patronizing me, dick."

All while his eyes were fixed on the road, he gave her a shove in return. "Stop hitting me, dick."

Lapsing into a fit of laughter at his feigned, over-the-top offense, she grabbed his hand. His skin was smooth and cool, a far cry from her clammy palms. As he interlocked his fingers with hers, the flutter returned to her stomach.

For a beat, she considered asking him if he'd planned to stay with her that night. As tired as she was, part of Amelia was still disappointed the two of them would soon have to separate.

However, the melancholy was interrupted when she caught a whiff of chemicals and decay leftover from the autopsy exam room. She needed a shower, and she was sure he did too—and not the type of fun shower that two consenting adults took together.

Amelia was dead set on a scalding hot, "peel the skin off her bones" pelting. Then, she'd slather her dried out self in fruity body lotion, curl up under her blankets, and drift off for the meager four hours of sleep she hoped to get that night.

Still, the thought of Zane's warm body against hers was tempting. A flush crept to her cheeks, and she was grateful for the low light.

As the car eased to a stop along the curb in front of Amelia's apartment building, she tried to ignore the pang of disappointment that came with realizing their time together was at an end. "Well, I'd ask if you wanted to come in, but I can still smell the autopsy room. Not much kills a mood quite like watching a murder victim being cut open, huh?"

Squeezing her hand, he flashed her a tired smile. "It also doesn't help that it's two a.m., and we've both probably been awake for almost twenty-four hours."

She was suddenly struck by a need to insert a sliver of optimism into their dialogue. "It's okay, though. I'm not going anywhere. Maybe we, uh…try again tomorrow night? After work?"

His expression became a full-on grin. "As long as you don't eat all that cake, I think that should work just fine."

Amelia's cheeks burned, but she ignored the sensation and feigned pensiveness. After the night's events, she'd almost forgotten Zane had brought her a belated birthday cake. "No guarantees there. I've been known to consume an entire cake for breakfast."

"I wouldn't be surprised if you actually did that."

She tried to think of a sarcastic rebuttal, but none came to her tired mind. "I love cake, but I don't think that'd be a good way to start the day. I'd probably just want to crawl back into bed after I ate it. Which, speaking of." As if to emphasize her comment, she yawned.

Even as Zane waved away the gesture like it was a pesky insect or a foul smell, he covered his mouth. "Stop it. You know that's contagious. I still have to drive home."

"You don't *have* to drive home." She offered him an exaggerated wink, though her comment was completely facetious.

With a matter-of-fact grin, he leaned over and wrapped one arm around her shoulders. "Yes, I do. There is no way in hell I could sleep while I smell like a damn cadaver."

Amelia chuckled as she returned the embrace, tucking her face into his shoulder. When she took in a breath to savor their closeness, sure enough, she noted the faint odor of rot. She couldn't be sure which of them was the source or if the smell was just stuck in her nostrils. Maybe she'd never get rid of the stench.

She tightened her arms around Zane before pulling away to face him. "I didn't say anything about sleep, but point taken. I feel like the smell of that autopsy room has been tattooed in my nose."

The corners of his gray eyes crinkled with mirth. "I know. It's in my nose too. It'll go away, though. Don't worry."

After Zane had tensed at her inadvertent comment about Russia, Amelia's heart felt ten times lighter at the easy smile on his face. She'd worried for a moment her lack of a filter had almost undone the trust they'd been able to restore over the past couple weeks. As he donned that brilliant smile of his, she realized her trepidation was unfounded.

The feeling was liberating, but so much fondness also came with a hint of foreboding. Her last relationship had ended at around the same time as her contract with the military. She'd enjoyed his company, but their time together had always felt light and airy. More like a reprieve from the treacherous world of dating than any real chance at a happily ever after. They'd ended on good terms and occasionally still exchanged a few friendly messages to catch up.

Was she ready for this? Was she ready to truly commit herself to someone?

Yes. She thought she was. Her certainty didn't make the

experience any less daunting, but the reward was worth the risk.

Tilting her head, she pressed her lips against Zane's for a kiss. As much as she wanted to lose herself in that moment, the persistent stench of death kept her firmly grounded in reality.

Before they separated, she looped her arms around his shoulders for one last, quick embrace. "Drive safe. I'll see you in the morning."

He kissed her cheek and gave her one of his showstopping smiles. "I will. Try not to eat all that cake, okay?"

She gave him a final squeeze. "No promises, but I'll do what I can."

He rested a hand over his heart. "That's all I ask."

As Amelia let herself out into the gusting wind, the cold cut through her coat like she was wearing a light sweater.

Get inside, Storm. Pronto.

Glancing up to the dark windows of her apartment, she could swear she spotted a hint of movement at the edge of the glass.

Her first inclination was toward paranoia, but she had to keep in mind she lived with a cat. The scratch marks at the bottom of the curtains hadn't magically appeared on their own.

She neared the building's front door, and an even deeper chill crept over her bones.

One way or another, she had to shake the constant anxiety that had followed her since the incident with Cynthia McAdam and Glenn Kantowski. Being scared of her own cat was no way to go through life.

No matter how hard she tried, she couldn't shake the nagging sensation that the one time she chose to ignore her paranoia would be her last.

7

As soon as Amelia stepped out of Zane's car, any semblance of warmth seemed to vanish. He had cranked up the Acura's heater, but the chill went deeper than just air temperature. Careful not to let the rush of negativity show on his face, he watched as she hurried along the sidewalk and let herself into the apartment building.

Even as the door swung closed behind her, he didn't let his neutral expression falter. He doubted she could see him as she ascended to the second floor, but he'd long since become accustomed to steeling his expression.

A light flicked to life in one of the picture windows, then went dark for a couple seconds before the glow returned. Months before he and Amelia had even met Ben Storey, they'd come up with a system to alert one another if they encountered trouble when returning home. If all was well, they would turn on the light, turn it off for a couple seconds, and then turn it back on again. Any other pattern meant the person inside was in danger.

Not that the technique had helped when a dirty Chicago police officer, Cynthia McAdam, had posed as a protective detail and kidnapped Amelia. McAdam had acted as part of Glenn Kantowski's plot to frame Amelia for the murder of Kantowski's former lover, City Councilman Ben Storey.

The obvious danger to Amelia's life might have ended when Kantowski was killed, but Zane still suspected there was more to the plot than met the eye. He hadn't mentioned as much to Amelia yet, partly because he didn't want to freak her out over his baseless paranoia and partly because she likely already held the same suspicions.

Rubbing his tired eyes, Zane freed himself from the musing and sighed. He didn't want to leave Amelia for the night, but he also didn't want her to notice him sitting in his car in front of her apartment.

In fact, he didn't know what the hell he wanted.

"A shower. I want a shower. I'm going home, get some sleep, and shake off this…whatever this is. Then tomorrow, I'm going to work and find out who in the hell slit Lars Poteracki's throat so deep you could see his spine."

With one last glance at the cheery glow of Amelia's living room window, Zane shifted the car into gear and started his short journey home.

Though the abundant illumination of the streetlamps indicated that he was the only occupant of the car, he couldn't shake the sense he wasn't alone.

He checked the rearview mirror, but there was nothing. Only the shapes of houses that had been rendered blurry by the snow whipping through the night air.

"No one's following me. Get it together, Palmer."

It was true. No person was stalking Zane. He was certain of that much. Picking out a tail had become second nature to him during his work in the CIA.

What loomed at the edges of his psyche was far more complex than a stalker.

As he rolled to a halt at a traffic light, his gaze was drawn to the expansive windows of a corner shop. The owner had closed for the night, and in the relative darkness of the store's interior, hundreds of colorful lights twinkled merrily along the branches of a tall pine tree.

A sharp gust of wind whistled past Zane's car, carrying with it a cascade of snowflakes. The sight was a beautiful holiday scene to most, but to him, the winter wonderland was a gateway for the phantom visitor who had climbed into the car as soon as Amelia had left.

Blood pounded in his ears, and the taste on his tongue turned bitter and acidic.

"Please! Let me go!" The woman's voice seemed to echo through the mostly empty Chicago street, but Zane knew only he could hear her. She was a memory. One that wouldn't stay buried.

Ten years ago, eleven days before Christmas, he'd learned the hardest lesson of his CIA career. Maybe the hardest lesson of his life, save the night his younger sister was killed.

Secondhand smoke lent a hazy, dreamlike quality to the twinkling lights of a stout Christmas tree in the corner of the room. A band of icicle lights hung above the doorway that led from the dining area to the living room. The festive décor made the wood paneling, dated fixtures, and scuffed flooring seem more like an old family home than a mobster's hideout.

Five of them had gathered around a sturdy, rectangular table to play poker to pass the time before their expected shipment was slated to arrive. Wind howled outside, and the nearby window rattled in its sill. A sliver of muddy daylight pierced through the slight opening between the dark curtains, but within another hour, the sky would be dark. In the month of December, sunlight didn't last long this far from the equator.

Here, in this godforsaken place, he wasn't Zane Palmer. He was Mischa Bukov, an up-and-coming foot soldier for the Russian mob based around the Sea of Okhotsk. Located just north of Japan and just west of the Bering Sea, their temporary outpost was a prime spot to conduct illicit deals in both Hokkaido and Alaska.

In addition to the illegal seafood business, which was far more lucrative than Zane had expected, the Okhotsk location was one stop in an elaborate, multi-national human trafficking ring. The CIA didn't often care about traffickers, but these traffickers were like a cancer that wouldn't stop growing.

No matter how much manpower Interpol and the FBI threw at the organization, no matter the number of arrests and convictions, the Russians and their allies never seemed fazed. Their influence extended to a variety of government entities around the world.

How exactly the Agency had become involved, Zane didn't know. Nevertheless, here he was. Playing poker with a group of hardened mobsters while they waited for a ship to dock.

"Mischa, you're a little blind." The dealer for this round spoke the words in Russian. Maksim Dragunov was a veteran with shrewd eyes and a bushy beard streaked with silver.

Despite Maksim's standoffish persona and constant frown, Zane had come to like the older man. As much as a covert operative for the CIA could like a Russian mobster, anyway.

Zane balanced his half-finished cigarette on the edge of a heavy glass ashtray and tossed a pair of white and black poker chips to the center of the tarnished table. Hunching back in his seat, he peeked at the cards he'd been dealt. An eight of hearts and an ace of clubs. Not great, but he'd seen worse.

The first round of betting hadn't yet made it back to Zane when the clatter of the front door drew their collective attention away from the game. A rush of frigid air billowed inside as a muscular man with a scruffy face and a fur-lined hat stepped over the threshold.

Unease tingled at the base of Zane's scalp. The man, Rurik Kopeykin, was the sergeant who'd been left in charge of their operation while the boss was busy elsewhere.

Like a pair of laser beams locked onto their target, Rurik's pale blue eyes snapped to Zane's. "Mischa. Get your coat. I need your help out on the docks."

Keeping his pulse and breathing carefully even, he stubbed out his smoke and pushed to his feet.

Maksim raised a bushy eyebrow. "Is the boat here?"

"No." Rurik hardly acknowledged his fellow sergeant. "This is for something else." His stiff posture and jerky eye movements reeked of either anxiety or ire. Zane couldn't quite tell.

Though Zane's unease had abated in the thirteen months he'd been undercover, any abnormality in the day-to-day actions of his peers still came with a lightning bolt of paranoia. The Agency had trained him well, very well, but dealing with actual, real-life undercover work was something no amount of training could ever prepare him for.

If he'd been made, he'd already be dead. He was a covert operative with the CIA, not a rookie detective infiltrating a small-time crime family in the States.

With every nerve in his body standing at attention, Zane shrugged on his coat and followed Rurik out into the gusting wind. As he passed through the doorway, he spared one last glance at the Christmas tree.

Snow crunched beneath their booted feet as fat flakes dotted their dark coats with splotches of white.

Brushing off his sleeves, Zane sped up his pace to fall in beside Rurik. "Is there a problem at the docks?"

The man's jaw clenched. "Not for much longer."

Rather than set Zane at ease, the ominous edge in Rurik's tone set off alarm bells. Not bothering to reply, Zane swept his gaze over the marina. Only a couple battered fishing vessels were moored to the dock. With another hour or two remaining before dusk, the others were likely still out on the water.

Not that any of the fishermen in this town were held to any of the multitude of national and international ordinances that regu-

lated commercial fishing. Everyone knew who really ran this industry.

Zane wondered if civilians back home would think twice about ordering crab legs if they knew the amount of blood that was spilled to keep their luxury dinners so cheap. Or if they were aware of the other trades that flourished alongside the illegal seafood business.

As Zane and Rurik descended a short line of steps to the boardwalk, Zane spotted the shape of a broad-shouldered man out near the edge of the nearest dock. At his side was a shorter, slimmer man, though in the blowing snow, Zane couldn't make out many of the either man's features.

Who in the hell were they? And why was his presence needed out here when there were no incoming boats? He'd half-expected Rurik to drag him out to help one of their people with a mechanical issue or manual labor—more grunt work for the new guy.

That didn't make sense, though. There were two other soldiers who'd been at the Okhotsk location for less time than he had.

For a beat, a pang of excitement pushed aside his mounting paranoia. Was he about to get a piece of new, actionable intel? He'd passed plenty of information over to the Agency already, but much of it was merely confirmation of what Interpol or the Feds had already learned.

He stamped out the glimmer of optimism before it could take root. He always prepared for the worst, and he didn't want to lose his edge by being lulled into a false sense of security.

The crunch of snow gave way to the thud-thud of his and Rurik's steps against the wooden dock.

As if he'd hit a tripwire, the grim realization struck Zane when they reached the halfway point. At the lessened distance, he recognized the tall man as another sergeant with a reputation even more brutal than Rurik's, but the second man...

Wasn't a man at all.

Thin shoulders shook in the sub-zero wind, and the ragged sweater hung awkwardly off the slender frame of a woman. Along with a pair of ripped jeans and stocking feet, a black bag covered her head. Zane thought he spotted a flutter of reddish blonde hair, but he wasn't quite close enough to be certain.

Zane barely managed to school his expression as he turned to Rurik. Rather than the anger and disgust that churned in his gut, he gave the other man a look of befuddlement. "Who is that? What in the hell is she doing out here?"

"Keep walking, Mischa," Rurik growled.

Even as Zane's heart sought to break free of his chest, he forced his feet to comply with the sergeant's request.

She was one of the girls they'd kept under lock and key at the edge of town—one who would soon be shipped off to parts unknown. She had to be.

The Sea of Okhotsk wasn't a place for families, particularly wives or daughters. There were a few grizzled women who operated shops in town, but they were likely more dangerous than Rurik or any of his men, Zane included. As proprietors of their respective establishments, they lived in town year-round.

The girls in the cabin north of the docks were a different story. A week ago, Zane had been tasked with bringing food and water to the captive women. He'd been aware of their presence before then, but actually seeing the group of young, malnourished girls had shaken him. The oldest of the bunch couldn't have been more than nineteen, and the youngest probably wasn't even fourteen yet.

Interpol had long suspected the Sea of Okhotsk was one of the traffickers' many stops, and Zane hoped his confirmation would lead to action. He had to believe someone would act. Why else would he be here?

During his second day tending to the cabin, he'd noticed one of the girls had sustained a cut to her forearm. He wasn't sure when the wound had been inflicted, but by the time he'd spotted it, it was deeply infected. She'd been scared to even speak to him at first, but he'd gradually coaxed an explanation out of her. He'd learned that her name was Katya, and one of Rurik's guys had *sliced her arm with a steak knife during a drunken, late-night visit for sex.*

Until then, Zane had assumed that Rurik, Maksim, and the rest of them were expected to adhere to a "hands off the merchandise" code of conduct.

Like so many other aspects of the Russian human trafficking trade, he'd been dead wrong. Apparently, Rurik had no issue allowing his most trusted colleagues to pay regular visits to the girls. When Zane had mentioned as much to Maksim, the older man had scowled deeper than Zane had ever witnessed. Spitting on the frozen ground, Maksim had offered a few choice words about his fellow sergeant and his entourage.

The following day, Zane had stuffed a handful of antibiotics, bandages, and ointment in his coat before he'd gone to check on the girls. His logic had insisted that their boss would be willing to invest the meager effort if it meant ensuring their so-called merchandise stayed intact.

He'd been so...so wrong.

Salt-tinged air whipped past Zane's face as he and Rurik stopped just short of the young woman and her burly keeper. The bulky man was Sergei Isayev, if Zane remembered right. He still wasn't sure of the girl's identity, but his stomach sank with each passing second.

Had one of the women at the cabin told Rurik or Sergei something about Zane? Were they hoping to earn favor with their captors by attempting to divert the mob's scrutiny to one of their own?

The idea was ridiculous. Those poor women were barely given enough food and water to survive, much less to allow them to come up with an elaborate plan to frame him. Not that he would blame them if they did.

Rurik's broad hand clamped around Zane's upper arm. The sergeant's soulless eyes latched onto Zane's as he pointed to Sergei and the girl. "You know her, yeah?"

In the same instant, Sergei ripped away the black bag, exposing a head full of strawberry blonde, corkscrew curls. Her bloodshot emerald-green eyes were as wide as a pair of saucers, and the dull afternoon light caught the tear streaks on her flushed cheeks.

Red-hot fury boiled in Zane's veins. If he took them by surprise, he could break Rurik's arm in three places and throw him into the sea before Sergei even brandished a weapon. The six feet that separated Zane and Sergei would bring him up close to the burly Russian. Though Sergei's bulk was almost entirely muscle, Zane had been trained by the CIA.

He could kill them both. Could throw them into the icy water and craft an elaborate lie to explain how they'd both gone overboard after a freak accident.

No matter how adept Zane had become at lying, no one would so much as entertain his tall tale. Others were undoubtedly aware of what was transpiring out here. If he fought Rurik and Sergei, he'd be as good as dead himself.

Even if he managed to get out of Russia alive, he'd have to face the wrath of the CIA. The Agency didn't have the authorization of the Russian government for this operation, and relations between the U.S. and Russia had always been strained as it was. If Zane was caught in the midst of a clandestine mission on foreign soil, he'd have to contend with repercussions on an international level.

His family would inevitably be dragged into the entire mess, including his stepfather, a high-ranking officer in the Air Force who'd been instrumental in Zane obtaining his position with the CIA.

Figuratively, his hands were tied. There was nothing he could do.

With a single gruff motion, Sergei shoved the girl to the ground. Both hands were bound behind her back, and as Zane reflexively jerked forward to catch her, Rurik's iron grasp tightened.

Zane's attention was fixed on Katya as her head bounced off the wooden dock with a nauseating thud. A cry of pain escaped her, and though Zane was grateful to hear she was still conscious, the relief was short-lived.

He caught the swift arc of Rurik's right hook in the corner of his eye. Wrenching away from the sergeant's hold with every ounce of strength he possessed, Zane barely managed to avoid the worst of the blow. Rurik's fist glanced off his chin, but the force of the punch snapped his head to the side and set him off balance.

In the heartbeat that followed, a whirlwind of doubts and what-ifs whipped through Zane's mind, his thoughts as choppy and dangerous as the grayish water of the harbor.

If he continued to fight back, he'd only piss Rurik off even more. Whatever point the man was trying to make, it was in Zane's best interest to let the man make it. He might win a fistfight, but in the long run, he'd be shooting himself in the foot.

Neither Rurik nor Sergei had brandished a firearm. They weren't here to kill him. If they were, he'd already be dead. He was on the boss's good side, and if their leader caught wind that Rurik had gone off on a wild hair and shot Zane in the head, Rurik would follow him to the grave.

When Rurik's next blow arced toward Zane, he made the conscious decision not to dodge.

Splotches of golden light exploded in Zane's left eye, pain lancing through his head like a living thing. The metallic tang of blood crept to his tongue, and the next thing he knew, he was falling.

The blare of a car horn ripped him out of the reverie with so much force that he almost jumped from his seat.

"Shit!" Dragging in a trembling breath, he raised his arm to wave a half-hearted apology to the driver behind him. "Yeah, yeah. I heard you. I'm going."

Though he hadn't moved from his seat, his voice was raspy, and his entire body felt weighted down with lead.

Tightening his grasp on the steering wheel, he fought

against the onslaught of memories threatening to overwhelm him.

Christmas.

Heavy snow.

Just like that day.

He couldn't say for sure what was wrong with him or why his brain short-circuited whenever he experienced significant snowfall in the month of December. Psychological circles might have diagnosed him with posttraumatic stress disorder, but he wouldn't know. He'd gone through plenty of counseling after the car accident that had killed his younger sister when he was a kid, but as an adult? Not so much.

Sure, therapists and doctors were bound to strict confidentiality laws, but while Zane had still been in the CIA, he hadn't trusted his secrets to remain secret.

The stigma of mental illness was bad enough for the general population, but when it came to those who served in roles like law enforcement and the military, society was often ass-backward. Ironic that those who witnessed the worst that human beings had to offer were the ones who were shamed the most for asking for help.

If a woman in the military, the CIA, or law enforcement sought counseling for her PTSD, she was viewed as overly emotional—a stereotype of her gender. And if a man in the same line of work was outed for receiving care for a mental illness, then he was a wimp. Men weren't supposed to have feelings, and women were chided for theirs.

Zane didn't *think* he'd ever bought into the sexist notion that men didn't have emotions, but why else would he be so hesitant to try to find a real solution for his own problems?

Looking up techniques to help with flashbacks and panic attacks was helpful to an extent, but at the end of the day, internet searches weren't any better than slapping a band-aid on a gunshot wound.

As he pulled into the parking garage, part of which was reserved for occupants of his apartment building, he almost considered turning around to go back to Amelia's place. He could grab clothes and be on his way in less than five minutes, and he could spend the sleepless night with her instead of tossing and turning by himself.

"No." He killed the engine for emphasis. "Let her sleep. This is your problem, not hers. She's got enough on her plate."

Zane stepped out into the drab concrete fortress. An orange hue from the streetlamps seemed to glitter off the snowflakes that whipped by the garage. Just the fleeting glimpse sent a jolt of unease through him. The radio announcer had advised tonight's precipitation was just a glimpse of what was to come over the next day and a half.

Short of pretending he had the flu and locking himself in his apartment, Zane wasn't sure how he planned to cope with the next forty-eight hours.

Stomach in knots, Zane set off for what he already knew would be a sleepless night.

8

As Amelia sat down to pull off her riding boots, her thoughts kept wandering. First to Zane, and then to the man whose autopsy they'd witnessed that night. A sliver of guilt stabbed at her brain as she pictured Lars Poteracki's pale, lifeless face. For the past half hour, she'd been so wrapped up in what was happening between her and Zane that the case had drifted to the back of her mind.

The sentiment was irrational. She couldn't focus every single second of her life on what had happened to the dead. Their stories were important, but she had to learn to commit herself to her work and still be present for the people who cared about her. Anything less was a disservice to everyone involved.

A relationship—if that's where she and Zane were headed—would be the ultimate test of her ability to balance her work and personal lives. As it stood, she had virtually no friends in the city, though Chicago *was* her hometown.

That's what happens when you date a mafia kingpin's son during high school. It's not a great way to make long-term friends.

Midway through replacing her second boot on the mat in front of the door, Amelia froze in place.

From her spot on a bench in the foyer, she scanned the visible portion of the living room and then the kitchen. A granite breakfast bar was complete with a trio of tall, cushioned chairs Amelia had purchased when she'd moved in a few weeks ago. The bar separated the living area from the kitchen, and a sleek, modern light fixture bathed the space in a warm glow.

Her knees creaked as she rose to stand—a leftover nuisance from her stint on the high school track team, plus half a season as a softball catcher. She was only thirty, but her knees had to be at least ten years older than the rest of her body.

One hand resting on the grip of the Glock holstered beneath her left arm, she started toward the living room.

Where in the hell was Hup?

Amelia's blood flowed like ice water in her veins. She'd come across the long-haired calico at the end of the first case she and Zane had worked together. The cat had belonged to the family of a young kidnapping victim, Leila Jackson. After testifying against the brutal Leóne family to put Emilio Leóne behind bars for a measly five years, Leila had accepted an offer to go into the United States Federal Witness Protection Program.

When the poor girl had realized she wouldn't be permitted to bring her beloved cat to her and her family's new home, she'd been beside herself. At sixteen, the kid had endured more hardship than most adults would ever be faced with in their entire lives. Rather than leave Leila to the heartbreaking task of handing her pet over to the humane society, Amelia had offered to take the six-year-old calico. She and the furry little lunatic had become best friends ever since.

In fact, aside from Zane, Hup was Amelia's *only* friend.

So…where the hell was she?

Concern coalesced in the pit of Amelia's stomach, and her heartrate increased as she unholstered her service weapon.

Hup had her shy moments, but for the most part, the feline required attention every second of every day. She'd even sit on the edge of the bathtub while Amelia showered, shielded from the water by only the plastic curtain.

If there was one aspect of Amelia's day she could guarantee, it was Hup trotting up to her when she returned home from work.

Glancing from the sectional to the entertainment stand and then to the dark hall at the other end of the room, Amelia gritted her teeth. No movement. No signs that any of her modest décor had been disturbed.

When she turned to the bowl of cat food at the end of the bar, she noted that the dish was full.

Granted, Amelia had fed her about an hour before she and Zane left. But the cat was a pig. At the absolute least, Amelia would have expected the food in the center of the bowl to have been eaten.

Instead, the dish was full.

Had Hup snuck out without her or Zane noticing? The cat could be sneaky when she wanted, but Amelia doubted that Hup's exodus from the apartment would have escaped both her *and* Zane's attention.

Fishing her phone from the back pocket of her jeans, Amelia unlocked the screen with her free hand. One finger hovering above the button to dial Zane's number, she took a cautious step toward the hall.

Almost immediately, an excited *meow* came from the open doorway of her bedroom, followed in short order by the barely audible patter of Hup's paws.

Of course the damn cat had been sleeping. She was a cat, wasn't she? Tilting her head back, Amelia heaved a sigh…

And almost jumped out of her skin when a man's voice cut through the relative silence. Reflexively, she snapped up both arms to level the nine-mil in the direction of the speaker.

"You mind putting that Glock down?" Alex Passarelli's request was so calm, so collected, he might as well have been asking her for the time.

"Alex?" She hardly heard her incredulous tone over the thunder of her pulse. "What in the actual *fuck* are you doing in here?" Though the query was pointed and her tone borderline hostile, she let her arm flop to the side as he emerged in the hall.

His jet-black hair was combed straight back from his forehead, and the healthy shine confirmed that he took care of his appearance. The front of his peacoat was unbuttoned, revealing a neatly pressed dress shirt tucked into a pair of tailored slacks. There wasn't much color in his attire, but he made monochrome look good.

Hands held out to his sides, he kept her fixed with an expectant stare. "Well?"

Just as she was about to ask for clarification, she noticed the weight of the Glock in her grasp. She tucked the weapon back into its holster. "Seriously, what are you doing here? And how? *How* are you in here? Christ, I already have a security system. Do I need to get a guard dog? Set up a trip wire?"

"Your neighbors might not like the trip wire very much." He lifted one shoulder. "As for the *how*? I deal with technology every day. Getting past an electronic alarm system is as easy as picking the right tool for the job."

As a squeaky meow drew her attention down to where Hup was weaving in between her ankles, curiosity burned at the back of Amelia's mind. "Did you feed my cat?"

Alex's gaze drifted to the feline. To Amelia's continued surprise, Hup turned around and trotted over to him. "She wouldn't leave me alone. She kept rubbing her face on my leg and meowing at me. I figured I couldn't be quiet and stealthy with a yowling feline attached to me, so I fed her."

"You broke into my apartment and fed my cat? Who does that? And can we circle back to the *why* again? If you wanted to sit down and have coffee, there are better ways to go about it."

He let out a derisive snort. "No, actually. There aren't. I've been trying to get ahold of you for the past month. Did you forget how to answer a phone or something?"

In the silence that followed, she studied Alex closely. Though he appeared as put together as always, his stance was tense, and shadows darkened the skin beneath his brown eyes.

Whatever could make a seasoned mafia capo nervous, she wanted no part in. Then again, *want* didn't have much bearing on her dealings with Alex and the D'Amatos. Their relationship was borne out of necessity, and nothing else.

Her brother had sold out to the powerful crime family, and the decision had led to his death. Not that Amelia thought the D'Amatos had pulled the trigger—she was confident they hadn't. Trevor's position as a Chicago homicide detective would have been invaluable.

Just because the D'Amatos were the lesser of two evils in the city didn't mean Amelia would align herself with them. She and Alex's history was just that…history. Luca Passarelli had made his stance on her presence clear nearly twelve years ago when he'd threatened her into leaving Chicago.

As her eyes bored into Alex's, she could still hear Luca's voice as if the confrontation had occurred yesterday.

With one hand clamped down around her throat, Luca had pushed up the skirt of her dress and groped between her legs with so much force he'd left bruises. He'd regaled the litany of different ways he intended to screw her if she chose to remain in Chicago. He'd gone in-depth about more than one of the depraved sex acts he intended to perform on her. His wife, Sofia Passarelli, was mafia royalty, and Luca had never been able to reenact the dirty fantasies with her.

"But the little whore who's fucking my son can take it, can't she? She can take it all." His breath had felt scalding against her skin as he'd fervently whispered each word.

She was welcome to stay in the city, he'd told her. The only stipulation was she'd be expected to cater to his every desire, all without alerting Alex or Sofia. And if she failed to hold up her end of the bargain, she'd meet a fate much worse than death.

What would she do if Luca was the one who'd decided to let himself into her apartment at two in the morning? She liked to think she wouldn't hesitate to shoot him, but she knew better than to underestimate her foe. Luca had been in the mafia world his entire life. There was no doubt he'd picked up a trick or two during all those years. Amelia was confident in her hand-to-hand combat skills, but she wasn't naïve or suicidal.

Shaking off the bad memory, she returned her attention to Alex. Fortunately, he looked nothing like his father. Where Luca's frame was broad-shouldered, almost what she'd expect from a linebacker, Alex was tall and leanly muscled.

Hell, if she saw the two of them side by side, she wouldn't even suspect they were related.

"I didn't forget how to answer a phone." Amelia was compelled by a sudden desire to finish this interaction and get Alex the hell out of her apartment. "I just haven't been keen on answering the phone when I know it's you."

He rolled his eyes. "Yeah, I noticed. Look, I'm not just here because I wanted to sit down and have a conversation about the Cubs, okay? I *need* to talk to you, and I think it's best if we don't risk being seen together."

"Instead, you'll risk being caught breaking and entering. That makes sense." She didn't mask her irritability.

Before she could add to the sarcastic observation, he snapped up a hand. "Let's just cut this shit out of our routine, okay?" He pointed to the living room. "I need to talk to you. You mind?"

She bit off a smartass retort and strode over to the couch. "You're lucky, you know that?"

His brows creased as he took a seat. "Funny, I was just thinking the opposite."

Amelia ignored the remark. "You're lucky I got home by myself. What in the hell were you going to do if my partner was with me? Hide in the closet all night?"

A sheen of ice seemed to creep over his face. "Partner, eh? What kind of partner comes home with you at two a.m. and spends the night?"

Her filter didn't kick in before she spat out a venomous response. "The kind you have sex with, Alex. You know adults are allowed to do that, right? Even if they work for the FBI?"

Pressing his lips together, he locked his scrutinizing stare on hers. In the moments that followed, a deathly silence threatened to swallow them whole. Part of Amelia wished she could vacuum up the words, but part of her wanted to throw them in Alex's face all over again.

Without averting his intent stare, he produced a couple folded pieces of paper. "Well, it's a shame you came home alone, then. I hope he's a good one."

All Amelia could do was blink at him. She'd anticipated a response filled with vitriol, but as best as she could tell, Alex's calm reply was genuine. "Yeah. He is." She pointed to the paper, desperate to change the subject away from Zane. "What's that?"

"This is what I've been trying to show you for the last month." Smoothing the sheet atop the coffee table, he didn't bother to explain further.

Amelia scooted to the edge of her seat to get a closer look at the image. The instant her gaze fell on the photo, the floor seemed to fall away from her. The thud of her heart against her ribs was so loud, she was almost certain Alex heard it. "Is that...Brian Kolthoff? And..." She had to force herself to say the second man's name. "Joseph Larson?"

"Yes. This is Kolthoff and Larson on the deck of one of Kolthoff's yachts, the *Light of Grace*. It was taken at the end of this summer, not long after you and your people raided the Kankakee County farm."

Licking her dry lips, she finally managed to pry her attention away from the picture. "Who took this?"

"A friend."

She should have known Alex wouldn't give her a straight answer. "I...I don't know what you want me to do with this. If this was taken after the Leila Jackson case, then technically, there's not much the Bureau can do with it. Legally speaking, Brian Kolthoff's an innocent man. Even if they've known each other for decades, Larson could argue that they didn't meet until this was taken."

Alex held up the second folded paper. "Guess we're lucky that's not the only one I have then, huh?"

Amelia could hardly believe her ears. "It's not the only...what?"

In response, Alex spread the second picture beside the first. The shot was another glimpse of Kolthoff and Larson, both of whom were blissfully unaware they were being watched. The two men were seated at an outdoor table, shaded by a wide umbrella as they ate. Joseph wore a shit-eating grin, clearly amused by something Kolthoff had said.

When Amelia peered closer at the print, she spotted palm trees and sparkling blue ocean behind a fence at the men's backs. "Where was this taken?"

"Key West, Florida. About two years ago, according to my source."

Annoyance fluttered at the edge of Amelia's thoughts. "Your source, huh?"

Alex's jaw tightened. "I can't tell you. Otherwise, I would've already given you a name."

Her curiosity wouldn't be quelled so easily. "So, it's someone in the D'Amato family? One of your guys?"

His expression changed so little, it could have been carved from stone. "Drop it, Amelia. This is the last time I'm going to ask. If you want my help, you'd damn well better understand it comes with a few stipulations. First and foremost, I'm not outing my people and my people's people to you. I don't care about our history. You're a Fed, and I'm… I'm not. The sooner you accept that, the better off we'll be."

"Fine." As much as she wanted to press him until he gave her some semblance of an answer, his tone left no room for debate. There were many aspects of life where she'd learned to live and let live, and the source of Alex Passarelli's information was one of them. "I'm still not quite sure what I'm supposed to do with these, though."

"Take them to your boss or your boss's boss. Give them to someone who can fire that prick. Kolthoff's been buddy-buddy with the Leónes for ages. If Larson's palling around with him, then I guarantee you he's in bed with the Leónes too. You said your office had a leak, didn't you?" He jabbed a finger at the pictures. "There's your leak!"

He was right.

The puzzle pieces all fit. Joseph had worked the Leila

Jackson case with Amelia and Zane, and he'd had access to almost the same files they had. And then, there was Carlo Enrico. Enrico had been murdered in prison before he could finger a corrupt CPD detective who'd partnered with Alton Dalessio for the kiddie porn ring they'd run out of the Kankakee County farm.

Everything made perfect sense, but that was precisely why Amelia had to watch her step. "Alex, I can't just waltz into the Special Agent in Charge's office and plunk these down on her desk."

Indignance flashed behind his eyes. "Why not?"

Amelia wanted to throw her arms in the air, but she refrained. "Corroboration. We're talking about firing a *federal agent*. This isn't like ousting someone from an office gig. The SAC's going to want a damn good reason to shitcan a guy who's been with the Bureau for more than a decade."

"And this isn't a damn good reason?"

Alex had a point, but Amelia wouldn't concede so easily. "What am I supposed to tell her? Am I just supposed to waltz in there and go 'hey, SAC Keaton, guess what my ex-boyfriend gave me? No, not that ex, this is the D'Amato capo's son I dated when I was in high school. Yeah, yeah, that's right. *That* D'Amato family. The one I never disclosed about knowing. Well, anyway, you see—'"

"I get it." Alex raised a hand to cut her off. "Can't you just tell her that someone mailed them to you? Or that you found them under your door?"

"I don't know. Maybe." She slumped down in her seat, her energy suddenly sapped. "But my gut is telling me I'm going to want to make sure I have all my bases covered. I know you said the second picture was taken two years ago, but I need a way to prove that. Otherwise, it'll be like I said earlier…" She left the thought unfinished.

Alex rubbed his temples. "Yeah, I can see your point. It's a little more complicated than I thought it would be."

"Look, if there's anything you can tell me that'll help me here." She held up a hand. "And I don't mean outing your source. If there's anything you come across that you can share with me, no matter how insignificant it seems, let me know, okay?"

Shoving to his feet, Alex nodded. "I'll keep an eye and an ear out. If Larson's been in the game for a while, there're bound to be breadcrumbs somewhere. No one stays completely hidden in this world."

Amelia ignored the ominous undertone hidden in Alex's observation. As she moved to stand, Hup bolted across the room to her food bowl. The cat's luminescent eyes followed the movement of the two humans as Amelia followed Alex to the foyer.

Hup was an awful guard cat, but Amelia didn't have time to train a puppy or even to care for a dog. She needed a better method to keep her apartment secure when she was gone.

Just before Alex reached the front door, she held up a finger. "One more thing."

Though his expression told her he was more than over this interaction, Alex turned to face her. "Okay?"

"Would you mind letting me know more about how you got past my security system? An email or something, you know? Just tell me what you'd recommend I use if I actually want to keep people out of here."

The corners of his eyes crinkled ever so slightly as he chuckled. "Yeah. I can do that. Just answer your phone next time, okay?"

She touched her hand to her forehead in a casual salute. "You got it."

As much as she wanted to put distance between herself

and the D'Amato family, Alex's revelation tonight had reminded her why she ought to reconsider before she burnt that bridge to the ground.

If she was about to wage war on Joseph Larson, she needed all the allies she could get.

9

Easing her daughter's bedroom door closed one inch at a time, Erika Brabyn tiptoed down the hall. For the second night in a row, her poor baby had woken up crying after a nightmare. The girl wasn't quite five, and Erika's heart broke a little each time Destiny told her about the frightening dreams.

As she reached the galley kitchen of the apartment she shared with her long-term boyfriend and Destiny's father, Erika let loose the shaky sigh she'd been holding. She was no stranger to sleep issues, including vivid nightmares that left her in a cold sweat.

Saying a quick prayer that the problem wasn't genetic and that her daughter was just going through regular growing pains, she pulled open a cabinet and retrieved a bowl. Three a.m. cereal was her guilty pleasure, though she could've done a lot worse for vices.

She'd *done* a lot worse, in fact.

Before Neil and Destiny, she'd been a runaway. After her first few nights on the street, she'd learned quickly she'd need a hell of a lot more than the three-hundred bucks she'd stolen from her miserable stepfather if she wanted to survive.

For a high school dropout with no employment history, finding cash was easier said than done. Under no circumstances was she willing to return home and subject herself to the suffering she'd endured the previous sixteen years.

Working the streets as a prostitute was still a damn sight better than her stepfather's nightly visits, or her mother's drunken beatings. How many times had Erika tried to tell that woman about what was happening, only to have her lash out for "trying to steal her man?"

Erika pulled a box of cereal from atop the fridge and shook off the memories. Her life now wasn't quite glamorous, but she had a roof over her head, food in the kitchen, and people who loved her. Clawing her way off the street hadn't been easy, but it had been worth the effort.

Switching off the kitchen lights, Erika scooped up a bite as she picked her way over a handful of toys to get to the couch. She considered searching for a show to watch until Neil returned home, but she was worried she'd somehow wake Destiny. And after all the rocking and reassuring she'd done to get the poor thing back to sleep, she didn't want to take the risk.

Instead, Erika ate her cereal in silence. She didn't mind the quiet. It gave her time to decompress and sort through her thoughts.

Not long after Erika had finished her cereal, the sound of the front deadbolt sent a jolt of surprise through her. Mentally cursing herself, she turned to face the door. The years of abuse she'd suffered, coupled with the time she'd spent on the streets, had left her jumpy.

She liked to joke about how she'd be frightened of her own shadow if it made noise, but the musing wasn't untrue.

As Neil emerged from the shadows of the short hall,

Erika's tension started to slip away. But when she spotted the weary expression on his face, a new type of worry took hold. "Hey, honey. What's wrong?"

Dragging a hand over his face, he sighed. "It's that obvious, huh?"

Erika felt a little crack in her heart at the worry on his scruffy face. "Something's been bugging you for the past couple nights. I can tell."

The cushion at her side sank as he dropped down to sit. "I'm sorry, babe. You know I hate to bring this shit home."

"Uh-huh." She set the bowl aside and took one of his calloused hands in hers. "If it's bothering you, then we should talk about it."

His face twitched in a slight smile. "That somethin' you learned in school?"

No matter how faint, Neil's smiles never ceased to bring warmth to Erika's heart. She lived for his and Destiny's happiness. "Kinda. Well, school and therapy. When I was still going."

As his expression started to fall, she squeezed his hand. Money was tight for their little family of three, and though the idea was counterintuitive, finances would be even more dire if Erika returned to the workforce.

She'd obtained her GED when Destiny was only nine months old, and now she was taking online courses at one of Chicago's many community colleges. Due to her life's circumstances, she'd been granted more than enough financial aid to fill her course load. In one more semester, she'd have an associate's degree in accounting.

Someday soon, once Destiny was in school during the day, Erika would find a job that paid more than the pittance she had made working in fast-food joints. When that happened, Neil would finally have breathing room to return to his career as a mechanic.

More importantly, he could quit his extra work on the streets of Washington Park. Sitting at home worrying herself sick was going to drive Erika to an early grave. She didn't understand how the wives and girlfriends of other drug dealers handled the stress. Some resorted to sampling the product their spouse sold, but that was a road Erika never wanted to travel. She'd stick with her middle of the night cereal.

One of Erika's contributions to their household was to offer Neil emotional support. "Is it about the thing you saw on Sunday night?"

He hadn't told her the whole story, but from the snippets he'd revealed so far, he'd witnessed a disturbing exchange. What counted as disturbing in his line of work, she didn't particularly want to know. But if it would help him, then she'd try.

Letting his head fall against the back of the couch, he fixed his blue eyes on the ceiling. "Yeah. It's that."

She'd come this far, and she wouldn't let him down now. "What happened?"

"After that dude…I think his name's Lars…after he hit me up, I went to find somewhere else to post up for the rest of the night. People were starting to dip outta that neighborhood, you know? So, I was just walking, minding my own business. I found this old building on Fort Street that I like hanging around. You can sit with your back to a cement wall, but you've still got two ways to split if stuff starts going bad."

Plenty of the general populace preferred to think of dealers as ignorant, gullible, strung-out, or flat-out stupid. But to survive, much less *thrive* in such a volatile industry took wits. Not only did Neil have to understand his customer base, but his situational awareness had to be top-notch. None of it was easy, and she hated he had to spend so much of his time close to danger.

More than a year ago, a ruthless trafficker, Kevin Ersfeld, had effectively waged war on the small-time dealers of Washington Park. He'd left a body count in the double-digits, and it took the city cops and the Feds to put him away.

Those had been dark days for Erika. Before then, Neil hadn't carried a firearm, just a hunting knife. When Ersfeld was at the height of his reign of terror, Erika had convinced him to set aside an extra chunk of cash to buy a handgun.

Erika touched his shoulder in a silent bid for him to continue.

Rubbing at the black scorpion tattooed at the base of his neck, Neil swallowed. "I was in that spot, and I hadn't gotten any customers yet. I saw that same cat, Lars or whatever his name was, coming down the sidewalk. I didn't think he was headed toward me, but I kept my eye on him just in case. And then…he sorta hesitated when he got to this alley. Same alley I'd just cut through to get to my spot."

Though Erika's chest was tight with worry at what he'd share next, she maintained her calm exterior and squeezed Neil's shoulder to remind him she was there for him.

Neil rested his hand on hers, but his eyes were fixed on the distance. "He started walking past the alley, and it seemed like nothing was gonna happen. Then, this other cat comes out of nowhere, and he puts a rag over Lars's mouth. It was like one of those kidnappers you see in *CSI* or some shit. Like a fucking movie! The dude must have had him in a death grip cuz Lars's flailing didn't seem to matter. Man, I was shook. I didn't know what the hell was going on. Made me think of that one cat, Ersfeld, you know?"

His muscles had tensed beneath Erika's gentle grasp. She was aware that plenty of violent confrontations occurred in Washington Park, and that Neil had seen his fair share of fights between users or even dealers. Whatever had happened to Lars had clearly affected him on a different level altogether.

She wanted to wrap both arms around him and squeeze, never letting go. For now, she settled for scooting closer to him. "What happened after that?"

His Adam's apple bobbed. "I'm not sure. I couldn't see too much. I was keeping my head down so they wouldn't see me either. After a couple minutes, I thought they were gone. But then this black car, one of those new Mazdas we were dreaming about getting someday, came around the corner and pulled into the alley. That's when…when I saw the other guy again. I'd gotten a little closer to see what the hell was happening, but he was wearing some kinda mask or something, so I couldn't see his face too well. Looked like a white guy, though. He just…dragged Lars's body and dumped him in the trunk." Wide blue eyes filled with anxiety met Erika's. "Who the hell does that shit?"

"I don't know, baby." Erika's effort to maintain a brave exterior had turned into a full-on battle. The life of a drug dealer wasn't filled with sunshine and puppies, but a blatant abduction was cause for concern. "Did you, uh…did you tell anyone about it? Was there anyone else there with you?"

His posture slumped. "No. There wasn't anyone with me. I memorized the license plate number, but…" he heaved a sigh, "what am I supposed to do with it? Call the damn cops? Tell 'em that the other night while I was slinging dope, I saw some cat get knocked out and kidnapped?"

"Of course not." Erika was certain Neil's sarcastic suggestion was a window into a moral battle he'd been waging since Sunday night. She also knew the guilt would eat away at Neil unless he found a way to deal with it. "Maybe you can make one of those anonymous tips, though? The ones where you don't have to leave your name or anything. Where you just tell them what happened?"

He wiped at his eyes as if the motion would erase the memory etched in his brain. "Yeah, maybe. Still…it feels like I should've done something."

Wrapping her arms around Neil's shoulders, Erika kissed his scruffy cheek. "You are doing something."

Though faint, a smile crept to his face. "What about you and Destiny? How were my favorite girls today?"

At the loving tone in his voice, Erika's heart was suddenly lighter.

Moments of reprieve were rare in their lives, and she'd learned to cherish each and every one.

10

Piping hot latte in hand, Zane stepped off the elevator and onto the sixth floor of the Chicago FBI field office. The building was quiet for eight-thirty in the morning, and Zane assumed the lack of foot traffic had to do with the looming blizzard.

His sleep had been fraught with nightmares. Closing his eyelids wasn't enough to blind him to Katya's fate. But by the time he'd pulled into the FBI's parking garage, he'd shaken off enough of the funk to adorn a convincing mask of normalcy. With the threat of two feet of snow hanging over the city's head, he wasn't sure how long he'd be able to maintain the façade.

His usual method of dealing with traumatic memories was to cordon himself off at home, away from the prying eyes of the world. But with Lars Poteracki's violent murder, he couldn't fall back on the unhealthy routine. Lars could no longer speak for himself, and someone had to help tell his story. Preferably in a courtroom, and with a guilty verdict for whatever sick bastard had carved a bible verse into Lars's chest and slit his throat clean through to the spine.

Zane softly cursed at the mental imagery. In an effort to chase away the bitter taste on his tongue, he took a sip of the peppermint mocha. The coffee was still far too hot for human consumption, but after fighting the urge to spit out the scalding concoction along with a slew of four-letter words, he returned his focus to the quiet office.

His footsteps were muffled against the drab gray carpet as he approached the zigzagging rows of cubicles belonging to the Organized Crime Division. Though he was usually at the office before Amelia, he'd received a text from her before he'd left his apartment. According to the message, she'd wanted to get a head start on Lars's case before the lake-effect snow rolled into town.

As Zane neared his and Amelia's desks, her head snapped up from where she'd been carefully studying the glowing screen of her laptop.

Despite his mental turmoil, the sight of those familiar, forest green eyes made his spirits a little lighter. "Morning, Storm. Find anything while I was on my way in?" He and Amelia were close, obviously, but he made a point to stick to some level of professionalism whenever they were in the office.

She pushed away from her desk and gestured to the screen. "Some good news on that piece of flesh found in Lars's teeth. Preliminary analysis shows it's human."

The word sent a slight shockwave through Zane's brain. "Human? Poteracki had *human* flesh between his teeth?"

Though slight, a glimmer of amusement sparkled in Amelia's eyes. "Yep. Dr. Francis noted it's something he's seen before in victims of violent murder. It's out of desperation. Poteracki must have bitten his assailant pretty hard when they were fighting."

A surge of anticipation pushed the remaining cobwebs of fatigue and sadness from Zane's mind. "Then that means the killer has to have a nasty bite mark somewhere on his body. I've heard of cases that've been broken wide open using dental records and bite mark wounds. It might not be enough for a conviction by itself, but it can definitely help steer us in the right direction. Was there anything else?"

"Yep. A big something else." She tapped the autopsy report. "Remember how Dr. Francis found very little livor mortis? Apparently, Lars was missing the majority of his blood volume. Dr. Francis confirmed that COD was from the head wound."

The puzzle pieces snapped together quickly in Zane's mind. "So, Lars's heart wouldn't have been beating when his throat was cut, so the blood loss wouldn't have come from that."

Amelia shot him a *bingo* wink. "Plus, there wasn't any sign of blood in Lars's lungs, which would have been present if he'd aspirated from the neck wound."

Dracula.

Zane mentally shoved the word away.

"Did the doc have any idea of where the blood could have gone?"

Amelia shrugged. "Nope. He doesn't believe being in the water would have caused the loss, especially since the lividity wasn't present." She wrinkled her nose. "Looks like it's our job to figure out what happened to it."

He clapped his hands together. "Fantastic. Just please don't tell me we'll have to interview anyone from the local vampire community."

He couldn't believe he'd really just said those words.

Amelia showed him all her teeth, then snapped them together a few times. "I'll save you from them, no worries."

Zane was more than ready for a change of subject. "What else is in the report?"

"They've put a rush on the DNA analysis from the skin in Poteracki's teeth, but we'll have to wait a day or two for it."

Modern technology made DNA testing faster than ever, but the process still required time. Fortunately, the FBI was equipped with a lab that was second to none.

Zane shrugged off his jacket, set the latte beside his keyboard, and rolled his office chair over to Amelia. Their seats were back-to-back, making it easy for them to collaborate while working a case. "Anything else in the write-up?"

Appearing thoughtful, she twirled a pen in the fingers of one hand. "Not really. They found a small baggie of heroin in Lars's pocket, but so far, all tox screens have come back negative. No indication of opiates in his system at all. He was as sober as a judge when he died."

"What are we thinking, then?" Already, Zane was glad to be back in some semblance of a normal routine.

Amelia lifted a shoulder and let it fall. "Could've been his first time using in a while. Maybe he went back to his old stomping ground, and someone fingered him for an informant."

"Or maybe he was jumped for some other reason. Could've been a territorial dispute. One of his old dealer friends thought he was encroaching on their turf and decided to shoot first and ask questions later, figuratively speaking. A lot of dealers don't have an issue with sampling their own product. Heroin might not make a person violent and unpredictable, but there are plenty of drugs that *do*."

Tapping the pen on her chin, Amelia leaned back in her chair. "Maybe, yeah. Meth can induce psychosis, even when the user isn't high. Could've been someone in the throes of a psychotic break, which would explain the violence and the… abnormality of the bible verse carved on his chest."

"It wouldn't be the first time religion has been part of a break from reality." Zane drummed his fingers against the desk. "Did you have time to get to anything else? I don't think either of us have had a chance to go over that case Poteracki helped with at the beginning of the year."

Amelia gave her wireless mouse a couple clicks, and a new page appeared on the laptop. "That's just what I was looking through now, actually. You got here right in time."

Zane didn't *feel* like he'd arrived at the office on time for anything. He stifled a yawn with the back of one hand, but before he could even start to respond to Amelia's comment, he caught sight of a familiar man in his periphery.

As Joseph Larson strode down the row of desks on the other side of the partition, the man's icy blue eyes snapped to Zane and Amelia.

The glance lasted only for a beat, but there was more than enough venom in that look to kill a dozen full-grown men. Zane didn't like to credit the creepy, wannabe rapist with much, but the guy sure could throw shade. Not to mention the dark cloud of discomfort and anxiety that seemed to follow him around like a lost puppy.

Though Zane was sure Amelia had noticed Larson as well, she gave no indication the creep's fleeting presence had registered with her.

Good. Ignoring him when we're in the office takes away all his power.

Well, until Spencer Corsaw officially stepped down from his role as Organized Crime's Supervisory Special Agent. Then Larson would no doubt throw his hat in the ring for the position. God help them if he succeeded in landing the spot.

Even if Zane hadn't known what Joseph did—and what he'd *tried* to do—to Amelia, the man wasn't leadership material. Speaking objectively, the Organized Crime Division would suffer with Larson at the helm.

Amelia's voice drew Zane back to her and the laptop.

"Lucky for us, Agent Donahue is an early bird. I talked to her a little bit before you got here. She's out in Portland right now, but she'll be flying back for the funeral in a couple days."

The west coast was two hours behind Chicago's time zone, and Zane wondered if he was the only one who'd slept in that day. "What did she have to say about the Ersfeld case that Poteracki helped with?"

Shifting her gaze back to the computer, Amelia's fingers flew over the keyboard. "She sent me everything she had on it so I wouldn't have to dig for anything. I asked her if she'd ever suspected, off the record, that Ersfeld might've been connected to something bigger, something like, say, the Leóne family."

Most information in an investigation made its way into the case files, but occasionally, the agent working the crime would have a hunch that didn't make its way into the official documentation. "What did she say? We didn't see anything that tied him to that family when we did our research last night. It'd be nice to hear confirmation from the agent who worked with Poteracki on the Ersfeld case. What did her gut say about it?"

"She didn't have any strong gut feeling one way or the other. For the most part, she thought Ersfeld was operating as a lone wolf. He wasn't the type who played well with others." Amelia maximized a new window on the laptop and scooted to the side to make room for Zane. "Ersfeld was a dealer and a trafficker, and his primary base of operations was Washington Park. There's a lot of information here, but it basically boils down to Ersfeld thinking he was Tony Montana from *Scarface*. He pushed all kinds of drugs, but his personal substance of choice was meth."

Zane's expression soured. "Just in case he wasn't unpredictable enough."

Amelia dipped her chin. "Exactly. According to all the statements I've read so far, Ersfeld was trying to take over Washington Park. He pushed drugs for the Leónes and for one of the cartels, but he wasn't closely affiliated with either of them. Not enough for the Leónes to take notice when he was arrested or even when he went to trial. Donahue said she thought it was because they knew Ersfeld was a loose cannon, so they kept him at arm's length."

"Then Donahue basically confirmed there's a low likelihood Poteracki was a Leóne casualty?"

Twisting a piece of hair between her thumb and forefinger, Amelia sighed. "Yeah. Good news and bad, honestly. I'd rather not have to deal with the Leónes, but it would've been nice to find some way to nail them after we lost that RICO case."

Zane couldn't agree with her more. For the time being, he'd take their distance from the Leónes as a win. "Then we've got Poteracki's only known feud with Kevin Ersfeld, who's been dead for nine months. Does Ersfeld have any family? Friends?"

Amelia clicked to a new web page. "A sister who lives in Canada with her wife and their three kids, and a father who's in a nursing home in that same area. Donahue said the sister and Ersfeld more or less hated one another. Ersfeld didn't approve of her 'lifestyle,' and she wasn't a fan of the fact her brother was a lunatic."

Zane fought the urge to roll his eyes. "You have to love some people's hypocrisy. Guess that rules out the avenging family theory, then. How about Poteracki's family? Anyone there who might've pissed off the wrong people?"

"That's what I was reading up on before I started going through the Ersfeld case, actually. I was trying to get a picture of what Poteracki's life was like before he died. Like I said, the tox screen didn't find any opiates in his system, but he had a baggie of heroin in his pocket."

A pang of sadness struck Zane as he thought about what Lars Poteracki's final hours must have been like. "Is the lab running a hair follicle test? That'll tell us if he'd used recently and if the substance had just metabolized from his bloodstream."

Amelia flipped through her tablet. "They did. It's a test that's usually done in under twenty-four hours, but they pushed it through with the rest of the analyses. Follicle tests can date back as far as ninety days, and according to our lab, Poteracki was clean for all of it. As far as Donahue knew, Poteracki had been clean since before he'd gotten out of prison two years ago."

"Then why did he have drugs in his pocket if he wasn't using again? Were the drugs planted? Was he going to relapse? Did something happen to trigger a relapse?" A sliver of guilt stabbed at Zane's heart, almost as if speculating on the reason for Poteracki's decision to buy heroin was speaking ill of the dead.

Neither Zane nor Amelia could understand what went through an addict's mind when they used after a period of sobriety, and Zane didn't feel he should speak on Poteracki's behalf.

However, his job required him to do just that.

The same hint of melancholy had manifested in Amelia. Drug abuse hit far closer to home for her than it did for Zane. Amelia's younger sister, Lainey, was an addict who'd recently been arrested for trying to smuggle heroin on a flight from Milwaukee to Chicago.

A flight she'd supposedly boarded with the intent to attend rehab and get clean.

As soon as the sadness had appeared on Amelia's face, it was replaced with the determined professionalism Zane had become used to seeing when they were at the FBI office or in the field. The job got to almost everyone, but they did their best to push through in the pursuit of justice.

The pen was back in Amelia's hand, her face turning thoughtful. "Something did happen. Poteracki's twin sister, Viola Poteracki, was killed in a head-on collision a little more than a week ago. Tox screen showed the other driver's blood-alcohol level was three times the legal limit. Viola was killed instantly, and the other driver died in the ICU a few hours later."

"That might very well explain the relapse. But his death? Are you theorizing this could be some weird form of revenge? Like the drunk driver's family blamed Viola for the accident for some reason?" The theory sounded farfetched even in Zane's head, and aloud, it was even more ridiculous. Then again, people suffering from grief didn't always think rationally.

Amelia pressed her lips together. "We'll have to keep it in mind, but my gut says no. I don't think the heroin in Poteracki's pocket was a coincidence. There's got to be some connection there."

Zane tapped an index finger against the armrest of his chair. "I don't think it's a coincidence, either. Let's put a pin in it for a second, though. While we're here, anyway. Did Donahue say anything about Poteracki's prison term? Did he make enemies on the inside?"

Amelia shook her head. "Not that she knew of. There's nothing in her notes about anything like that, either. Poteracki stopped using about six months before he was released. He hadn't exactly been a problem beforehand, but in that half-year, he was a model prisoner. They released him early for good behavior."

Silently, Zane lifted an eyebrow for her to continue. He

might not have been privy to specifics, but he knew Poteracki's story didn't end there.

Drumming the cap of the pen against her open palm, Amelia glanced back to the screen. "Poteracki was clean for about six months before his release, but he went right back to dealing when he got out. From what Poteracki told Donahue, he'd tried to get a job at a few places. He'd been an industrial contractor before he went to prison but couldn't get back into the industry with a felony on his record."

There were plenty of valid reasons an employer would reject a prospective worker for their criminal history, but Zane knew all too well that the system could be unjust for reformed men and women like Lars Poteracki.

Zane heaved a sigh. "A tale as old as time. A prisoner's released and can't find work on the outside, so they recidivate."

"Which is exactly what happened to Poteracki." Amelia gestured back to the laptop. "About six months after he was released, he was popped by Agent Donahue during an undercover operation."

Recollection struck Zane. Agent Donahue had posed as a low-level drug dealer and had gradually worked her way into an Irish drug smuggling ring. "I remember hearing about that."

"Donahue was trying to track down Ersfeld when she came across Poteracki, so Poteracki agreed to work with her as an informant. He had a web of contacts in Washington Park, and none of them liked Ersfeld. Poteracki wanted a way out of the life, and everyone wanted Ersfeld gone. Honestly, it sounds like it was a win all around."

More importantly, it meant the dead informant didn't appear to have left behind any obvious bad blood. Zane and Amelia were going to have to dig deeper if they wanted to find who'd harbored such a substantial grudge. Though the possibility remained that Poteracki had been the victim of a random killing, statistically speaking, it was the least likely scenario. In the majority of homicides, the victim and perpetrator knew one another.

After a moment of quiet, Zane returned his gaze to Amelia. "We've got three main theories. One, someone related to the drunk driver who killed Viola Poteracki had a misguided vendetta with Lars. Two, one of Ersfeld's old pals wanted Poteracki dead. And three…"

Zane trailed off, and Amelia took her cue to finish the sentence. "He got in a fight with the dealer he bought the heroin from. But then why wouldn't the dealer take the baggie back? They'd have to know there's a possibility it can be traced back to them."

Zane held out his hands in a gesture of helplessness. "Only one way to find out. Sounds like we need to head to Washington Park before all this snow buries us in the office for the rest of our lives."

Amelia reached for her handbag. "Good point. We should get started sooner rather than later. We can swing by Poteracki's apartment and see if the CSU found anything there overnight."

Mentally crossing his fingers, Zane followed Amelia's lead and stood.

God, he hoped they didn't have another Kevin Ersfeld on their hands.

11

Being back in Washington Park, so close to where I'd knocked Lars Poteracki unconscious and loaded him into the trunk of my car, was just short of exhilarating. The area was rife with sinners—drug dealers, users, prostitutes, pimps—and I had to remind myself my mission wasn't to cleanse every single one of them. I only had to take on a chosen few for my work.

For today, I'd taken shelter in a condemned rowhouse to conduct my surveillance. Clusters of leaves and debris had collected in corners and along the baseboards of the graffitied walls. On my way inside, I'd spotted a handful of discarded syringes on the rotting kitchen counter. Based on the lack of dust and grime coating the needles, they had been left here recently.

Though most of the windows in the place were broken, I peered through the gap between boards that covered one that had been left intact.

In any other part of the city, the sight of a grown man crouched in an abandoned house, staring out over an intersection, would have piqued suspicion. But in this particular section of Washington Park, the unusual was the norm. Just because no one else was in the house with me didn't mean squatters wouldn't show up later in the day, after they'd completed their scores.

From my vantage point through the boarded-over window, I made note of the steel gray sky. A mass of darker clouds loomed on the horizon, reminding me the city would soon be coated in a thick, white blanket. Much of Chicago's operations would come to a standstill after the two feet of snow fell, but there was one industry that never stopped, that never so much as slowed.

The sinners.

The dealers, users, and prostitutes.

While the rest of civilized society would hole up in their homes, the deviants would still wander the streets.

And so would I. Not even ten feet of snow would stop me from my mission.

The distant figures of an approaching man and woman drew me back to the present. Even from almost a block away, I could tell right away the pair wasn't the typical riffraff.

A mixture of emotions jolted through me. Could it be?

The small cluster of people who'd been mingling around the lot across from my post had also taken note of the newcomers' arrival. Several men and women split off from the group—presumably drug dealers looking to take cover in case the man and woman were cops. The sinners were like cockroaches when a light was turned on.

As for the man and woman, I peered closer and knew my instincts were right. They almost certainly *were* cops. Maybe I was just paranoid, but I could think of no valid reason a well-dressed couple would be walking the streets of a neighborhood like this one.

I couldn't be sure how, but Lars Poteracki's death must have led them back to Washington Park. To the same neighborhood where Lars had bought his filthy drugs, and the same neighborhood where I intended—no, was required—to acquire my next sacrifice.

Making sure to keep my surroundings in mind, I hunched down a little lower and followed the couple's approach. The pair paused at the streetlight catty-corner to my location. I half-expected the remaining deviants to disperse, but the foolish creatures held their ground.

When the man and woman finally crossed over to the men who remained smoking their cigarettes, recognition dawned on me.

I'd seen this duo before. Last night, in the news video. They were the well-dressed pair I'd studied so closely.

The Feds.

Scowling, I ignored the thought. Federal Bureau of Investigation or not, my work would continue. I was sure if the two agents knew what I was truly doing, they'd support my endeavor.

How could they argue with me? I was trying to make their jobs *easier*.

Unless they're dirty.

Surely, the Lord wouldn't permit such vermin to walk among those whose duty it was to protect the innocent. He wouldn't allow anyone from stopping me from fulfilling His mission.

No, I couldn't concern myself with that right now. I clenched my hands into fists. My mind was wandering again, and I needed to focus.

The posture of the two smokers had gone rigid, but as far as I could tell, their faces were calm. To my disdain, the Feds had positioned themselves with their backs to me, so I couldn't determine if they had flashed badges or not.

Holding my breath as I strained my hearing to its limits, I

rested my cheek against one of the splintery boards. My ear touched the cold glass, and goose bumps rose on my arms.

I could hear them, but I couldn't make out a single word. If this window was broken like the rest, I might have caught a word here or there. For the most part, the whine of the wind drowned out their faint voices.

A thought occurred to me, and a board groaned in protest as I shifted my weight to glance to the back entrance of the dilapidated house.

If I went outside, then perhaps the nosy agents would come talk to me next.

No. Too risky.

I nodded to myself. Even to the untrained eye, I stuck out in this neighborhood. I kept my body in prime physical condition, and I maintained a strict hygiene regimen. There was no way the obvious difference between my appearance and that of a squatter or user would go unnoticed by the Feds.

Besides, my curiosity took a back seat to the real reason I'd come to Washington Park today.

I had my next target, and now it was only a matter of time before he became part of my grand plan.

12

Zane shot Amelia a knowing glance as the taller of the two men took off in the direction of a run-down apartment building. They'd been in Washington Park for all of ten minutes, and already, they'd effectively been told to piss off and mind their own business. Zane didn't want to be pessimistic, but their trip was off to an inauspicious start.

Old buildings in varying stages of disrepair lined each side of the street. He and Amelia stood at the edge of a vacant lot—or it would be vacant if it weren't for the shell of a basement leftover from when a house was demolished. Based on the debris and graffiti that had accumulated in the veritable pit, the old home had been knocked down years ago.

The shell was reminiscent of the rest of the neighborhood, at least as far as Zane could see. He and Amelia had parked a few blocks away in hopes that approaching on foot would be less conspicuous. They'd both changed into street clothes—t-shirts and jeans under their coats—but they were well aware the transformation wasn't enough for them to blend in with the folks who called the area home.

Amelia blew a raspberry, returning his focus to her. "The

normal routine isn't working so well tonight. Nobody's talking."

Zane held up his hands in resignation. They'd changed clothes, but people from the streets could apparently smell the law on them from several blocks away.

"Something's got them spooked, for sure."

Amelia cursed and tightened her gray trench coat. "Want to split up?"

Before they'd taken the L to Washington Park, Zane and Amelia had scoped out the area around Poteracki's apartment. Though there were a handful of locations that could potentially turn shady once the sun went down, they hadn't spotted any activity suspicious enough to warrant immediate investigation. Poteracki's access card for the L indicated he'd left his place the night of his death but hadn't revealed his destination.

Zane waved a hand in the direction perpendicular to where the two smokers had gone. He and Amelia had a lot of ground to cover and not a lot of time to cover it. "Yeah, divide and conquer, that's a good idea. I'll take this direction and see if I can find anyone who looks…friendly."

A smile twitched on Amelia's lips. "All right. I'll go the other way. Past that condemned house. Which, by the way." She narrowed her eyes at the decrepit home. "I swear I saw something in one of those windows. There's probably a squatter in there."

As he followed her gaze, Zane searched each window for any sign of activity. "People tend to forget squatters exist, including when they're committing a crime. It could be a good place to start if there's anyone there."

"I was thinking the same thing." She jammed both hands into the pockets of her knee-length trench. "Well, good luck, I guess."

Zane chuckled at her dry tone. "Call me if you need

anything. You've got my spare key, so we can meet back at the car when we're done."

Tapping one hand to her forehead in a casual salute, Amelia set off in the direction of the two-story home and the squatter that may or may not inhabit the place.

Like they had so often lately, Zane's good spirits seemed to walk away right alongside Amelia. The cold hand of anxiety wrapped its fingers around his heart, leaving his mouth dry and his palms clammy.

This snow needs to just hurry up and happen. The sooner the holidays are done and over, the sooner I can bury all this shit again.

He doubted burying the memories of Katya was the proper method to cope with symptoms of posttraumatic stress disorder, but he still hadn't figured out another approach. He'd briefly considered meeting with one of the numerous Agency psychologists to find some relief. But his self-loathing for his own actions made revealing the story to a therapist out of the question.

Without professional counseling, Zane had turned to the internet in search of self-help measures to help combat the memories that haunted him. Clenching and unclenching his hands, he took in a deep breath of frosty air and slowly counted to five. As he exhaled, he forced his focus back to the apartment buildings and houses that lined the street. The skeletal branches of trees scraped against roofs comprised of patchwork shingles, as well as the peeling paint that remained on splintering siding.

Not all the residences were condemned, but the places where people lived weren't in much better shape than those the city had deemed unfit for human occupancy.

He walked for a few more blocks until he spotted a trio of young women stationed at the edge of a corner lot. The three-story apartment building cast a shadow over the side of the street where Zane walked, but the girls were just outside the gloom. He figured the three were prostitutes, and he hoped their pimp wasn't nearby.

Before the women noticed Zane, a silver sedan pulled to a stop at the curb. One of the three, a petite redhead, approached the vehicle, her hips swaying side to side.

Working girls working it hard.

As the redhead sauntered around to let herself in the passenger's side of the car, the taller of the two remaining women turned to face him.

A gust of winter wind rustled the strawberry blonde curls that framed her fair face. She couldn't have been much older than seventeen or eighteen.

Katya.

Panic and dread surged through Zane's veins like a microscopic parasite eager to devour him from the inside out.

Though he wanted nothing more than to turn on his heel and sprint back to his car, to find a hole to live in until the holidays passed, he forced one foot in front of the other. The task was Herculean, like he was plodding through quicksand in an Amazonian jungle.

His stomach lurched.

Christ, he needed to get ahold of himself. There was a reason he was here, and it didn't have a damn thing to do with the Sea of Okhotsk or the Russian mob or the damn CIA.

Grounding, isn't that what Amelia was talking about a few weeks ago? Something she said her sister-in-law told her about, or she told her sister-in-law about, one of the two.

Five things you can see. The run-down apartment building, the silver sedan pulling away from the curb, the four-way stop sign, the dead grass, trees.

Four things you can feel. He stuffed one hand in his pocket and brushed his finger against the silky material lining his coat. He paid attention to the way his feet hit the sidewalk. As he touched his unshaven cheek and brushed his fingers against the material of his dark wash jeans, he struggled to recall the next step.

Was it three things he could taste? No, that was ridiculous. Unless he was eating a full meal or trail mix, he was unlikely to pinpoint more than one flavor at a time.

Not that it mattered. He hadn't stopped walking, and he realized with a start he was only fifteen or twenty feet away from the two working girls. At the lessened distance, he noted the bright green hue of the blonde's eyes.

Emerald, like Katya's.

Get up, Mischa.

He heard Rurik's voice as clearly as the day the Russian had laid him out on the dock at Okhotsk.

With a paranoid glance over his shoulder, as if Rurik's ghost might have traveled all the way from Russia just to haunt him, Zane fought against a renewed bout of nausea.

Three things you can hear, *not taste.* He clung to the sudden remembrance like a life raft. The ever-present drone of Chicago's traffic filled the air, along with the fading hum of the silver sedan's engine, and a barking dog in the distance.

Swallowing hard against the bile that stung the back of his throat, Zane kept his expression carefully neutral as he neared the girls.

Two things you can smell. He caught a faint whiff of the product he used to style his hair, as well as the stale scent of exhaust that always seemed to permeate Chicago's air.

One *thing you can taste. Not three.* Though it had almost been overpowered by the threat of stomach acid climbing up his throat, traces of the peppermint mocha latte were still on his tongue.

"You need something, Mister?" The girl with the

corkscrew curls had posed the question, and to Zane's relief, she sounded nothing like Katya.

His heart still thundered against his ribs, but the desperate grounding effort seemed to have worked. "Yes, actually."

The women exchanged puzzled glances.

Zane ignored how his statement came across, considering the fact he was speaking to two prostitutes. "I'm not here for sex."

With an indignant huff, the second girl, a young woman who was likely in her early to mid-twenties, crossed her arms. "What the hell are you here for, then? You a cop?"

In small increments, Zane's composure had begun to return. He offered the dark-haired girl a slight smile as he produced his badge. "Something like that. I'm Special Agent Zane Palmer with the Federal Bureau of Investigation."

Both girls' eyes went wide, shock clearly written on their faces as they stared at his identification.

Licking her lips, the blonde slowly shook her head. "Look, mister…Agent, I don't know nothin' about whatever the hell you're here for. We ain't doing anything wrong. We're just minding our business. This place is condemned." She waved at the decrepit apartment building. "Nothing wrong with standing out here talking to my friend. We're not loitering or anything."

The second woman nodded vehemently. "That's right. Whatever you're lookin' for, you're lookin' in the wrong place."

Their obstinance, although commonplace among witnesses, helped Zane tether himself to the present.

Feigning a resigned sigh, he tucked his badge back into his coat. "Listen, ladies. You saw my badge, and you know I'm not a city cop. I'm not some detective from Vice who's here to arrest you or some shit, okay? Let's just establish that right now. I'm not here for you, or for your pimp, or for any of his friends."

The blonde worried at her lower lip, her knuckles turning white where she grasped the strap of her handbag. "What *do* you want, then?"

Pulling up the photo from Lars Poteracki's state ID card, he held the device out to the brunette. He hoped to keep his attention off the young woman who reminded him so much of Katya. "I'm looking for any information about this guy. I just want to know if you've seen him around here lately, or if you know anything about whether or not he might've been here a couple nights ago."

The girl's jaw clenched. "What's in it for me?"

Zane would've been surprised if she'd offered any information for free. He quickly pocketed the phone and pulled out his wallet to show the small stack of cash he'd pulled from an ATM before he and Amelia had left for Washington Park.

Both women perked up at the sight, as he'd hoped.

He held his hands out to his sides. "Any information you can give me, I'll pay you for it. All I ask is that you look at this person's picture, okay?"

Dark Hair's expression soured. "Why should we believe you?"

There were a couple different approaches Zane could use to try to get the girls to talk to him, but so far, he'd gathered the pair were out on the street just trying to survive. Both women were young, and neither appeared to be a user. Which, in his experience, likely meant they were less jaded than some of the more experienced working girls.

"Fair point." He plucked a handful of twenties from the wallet. "You've got to give respect to earn it, right? I suppose the same goes for trust."

When the girls exchanged glances this time, some of the

tension finally left their postures. Zane gave them each sixty dollars before he pulled out his phone. As he handed the device to the blonde, Dark Hair scooted closer to peer over her friend's shoulder.

A crease formed between Dark Hair's sculpted brows. Her chocolate brown eyes shifted back to Zane as she shook her head. "I don't recognize him. I haven't been around this area much lately, though. Who is he? Are you looking for him or something?"

Based on her even expression and matching body language, she was telling the truth. "His name is Lars Poteracki. I'm not looking for him. He's dead."

For a beat, the blonde's face contorted with panic. "Dead? What do you mean? Like a heart attack or…?"

"Murdered. Brutally." Almost reluctantly, Zane pinned her with an expectant stare. "You recognized him, didn't you?"

Any remaining color drained from the blonde's cheeks. "Kinda. I mean, I don't know his name or anything. But I saw him a couple nights ago."

Anticipation flooded Zane, and he almost forgot about her resemblance to Katya. "Do you remember which night? It's important."

"Uh, yeah. Yeah." She looked to Dark Hair, who nodded for her to continue. "It was, uh…Sunday. Sunday night, pretty late. I'm not really sure what time it was exactly, but close to midnight."

"Did he say anything to you? Did you interact with him at all?" Zane hoped that Lars wasn't one of the creeps who scoped out Washington Park for underage prostitutes.

"No." She closed one hand around the strap of her purse. "He didn't talk to me or anything. I was a few blocks north of here." She gestured behind herself. "And that guy, the one in your picture, he hit up some dealer across the street."

Now they were getting somewhere. "Do you know the dealer? Does he have a name?"

Pressing her lips together, she shook her head. "I don't know his real name. Don't think anyone does. He goes by Scorpion because of a tat on his neck. But he's not…he wouldn't *kill* anyone. No one's got a beef with Scorpion, you know? He just minds his business, doesn't step on anyone's toes. At least that's what the other girls around here say about him."

Zane held up a hand. "I'm not saying I think he killed anyone, but he might be a witness, even if he doesn't know it. Do you know what he looks like?"

Though Zane wasn't entirely sure he believed his own rationalization, the comment seemed to set the girls at ease. If they thought Poteracki's killer was an outsider, they'd be more likely to give any information they had. Only when the party in question was part of the group did loyalty impact a person's decision to tell the truth.

The blonde tugged at the collar of her thin peacoat. "Um, yeah, a little. He's young, probably in his twenties. He's white and has dark hair, but he's usually wearing a ballcap. Usually wears a hoodie and a leather jacket, and he's not that tall, but he's not real short, either. I've never been up close to him, so I'm not sure about much else."

As Zane asked a few more questions and then thanked the two girls for their cooperation, he mentally crossed his fingers that no suspicious characters had witnessed their interaction with an FBI agent. The immediate area appeared to be abandoned, but he knew better than most that prying eyes could hide in the most unexpected places.

13

Stretching both arms above her head, Amelia turned her gaze to the wall-spanning window of the little conference room. Fat snowflakes drifted lazily toward the earth, the rate of snowfall having increased since she and Zane returned to the field office only a half hour earlier. Then again, with lake-effect snow, a shower could become a blizzard in a matter of minutes.

Though the FBI office wasn't much busier than it had been when they'd left for Washington Park, Amelia had taken it upon herself to commandeer a room where she and Zane could conduct their research in peace. Plus, when it came to sharing their discoveries, a projector made life much easier.

Not like anyone's here today that would even notice we're in this room. Everyone's working from home and getting ready for fifteen feet of snow.

Adjusting her striped cardigan, Amelia glanced to the door. The blinds were pulled shut, blocking her view of the desks that belonged to Organized Crime.

After contacting the city transit authority to get ahold of security camera footage from the L on the night Lars Poteracki was killed, Zane had offered to procure coffee for the two of them. Hopefully, they wouldn't be at the office much longer. The last place Amelia wanted to be stuck was in the same building as Joseph Larson.

Well, provided the man was still here. She hadn't caught a glimpse of him since that morning.

She brushed off the thoughts like she was getting rid of a pesky fly. Her and Zane's fieldwork—the fruitless trip to Poteracki's apartment, the visit to Washington Park, and the time they'd spent retracing Poteracki's most likely route from the L to the location he was spotted interacting with the dealer called Scorpion—might have been done for the day, but there was still plenty of tedious research ahead of them.

Since Zane had taken over the hunt for the security footage from the L, Amelia had decided to run the specifics of Poteracki's murder through ViCAP. The Violent Crime Apprehension Program was a database available to law enforcement personnel around the country.

Investigators could input the details of various violent crimes, and then the information was available for LEOs around the country to use as a search tool. Considering the specifics of Poteracki's murder, such as the bible verse carved on his chest, Amelia wondered if they'd be able to find other homicides with the same modus operandi.

As blinds clattered against glass, Amelia's attention shot to the door. Paper cup in each hand, Zane shouldered open the door and shot her one of his patented grins. "Hey, I got you the salted caramel mocha you asked for. Do you know how many calories are in these things? I mean, I do, but I forget sometimes."

Rolling her eyes in feigned exasperation, Amelia accepted the drink from his outstretched hand. "Do I look like I care how many calories are in them? Besides, you're not really in a place to judge my diet. I saw that peppermint mocha you were drinking earlier. These drinks sometimes are the only thing keeping me going. They're packed full of caffeine, and they're delicious. It's probably better for you than an energy drink anyway."

Chuckling, he pulled out a chair and dropped to sit. "Fair point. Honestly, I don't really care how many calories are in them." To prove his point, he took a long sip. "Hey, I got an email back from the transit authority about the video from the L. We know when Poteracki got on, and we should be able to follow him until his stop. Which we're assuming is Washington Park, but this'll confirm."

Amelia grabbed a remote and turned on the projector. "This is a good start. I had just started to run the crime scene details through ViCAP to see if anything turns up, but let's take a look at the security cameras first."

"I'll email the link to you." Phone in hand, one of Zane's eyebrows arched. "Are we thinking this might be a serial killer?"

The idea had crossed Amelia's mind, but she wasn't entirely sold on the theory just yet. "It's possible, but it could just as easily be a hitman. And if it's a hitman with this specific MO, ViCAP will tell us if he's been around for a while. We can also check to see if he's been active in another part of the country."

Zane sipped his drink. "Serial killers are just…something else, you know? After Cedarwood and Dan Gifford, you'd think I'd have a better understanding of how they work. Instead, I think I've just got more questions. And serial killers all seem so creepy."

"I don't disagree with you. Traffickers are pretty easy to understand. They want money and power, and they don't care how they go about getting it. Serial killers, though.

Different beast entirely." She waved a hand to dismiss the discussion. "What time did Poteracki board the L?"

"Quarter 'til ten p.m., on the nose."

The trains themselves were outfitted with cameras as well as the common stops. Amelia selected the feed from the stop closest to Poteracki's apartment, and she started the video a full thirty minutes before the man's card told them he'd boarded. She sped the feed up to double-speed at first, gradually slowing as the clock neared nine-forty-five.

Straightening in his seat, Zane pointed at the screen. "There. That's him."

"He's alone." Amelia paused the recording, studying where Poteracki had just come into view at the edge of the screen.

In silence, Amelia and Zane watched the man stand next to a bench as he waited. No matter the number of victims she watched on security recordings, Amelia never got used to the sight of a dead person come back to life. She'd watched Dr. Adam Francis crack open Poteracki's chest with a pair of surgical pliers. She'd seen a parasitic lamprey slither out of one of the guy's nostrils.

But here he was. Standing beneath an awning as he waited for the L. An older woman sat on the other end of the bench at Lars's side. Other than white curls, little of her features were visible.

Ever the diligent one, Amelia scooped up her notepad and scribbled out a rough description of the woman, as well as timestamps. Though she doubted they'd be able to identify her, Amelia wanted to ensure she covered all her bases. If they ran out of leads, as they often did, she'd be prepared with a backup strategy.

She didn't know what in the hell that strategy was, but she'd cross that bridge when she came to it.

As Poteracki made his way onto the train, Amelia waited

intently to see who, if anyone, might have been following him. But other than the old woman and a mother and her daughter, there was no one. Apparently, Poteracki's stop wasn't a popular one at ten p.m. on a Sunday.

"Any of those people look like they were stalking our vic?"

Amelia didn't realize how quiet the room had become until Zane's voice shattered the silence. "Guess we'll find out." She switched to the video feed from the transit authority of the interior of the train's car, maximized the recording, and pressed play.

Even as Amelia's eyes darted from one passenger to the next, waiting for a suspicious movement, she spotted nothing out of the ordinary. The men, women, and children on board were all about as low risk as they came. Amelia sincerely doubted that a grandmother had overpowered Poteracki and nearly decapitated him.

To her chagrin, the entirety of Poteracki's trip was uneventful. When he departed the train in Washington Park, only the old woman followed. Switching to the correct video feed again, Amelia checked the exterior camera to determine whether Lars and the woman had taken off in the same direction, but yet again, her hopes for a witness were dashed.

She slumped back in her chair and blew out a sigh. "Nothing on the L, then. We can look over it a few more times, along with the video we didn't review, to see if we missed anything, but I don't think we did. Poteracki got onto the train by himself, and he left by himself."

"I'll send out requests for security camera footage from the businesses we saw when we were walking through Washington Park today. Maybe one of them will catch something that wasn't on the L."

Their list of tedious searches was growing with each

second. "Good idea. Let's see if we get something from ViCAP at least."

Zane rubbed his chin, his focus on the projector screen as Amelia returned to the digital database. "Any luck on finding this Scorpion guy by chance?"

"None so far." Amelia kept to herself the thought that searching for a generic description of a young white guy with a scorpion tattooed on his neck was like sifting through the entire world's supply of hay while looking for a single needle. If Scorpion's street name wasn't registered in the Bureau's database, nor the CPD's, then she wasn't going to find him.

Zane's thoughtful expression deepened as he leaned back in his chair. "She did say he looked young. Could be that he's not in the system, or he doesn't have much of a reputation yet. Those girls said he tended to mind his own business and keep to himself."

"Flying under the radar." Sometimes the most inconspicuous people were capable of atrocities, but Amelia knew she didn't have to remind Zane. Despite the prostitutes' characterization that the man was harmless, Scorpion was currently at the top of their suspect list. They just didn't know who in the hell he was.

The room lapsed into silence as she finished entering her query into the ViCAP database. Like any search engine, ViCAP threw a wide enough net to capture any result that might have been relevant but may not have been an exact match. Only a pair of trained, human eyes could truly rule out all the extraneous possibilities.

She'd begun the search with just Northern Illinois but soon realized none of the handful of results were similar enough to Lars Poteracki's murder.

One, the killing of a man in West Garfield Park two years earlier, was close, but not quite the same. The victim had been stabbed forty-three times in the chest and abdomen, and the killer had carved a cross into his forehead. However, the various discrepancies, coupled with the fact the perpetrator was serving a life sentence after confessing to the crime, was more than enough to tell Amelia the homicide was unrelated.

Scooting closer to the table, Zane propped his elbows on the surface and balanced his chin on the back of his hand. "Nothing in Northern Illinois, it's looking like."

Amelia couldn't hold in her sigh any longer. As much as she loved investigative work, she could do without sifting through false positives in digital searches. "Looks like it. I'll try expanding the search radius bit by bit. I don't want to wind up with a hundred cases that are sort of similar but aren't actually related. I also don't want to make the search so specific that it misses something that's actually relevant."

"Like if the victim wasn't found in a body of water, or if they didn't have the defensive injuries Poteracki possessed." Zane drummed his fingers on the table. "Even with just the bible verse and the near decapitation, it's a pretty specific crime. Specific enough to be a hitman's signature, without a doubt."

As Amelia expanded the radius to any location within three hundred miles of Chicago, she scanned the results for another case that involved a bible verse.

The bible verse on Poteracki's chest was the most distinctive aspect of the murder, and as such, was most likely to tie his death to previous killings.

Anticipation thrummed in her veins as she pulled up the summary of a homicide dated back four years. "From Terre Haute, Indiana. Case is currently unsolved."

Zane perked up at the word. "Was there a bible verse?"

"On his chest, just like Poteracki." Any lingering tiredness from the tedium of an afternoon's worth of internet searches evaporated. "Vic's name was Greg Beard. He was found in an alley, throat slit, wallet and cash still in his pocket." Amelia blinked in disbelief a few times before she read the next line. "This wasn't part of my search, but it says here that he had a rap sheet."

"Poteracki also had a rap sheet." Zane's focused gaze turned intent. "Drugs, it looks like. Shit, we could be dealing with a hitman."

Amelia minimized the window and navigated to the next search result. "This one's more recent. From Milwaukee, a little more than a year ago. Thomas Maddox was the vic, and guess what?"

"He had a rap sheet."

Cautious triumph filled her. "Yep. Bible verse carved on his back instead of the chest this time. Throat slit, same as Poteracki and Beard."

Zane whistled through his teeth. "Three guys. All within the same region. There's no way this is a coincidence. And if all these guys have rap sheets, then we could definitely be looking at a contract killer."

Amelia had already begun to type out a request for the full case files of the two men. "There were a lot of search results too. I bet there are more that fit this MO."

Additional cases that matched Poteracki's murder meant more opportunities for evidence, but it also meant they were dealing with a more dangerous killer.

Worse still, they were facing a more *experienced* killer. If the man had already left a trail of victims in his wake, there was no telling how many more would fall before he was finally caught.

14

Readjusting the messenger bag over her shoulder, Cassandra Halcott stepped into the waiting elevator. She'd become accustomed to four or five-inch heels ever since she'd landed her spot at the U.S. Attorney's office, but today, the flat soles of her riding boots reminded her how damn short she was.

Well, technically, five-four was average for a woman. But her boss, Simone Julliard, was close to six feet, and plenty of the female cops and federal agents she worked with were closer to the five-eight range. Usually, high heels eliminated the gap entirely, but Cassandra wasn't about to be caught in a blizzard wearing a pair of pumps.

With her brown riding boots, dark jeans, peacoat, and knitted beanie, Cassandra appeared as if she was on her way to go hiking, not discuss an upcoming trial with a pair of FBI agents.

Even though Dan Gifford—also known as The Fox Creek Butcher—had accepted a plea agreement to save himself from the death penalty, one of the guy's so-called clients, a

Russian mobster named Yuri Antonov, had hired an attorney from a renowned defense firm in Chicago.

Cassandra was familiar with the lawyers who worked there, and after only a year in the U.S. Attorney's office, she could say with confidence that she'd come to hate almost all of them. To be sure, she steadfastly believed every person charged with a crime deserved a competent defense. But sometimes, the number of motions thrown around by wealthy lawyers and their expensive firms became ridiculous.

Each and every one of those balding, self-aggrandizing pricks in their tacky, expensive suits knew what they were doing when they filed an unnecessary motion. They were wasting Cassandra's time, throwing away taxpayer dollars in an attempt not only to truly defend their client but also to inconvenience a prosecutor whose workload was already ten times larger than theirs.

Not to mention that only the rich could afford their services, and well...the entire dynamic left a bad taste in Cassandra's mouth.

And so it went with Yuri Antonov.

Cassandra knew what the monstrous Russian had done to an innocent, college-aged girl named Willow Nowland, and she could imagine what the sick fuck would do to her if he had a chance. She'd been in an interrogation room with the creep so many times she'd lost count.

His presence had unnerved her a bit at first, but now, Antonov didn't faze her. Sure, he'd rip out her throat with his bare hands if he could, but Cassandra wasn't a stranger to violence. She knew how to use a knife and a firearm, and she could defend herself—even from a monster like Antonov. In some respects, she'd be just as glad to kill him as he would be to murder her.

Gritting her teeth, she tightened her grip on the strap of

her messenger bag and turned her focus to the panel of numbered buttons beside the elevator door. The Violent Crimes Division, the section of the FBI that housed the two agents she was scheduled to meet with today, was on the *fifth* floor of the ten-story building.

On the *sixth* floor, however, was Organized Crime.

In Organized Crime was Joseph Larson.

The corner of her mouth sank at the thought of his name. As if compelled by a supernatural force, she reached out and tapped the button numbered six.

According to her research from the night before, Montanelli's Steakhouse was an upscale restaurant located conveniently across the street from a four-star hotel. Cassandra had even checked the menu to discern whether or not the price of Joseph's bill could've been spent on only one person.

Considering that a massive, sixteen-ounce ribeye, two sides, a salad, and a drink went for fifty bucks, she doubted Joseph had racked up a bill totaling nearly one hundred dollars by himself.

Just as well. Joseph Larson had already started to wear on her. They had a fair amount of common ground, but not enough that Cassandra had ever truly envisioned a long-term commitment with the man.

Should have thought of that before you started fucking around with someone you work with, Cassandra.

She held back a groan. The least she could do now was find the other woman and warn her. Maybe she should be upset with Joseph's mistress, but nothing was further from the truth. It wasn't the other woman's fault Joseph was a cheating ass.

As the silver doors of the elevator slid open to reveal the sixth floor, Cassandra's mind immediately went to Amelia Storm. She didn't *think* a person as put-together as Amelia would go for a fling with a coworker. Then again, when Joseph turned on his charm, he could be quite convincing.

Cassandra would know. She had the same knack.

Never bullshit a bullshitter, Joseph.

Squaring her shoulders, she set off down the hallway in search of either Amelia Storm or Zane Palmer. As long as she was at the FBI office, she might as well try to get a little information from one of Joseph's coworkers.

Though the effort had taken some time, Cassandra had gotten over the reflexive cringe whenever she crossed paths with Zane. They'd met through an online dating app earlier in the year, not long after they'd both wound up in Chicago for their respective jobs.

Aside from a few nights of harmless fun, the relationship hadn't developed into anything noteworthy. Zane was one of the good ones, though. He didn't hold their fling over her head, nor did he look down on her, as men were so often prone to do to women who sought out a little no-strings adult fun. After a few face-to-face interactions around the FBI office, any lingering awkwardness between them had vanished.

As Cassandra rounded the corner just past the elevator, she spotted Amelia Storm at the end of a hall that separated the rows of cubicles from a handful of conference rooms. Waving a hand to get the other woman's attention, Cassandra increased her pace to a trot.

Amelia's attention snapped up from her phone, surprise etched on her face. "Oh. Hey, Cassandra. What're you doing here?"

No bullshit, always right down to brass tacks. Cassandra doubted Amelia cared much for her ever since the Ben Storey case, but she always appreciated the agent's down-to-earth demeanor. It was refreshing after dealing with lawyers, who were anything but straightforward.

Cassandra jerked a thumb over her shoulder. "I just got off the elevator. Figured I'd stop by here quickly before I head down to Violent Crimes. We're about a week away from Yuri Antonov's trial, finally."

The glimmer of skepticism in Amelia's green eyes told Cassandra the woman knew there was more to the visit. "Steelman and Cowen were handling the Antonov case, weren't they? They're good agents."

"Yeah, that's who I'm here to see. Trial preparation, you know?" She glanced around to ensure Joseph wasn't hiding in plain sight. "I was just wondering if I could ask you something before I go down to the fifth floor." She gestured to the nearest shadowy doorway. "In private."

Amelia's jaw clenched, and her blatant skepticism bordered on suspicion. Not that Cassandra could blame her. "Okay. Sure."

With an appreciative half-smile, Cassandra ducked into the dim copy room. As Amelia followed, Cassandra did another cursory examination to confirm they were indeed alone.

The decision to ask the FBI special agent about her former case partner was spur of the moment, and Cassandra hadn't thought over a single word she was about to say. Though conversation and public speaking came naturally to her, the *thud-thud* of her pulse belied the anxiety she was trying to bury.

Might as well get right to it. Just act like you're worried about Joseph. This is a hard job, so I'm checking to make sure he's okay. That makes sense, right?

She sure hoped so. The last thing she needed was one of Joseph's colleagues giving him a heads-up about his girlfriend's snooping.

Clearing her throat, Cassandra turned back to the agent. "I was wondering if you and Joseph had been partnered up on any cases lately? Anything since the Carlo Enrico murder?"

Though Amelia's demeanor remained even, her posture stiffened, and the hand at her side clenched.

Shit.

Cassandra needed to be careful. She had no idea what would elicit such a powerful physical reaction from a woman like Amelia, and if she wasn't propelled forward by an insatiable curiosity and a growing sense of resentment for Joseph, she'd have been liable to let the subject drop.

But Cassandra had been cheated on and used in the past, and she wasn't keen on allowing the trend to continue. If Joseph was screwing someone else, then Cassandra would dump his ass so quickly and decisively his head would spin.

Before Amelia could reply, Cassandra held up both hands in a show of surrender. "Sorry, I know that came out of nowhere. I'm just…he's been acting a little weird, and I don't know any of his friends. You're the closest thing to a friend of his that I know."

The agent's jaw tightened…another curious reaction. "I wouldn't say we're friends. More like work acquaintances. We used to be partnered up on cases quite a bit back when I first moved to Chicago, but not so much lately. I'm not really sure what he's been working on, honestly. I figured you'd know better than me."

You and me both.

Cassandra bit back the sarcastic response. "Well, like I said, he's been acting weird lately. I just wanted to make sure everything was going okay at work. Your job is stressful, and I know that can take a toll on someone."

For the first time since the mention of Joseph, Amelia's expression softened. Not much, but enough to assure Cassandra she wasn't about to get punched. "Whoever he's been partnered up with would definitely be a better person to talk to than me."

The next question spilled from Cassandra's lips before she could think it through. "Did you know Joseph's ex? They would have been dating when the two of you were working together more closely. I think her name was Michelle?"

Any tension that had begun to subside returned in force. Cassandra ascertained Amelia was working to keep her expression neutral, but her body language insisted she would have been more comfortable walking through a fireworks factory holding a lit candle.

Clearly, there was more to the Michelle story than Cassandra realized.

As Amelia rolled her shoulders, the cool composure returned to her stance. The question had caught her off guard, but Amelia Storm had never struck Cassandra as a woman who *stayed* off-kilter for long. "I didn't know Michelle, no. I didn't even know he was dating anyone at all when the two of them were together. I don't think their… relationship was that serious. Or, at least it wasn't serious to him."

A less keen observer might have missed the simmering vitriol in Amelia's voice when she said the word *him*, but not Cassandra. Spotting people's tells was quite literally part of her job.

"Gotcha." Cassandra forced herself to smile and lighten her tone.

Amelia didn't smile in return. An emotion that appeared closer to concern marred her pretty features. "Actually, I'm not sure—"

"Never mind." Cassandra held up a hand, embarrassment heating her cheeks. "Thanks, Agent Storm. I appreciate you humoring me." What had she been thinking? She should have never approached the agent like she was some teenager gossiping with her friend. "When I was a kid, my mom always used to tell me I worried too much. And you know that had to mean something since it was coming from my *mom*. You know, the woman who's supposed to worry about me."

Several long seconds went by before the agent let out a quiet chuckle, much to Cassandra's relief. "Nothing wrong with that. I hope everything works out okay."

There was still an air of mistrust between them, but as far as Cassandra could tell, the remark was genuine. "Thanks. I'm sure it will."

One way or another.

For the first time since she'd started poking around in Joseph's personal life, a sliver of dread wedged its way between her ribs like a knife.

Rather than set her mind at ease or provide answers to her questions, the discussion with Agent Storm had done the opposite.

Why had the agent seemed hesitant to discuss Michelle? Why did her stance grow so tense when Cassandra simply mentioned Joseph? Was there bad blood there that Cassandra didn't know about? Had Joseph screwed around with *Amelia*?

All she knew for sure was she had more digging to do, and she wouldn't stop until she had the whole truth.

❄

As I finished washing my hands, I reached to the stainless-steel dispenser for a handful of flimsy paper towels. The restaurant chain where I worked made money hand over fist, but apparently not quite enough to stock the stores with high-quality paper products. Cheapskate management was the norm at just about every restaurant, I'd learned.

From Terre Haute to Detroit to Milwaukee, they were all

the same. Cut the costs in every conceivable location, starting with the damned paper towels.

It didn't matter.

Restaurants such as these were the perfect venue for me to provide cleansing to the masses. Lars Poteracki, along with many other sinners of his ilk, had given their lives so that I might deliver their blood to the innocents to keep them free of sin.

Once I'd prayed over Lars and freed him of his sins, I drained as much of his purified blood as I could. Every drop counted.

Not nearly as many people attended Sunday church services anymore, but I'd found a way to bring the blood of Christ to them. Of course, Lars Poteracki was a far cry from the savior himself. But after my ritual, which was shown to me by the divine, the blood held the power to cleanse. To keep the masses free of the sins that had dragged Lars to the pit.

Glancing over my shoulder to the rest of the kitchen, I balled up the paper towels and tossed them into a newly emptied trash can. At two in the afternoon, the lunch rush had finally tapered off, allowing for the downtime for dinner prep. Many of the early shift workers had gone home for the day, leaving something of a skeleton crew for the mid-afternoon hours.

A pair of college-aged guys stood beside the hot line, chatting about some sporting event they'd attended the night before. The shorter of the duo— a kid named Armando who was studying botany, if I remembered right—reached for a metal ladle to stir absentmindedly at a container of alfredo sauce while his friend spoke.

Our manager had wandered off to her office, presumably to catch up on scheduling and other administrative duties.

Aside from a middle-aged man on his break and the front-of-house staff, we were the only ones here.

It was the perfect time for me to accomplish my task.

Tugging on the long sleeves of my uniform shirt, I smiled and waved to the college kids. "Hey, guys. How was lunch rush today?"

Armando lifted a shoulder and looked to his friend, Derek. "Pretty busy for a weekday, which was weird. It was probably because of the weather. They all had to come get their pasta and breadsticks before we're buried in two feet of snow."

I grinned. The restaurant staying open in the face of the storm hadn't come as a surprise, but I'd been pleased with the decision. "Probably." I gestured to the far wall that held our stoves, as well as the door to the walk-in cooler. "I'm going to get started on dinner prep. Let me know if you guys need any help."

Armando and Derek returned my smile. As I turned to make my way to the back of the kitchen, they resumed their conversation.

They suspected nothing.

As I set about heating up a large batch of marinara sauce, I stole a glimpse beneath my sleeve. After four years, I'd come close to perfecting my transportation of cleansed blood. I ordered IV bags online, and then I taped them to my arm after they'd been filled.

No one was ever the wiser. As long as I mixed the concoction into a type of food where the average person's pallet wouldn't pick up on the tinge of iron, such as a tomato-based sauce, consumers weren't aware of what they were consuming.

With a quick scan of the immediate area to ensure no eyes were on me—including making sure my back was turned to the security camera mounted in the corner of the room—I picked up a serving spoon and stirred the marinara I'd just dumped from a bag into a rectangular metal container.

At the same time, I unfastened the plastic that held the blood inside the IV bag.

A rush of euphoria washed over me as the crimson liquid dribbled down into the sauce. For that moment at least, I was at peace. I knew my purpose in life, and I knew I was doing as the Lord asked.

The IV bag up my sleeve was the last of Lars Poteracki's cleansed blood, but that was no issue for me.

I'd already settled on my next target.

15

After the bizarre conversation with Cassandra, Amelia returned to the little conference room she and Zane had borrowed for the afternoon. Easing the door closed behind herself, she turned to the window to take stock of the weather. The gray sky had darkened a couple shades, and the lazy snowfall had taken on a frenzied pace. If she and Zane didn't leave the FBI office soon, they'd be facing a questionable drive home.

Considering the unexpected questions from Cassandra Halcott, Amelia most definitely didn't want to get stuck at the field office. She'd only been away from her desk to use the bathroom and stretch her legs, and part of her wondered if the lawyer had truly run into her by chance, or if she'd been lying in wait to spring the question.

To be honest, the mention of Michelle Timmer had given Amelia quite the jolt. She felt terrible that she'd barely thought of the forensic tech until Cassandra mentioned her.

Amelia made a note to follow up with the Chicago PD about Michelle's case. What was the status of their investigation? Was the case still open? Amelia hated that she hadn't taken the time to follow up.

Of course, she'd been a little bit busy catching bad guys and trying her best not to be killed, but still…guilt settled on her heart. Michelle was one of the FBI's own.

She added three exclamation points at the end of her *"Follow up on Michelle Timmer"* note.

As Amelia took her seat at the small, circular table, she absentmindedly twisted a piece of hair around her index finger. Zane had also gone to take a short break, leaving Amelia alone as she contemplated her run-in with the Assistant U.S. Attorney.

She still wasn't sure who in their right mind would genuinely be concerned for Joseph Larson's welfare. Aside from the handful of times she'd pissed him off, Amelia had hardly ever seen the guy's veneer crack. Though the work they did at the FBI deeply affected most agents, Amelia was confident Joseph's brain was wired differently.

Especially now that Alex had given her the photo of Joseph Larson and his apparent bestie, Brian Kolthoff.

At the beginning of the summer, Amelia and Zane had worked the kidnapping case of a girl named Leila Jackson. Leila had been snatched off the street of her seemingly safe hometown of Janesville, Wisconsin. At only twelve years old, the girl had been sold into the underaged sex trafficking industry. Eventually, when Leila's body matured and she could no longer pass for a child, the creeps who'd held her captive decided to sell her to someone else.

That someone else, of course, was none other than a prominent León family capo, Emilio Leóne. Emilio's cousin was the head of the entire Leóne operation, and Emilio himself had run the family's prostitution ring. Though Leila was only sixteen when Emilio bought her, due to her appearing closer to twenty than sixteen, he was quick to send her out to work the streets.

What Emilio hadn't counted on was Leila's indomitable spirit. The poor girl had lived in hell for four years, but she'd still fought back when Emilio's men tried to get her to bend to their will. After falling into Emilio's bad graces, the Leóne capo made the decision to cut his losses and sell the obstinate teenager to a private buyer.

To Brian Kolthoff, then known only to the FBI and the Leónes as The Shark. Kolthoff was a multi-billionaire who'd made his fortune in venture capitalism and who now commanded a cushy position as a Washington D.C. lobbyist.

So, naturally, the charges brought up against Kolthoff hadn't stuck. The man had a prestigious law firm on retainer, and the attorneys had been quick to secure bail on the condition that Kolthoff wear an ankle monitor and stay within the city of Chicago. Hell, he couldn't have spent longer than an hour in a prison holding cell before he was sprung loose.

Even though Amelia had quite literally caught him in the process of buying an underaged sex slave, Kolthoff had dodged every single charge thrown his way. He'd claimed he thought Leila was an escort, and he'd merely paid for her to accompany him to a social event. And he *surely* hadn't known she was underage.

Amelia scoffed out loud at the memory, and she used the sound to pull herself back to the conference room and away from the past. Whoever had said money couldn't buy happiness was apparently unaware of the holes in the U.S. justice system.

Amelia scooted up to the table and opened her laptop. Kolthoff was a free man, and there was little Amelia could do about him right now.

Joseph was a different story. If she could find a way to definitively prove Joseph Larson and Brian Kolthoff had been affiliated since before the Jackson case, she could use that as ammunition against Joseph. His relationship with a major suspect in an investigation, and his failure to disclose that friendship and recuse himself from the case, were potential grounds for termination.

Amelia doubted the FBI would be able to bring up criminal charges, but for the time being, she'd settle on Joseph getting shitcanned. The wannabe rapist deserved worse, but like the saying went, revenge was a dish best served cold.

Besides, she had a case to work. Someone had brutally murdered a former FBI informant and had dumped his body in Lake Michigan. Though none of Lars's immediate family were alive, the poor guy still deserved answers.

Just as Amelia had finished typing in her password, blinds clattered as Zane shoved open the door.

As Amelia swiveled in her chair to face him, the dark thoughts about Joseph Larson, Leila Jackson, and Brian Kolthoff weren't so oppressive. "Hey, how was your break?"

He scratched the side of his scruffy face. "Short. I ran into SAC Keaton. She wants us in one of the briefing rooms for a department meeting."

Amelia's contentment wavered as she pushed to her feet. "For this case?"

"No." Zane stepped aside so Amelia could follow him out into the hall. "She didn't say, but it sounded like it was something more…administrative, I think the word would be."

"If someone's stealing people's lunches again, I swear to god." She left the threat unfinished and huffed. Even in the heart of the damn FBI, people were still ballsy enough to take their coworkers' food. Truly, lunch theft was an issue in every office job known to man.

"There's a reason I stopped bringing my lunch." Zane's expression turned thoughtful as they started toward the briefing room. "Well, a couple reasons, but that was one of them. And I'm too lazy to cook."

"I've told you fifty times, you need to get a crock pot. I don't know what adult *doesn't* have a crock pot. You throw a bunch of food in it, turn it on, and in six hours, you've got meals for days."

He wrinkled his nose. "But then I have to wash the dishes. That's the part that gets me, honestly. It's not the cooking. That's fine. It's the dishes after that I can't deal with."

Amelia and Zane had discussed their culinary abilities plenty over the past six months, and her suggestions were always met with Zane's disdain for washing dishes. When Amelia had pointed out that his apartment was, indeed, equipped with an appliance that would clean the plates and forks for him, he revealed that he hated unloading the machine almost as much as manually doing the dishes.

Try as she might, Amelia couldn't wrap her head around it. Everyone had their quirks, though. Amelia was terrible about getting her mail, and Zane hated any form of kitchen cleanup.

Their short conversation drew to a close as they approached the space that had been creatively dubbed *Briefing Room A*. Through the open doorway, Amelia caught a glimpse of the Special Agent in Charge, Jasmine Keaton. She stood in front of a whiteboard, and to her side was another familiar face. Supervisory Special Agent Spencer Corsaw maintained the same vintage-inspired hair style—parted to one side and slicked back with a product that made it shine under the harsh fluorescent lights.

With his neatly pressed black suit, matching dress shoes, and silver striped tie, Spencer looked like he'd just stepped out of a time machine from the 1960s. Or the set of *Mad Men*. One of the two.

As Amelia and Zane stepped into the room and offered

their greetings to the SAC and SSA, Amelia glanced over the few other occupants. Organized Crime was comprised of a number of special agents, but presumably due to the weather, only three others were present.

Though Joseph's icy blue stare inevitably drifted to Amelia, she ignored the man's presence and kept her focus on SAC Keaton and SSA Corsaw. Other than Joseph, Special Agent Jacob Alvarez and his partner on the cartel taskforce, Kavya Bhatti, were in attendance.

Throwing a questioning look to Zane, Amelia dropped down to sit on a cushioned, leather bench beside the door. He nodded his understanding, closed the door, and took his spot beside her.

Joseph's attention had shifted elsewhere, but Amelia was still stricken by a crawling sensation on the side of her face and neck. Just knowing the man was within her line of sight was enough to set her on edge.

This had better be quick, and it better be good.

As if she could read Amelia's mind, SAC Keaton stepped away from the whiteboard and clapped her hands together. The quiet chitchat from the gathered agents went silent, and the SAC gestured to the window. "As I'm sure you've all noticed, the weather is starting to get worse. I sent out a notification this morning advising that anyone who was able could work from home, but I appreciate those of you who came in today."

Amelia was starting to wish she hadn't and that she and Zane had met up outside of work to go to Washington Park.

SAC Keaton lifted a hand, looking like she was staving off questions from a mob of reporters. "Don't worry. I didn't interrupt your afternoons just to tell you it's snowing." She sidestepped and beckoned Spencer forward. "I'll let SSA Corsaw take it from here."

Appearing uncharacteristically nervous, Spencer rubbed

his hands together. "Thanks. Well, as some of you might've already heard from the rumor mill, I've been planning to step down from my role as Supervisory Special Agent for some time now. And if you hadn't heard about it, then now you know. I've decided to take my career in a different direction, and once a replacement is found for my position, I'll be transferring over to the Intelligence Analysis team."

The move made sense, at least as far as Amelia could tell. Spencer was a logical person, and he was smart. Intelligence analysts were the backbone of many of the Bureau's investigative departments, including Organized Crime and Counterterrorism.

Plus, the job was far quieter and less risky than field work. Amelia couldn't blame Spencer if he simply wanted a more peaceful existence.

As understanding as she was of his decision, and as much as she hoped the transfer would bring him happiness, all her optimism flew out the window with Joseph's reaction.

A self-assured smile crept over the man's clean-shaven face, his pale eyes glittering with something that resembled anticipation.

Shit.

With more than a decade of FBI experience, plus his tenure in the military beforehand, Joseph seemed like a frontrunner for the position. Even though Amelia knew the bastard was far from leadership material, he'd always projected and maintained an air of competence. If he hadn't, he wouldn't still be working for the Bureau.

While SAC Keaton explained how the interview process would work, as well as a handful of other housekeeping items, Amelia racked her brain for anyone in their department who'd truly rival Joseph.

Zane? Amelia knew Zane hadn't actually worked for the

FBI for the past thirteen years, but on paper, he had more FBI experience than Joseph.

But what would that mean for the two of them and their…relationship?

It'd be fine. You'd transfer to a different department, just like Spencer's doing. Go to Violent Crimes with Steelman and Cowen, or Victim Services.

No, that solution didn't sit well with Amelia. First of all, she had no idea if Zane even wanted a leadership role at the FBI. He'd never struck her as a fan of office politics, and she didn't want to force him into a role he hated just because she was worried Joseph might ascend to become their boss. Plus, there was no guarantee Zane would land the gig.

Kavya Bhatti had been with the Bureau for…how many years? Six? And her partner, Jake Alvarez, had four years of experience.

Amelia gave herself a mental shake.

She couldn't risk spinning the proverbial wheel. Another agent might beat Joseph out for this promotion, but what about the next? What about the day Joseph decided to pine for Jasmine Keaton's job?

Straightening her back, she maintained a carefully blank expression.

There was only one course of action that was acceptable now.

She had to corroborate the photo Alex had given her. She had to take away Joseph Larson's badge, and his power, for good.

16

By the time Neil Rosford arrived at his favored spot in Washington Park, the snowfall had rendered visibility less than a couple blocks. He hated when the weather impeded his vision. The corner lot and its decrepit, abandoned three-story apartment building were the perfect location to spot people well before they reached him.

Looming trees and buildings lined the street, providing him a sheltered vantage point to watch for suspicious characters. He'd also memorized the immediate area, and he had multiple paths of escape if anything went south.

But when he couldn't see past the damn block, the entire purpose of his station was defeated.

As he heaved a sigh, his breath formed a thin cloud before it was whipped away on the cold wind. After what he'd seen the other night, he didn't want to get stuck anywhere he could be caught off guard.

Neil had never known Lars's last name until he saw the guy in the news. Poteracki sounded Polish, but Neil always figured the tall, lean man with shoulder-length blond hair and bright blue eyes was Scandinavian.

Hunching against the cold, blowing wind, Neil pushed aside the inane thought and scanned the immediate area. No customers had approached him yet, but despite the weather, he knew they'd show up soon. He didn't want his mind to wander too far while he worked.

But forgetting Lars Poteracki's abduction wasn't quite that simple. Neil had no reason to think he, personally, was in the shit with anyone in the neighborhood. Ever since he'd started slinging drugs out here, he'd kept his head down, and he'd stayed away from other dealers' businesses.

The portion of Washington Park where Neil sold wasn't the most lucrative, but it was enough to pay his and Erika's bills—barely. Unlike so many of the kids Neil saw trying to prove themselves as some sort of badass, to climb their way up the hierarchy of illegal drug trafficking, he didn't care.

Barely paying his bills was enough. Anything more would be taking on additional risk, and that wasn't why he was here.

Neil didn't *want* a position of authority in this world. Anyone who called shots around here ended up dead or in prison.

Was that what had happened to Lars? Had he pissed off the wrong person?

In a sense, Neil hoped that was the case. If Poteracki had gotten on the bad side of one of the city's organized criminal enterprises, then Neil had nothing to worry about. Sure, Lars's death didn't sit well with him, but he'd mind his own business if it meant he'd keep his head attached to his body.

Cops had pulled Lars's corpse out of Lake Michigan last night. Though not many details had circulated yet, there was enough information in the article Neil had read on his phone to shake him.

Lars's throat had been slit, and the wound was so deep the spine was visible. None of the reports were sure of the motive behind the killing, but considering Lars's criminal record, they'd all jumped to the same conclusion.

Drugs. A feud. A territorial dispute.

Never mind that Lars had been out of the game for almost a year. Ever since Ersfeld went down, Lars had disappeared from Washington Park.

At first, Neil had thought the guy had been sent to prison alongside Ersfeld. Then, one day, he was making a late-night grocery run when he spotted Lars stocking the cereal aisle.

He'd gotten out. He'd left behind this cursed life and found a way to make it work legitimately.

The sight had given Neil a much-needed shred of hope for his own future. As long as he could make ends meet until Erika finished her degree, they'd be fine.

Now, he wondered. Had Lars truly left behind the lifestyle? If he had, then why the hell was he in Washington Park buying heroin from Neil the other night?

Had he relapsed? Or was Lars's reappearance to score part of something bigger, like the start of a new gang rolling into the area?

Neil shivered and shifted his weight from one foot to the other.

I only need to be shook if I did something to piss someone off. And I didn't. I know I didn't. Whatever Lars did was his issue. Not mine. I ain't said a damn thing to the cops about what I saw. Whoever killed Lars has got no reason to gun for me next.

The logic was sound, but it did little to assuage Neil's rampant paranoia.

A familiar man emerged from an alley, and though the presence of a heroin addict wouldn't do much to calm a regular person's nerves, the repeat customer grounded Neil back in reality.

Daylight waned, and more buyers came and went as the hours passed without incident. Neil allowed himself to fall back into his regular routine, but he was still acutely aware of the handgun tucked in the waistband of his pants. More aware than usual.

Maybe this was what soldiers in Iraq felt like during their tours of duty—their senses on high alert, ready and waiting for the shit to hit the fan at any moment.

He snorted to himself at the thought. Yeah, right. He was a drug dealer, and he knew he couldn't compare what *he* did with the experiences of anyone serving in the U.S. military.

Stop it. Focus. Don't let your guard down because you're getting bored.

Shifting his weight from one foot to the other, Neil glanced around the neighborhood. He hadn't seen a customer in more than twenty minutes. Perhaps he was due for a change of scenery.

Only a few hours had passed since the snow had started, but there had to be at least six inches on the ground already. When this part of Washington Park was covered in snow, Neil could almost trick himself into thinking the area was welcoming. The roofs of condemned houses and apartment buildings were blanketed in a layer of pristine white, like a sheet cast over a broken piece of furniture to hide it from view.

He wouldn't miss this place when he was gone. Slinging dope was a means to an end for Neil and not a way of life like it was for so many of the other dealers who frequented the area.

The quiet crunch of footsteps on snow jerked his attention to the approaching figure of a man. His face was downcast, almost as if he hadn't even noticed Neil, and he'd stuffed both hands in the pockets of his leather jacket. He was clad in black cargo pants, coat, and a hood that obscured most of his facial features in the low light. Such a getup wasn't unusual for Neil's buyers, but this man was…different.

His leather jacket appeared to be new, and his pants weren't the disheveled, ripped garments he often saw on the local homeless population. Neil didn't recognize *all* his customers on sight, but he'd committed the repeat buyers to memory. Whoever the newcomer was, he hadn't bought dope from Neil before. Neil would have remembered someone like him.

As the man in black drew nearer, Neil inched his hand toward the weapon tucked in his jeans. "You lookin' for something?" He kept his tone stern but not quite hostile.

A pair of flat, green eyes snapped up to meet Neil's. "Yes, actually."

Unease slithered down Neil's spine like a living thing. As the finger of one hand brushed against the textured grip of the handgun, Neil swallowed the sting of bile at the back of his throat and straightened his shoulders. "What can I do for you?"

In a swift movement with fluidity and purposefulness Neil hadn't expected, the stranger pulled a hand from his coat to brandish a matte black handgun. "I'm going to need you to show me your hands. I know you're armed. Come on, nice and slow."

Terror clamped down around Neil's throat like a vice, but he clenched his teeth together to keep his composure from faltering. The man hadn't identified himself as a cop...*yet*. However, cops weren't the only people who showed up in this part of town to brandish weapons and threaten drug dealers.

There were those in Washington Park and around the entire city who made their living by robbing dealers. Some called them stick-up boys, and others had a list of other names that were far less kind.

Swallowing, Neil inched his hand away from the nine-mil. Just as the stranger had requested, he held both arms out to his sides, harmless. Defenseless. Vulnerable.

None of those were sentiments Neil ever wanted to experience, especially out *here*.

No matter how hard he racked his brain, he realized he had no choice.

He could aim and fire a handgun well enough, but he wasn't Wyatt Earp or Doc Holliday. The man in black wasn't here for a high noon standoff in the Wild West. And if he was, Neil wouldn't have stood a chance.

How was he supposed to defend himself when the other party *already* had their weapon drawn?

Simple. He couldn't.

Shit.

Making an attempt to whip out his nine-mil in time to land the first shot was a death wish. He always posted up in this corner lot because it offered a handful of different escape routes, but he'd never truly considered how useless those paths were when he had a gun pointed at his face.

All he could do now was adhere to the stranger's demands and hope the man was only interested in leaving Washington Park with his product and not his life.

The stranger gestured Neil forward with his free hand. "Come on. Off the stoop. No fast movements."

Gritting his teeth, Neil slowly descended the two steps to the snow-covered sidewalk. Only five feet of distance remained between him and the stranger, easily close enough for the man to land a lethal shot if Neil made any sudden movements.

The man stepped to the side and motioned Neil forward. "Come on."

"Where are we going?" Neil inwardly cringed as the words left his mouth. He didn't *want* to know the answer to the question, but he also knew he was better off with more information.

"I'm parked around the corner. We're going for a drive." The man's words were as calm as if he were placing an order at a fast-food joint. His shrewd stare didn't waver as Neil took one agonizing step after another.

Blood pounded in Neil's ears as he reached the sidewalk in front of the apartment building. First, Lars Poteracki was abducted right in front of Neil, and now a strange, clean-cut man wanted Neil to go for a *drive* with him?

Were the two incidents related? Was this the same man?

Was he here to kill Neil for witnessing the event?

Neil's mind was weighted down with the cacophony of his thoughts as he forced one foot in front of the other. Though he couldn't see the gun pointed at his back, he could *feel* the weapon's presence.

His gaze darted around the dark neighborhood as he walked, desperately searching for a safe exit route or another person, but nothing seemed promising.

Not that witnesses mattered much around here. Bystanders kept to themselves, and no one talked to the cops unless they were bailing themselves out of trouble. The irony of his decision not to report Lars's kidnapping to the police wasn't lost on him.

As they rounded the corner of the apartment building, Neil's attention shot to a black, late-model Mazda.

The same car that had abducted Lars Poteracki.

His footsteps faltered, and the strange man at his back made a threatening noise in his throat. Straightening his back, Neil dug deep to conjure up some semblance of his composure.

He wants to make sure I won't rat him out. That has to be it. Maybe I should ask him about it. Tell him I haven't said anything to anyone and that I'll keep my mouth shut. Maybe that's why we're going for a drive.

A twinge of hope pierced through Neil's anxiety.

Could that be it? Could the stranger want to *go for a drive* because he wanted to make sure Neil wouldn't talk?

As much as the thought of Lars being brutally murdered weighed on Neil's psyche, he *would* keep his mouth shut. For the sake of himself and for his family. He wasn't a snitch. Snitches got killed in this neighborhood.

The Mazda's taillights flashed red, followed by the *click* as the latch for the trunk disengaged.

Red-hot panic swelled in Neil's chest. The trunk?

Before he could think through the decision, he whirled around on one heel to face the stranger.

Doing his best to ignore the threatening sight of the handgun, Neil met the man's listless eyes. "Look, you don't have to do this. I don't know what you think…or what I saw, but I won't say shit, okay? I ain't no snitch. Whatever business you had with Lars Poteracki was your own thing. I ain't going to stick my nose in that."

With the matte handgun, the stranger gestured to the trunk. "Get in." Again, his voice was so casual and emotionless, he could've been ordering from a dollar menu.

He wants to scare me. He wants to make sure I won't talk.

Even as far removed as Neil tried to stay from the world of drug trafficking, he was still familiar with the intimidation tactics utilized by those further up the food chain.

They wouldn't settle for sternly requesting that a witness remain silent. They'd want to scare that person shitless, to make sure they knew what they were in for if they changed their mind and decided to go to the cops.

Just do what he says. Let him know you won't talk. You might get roughed up a little, but it'll be fine. It's what guys like this do.

Neil's mind whirled in indecision. He knew he could be

playing right into the hands of the person who wanted to murder him, but honestly, what choice did he have?

There were no onlookers, so if Neil tried to fight back or run, the stranger wouldn't hesitate to put a bullet in his back.

If he heeded the man's command and got in the trunk, then...

Then he at least had the *possibility* to live to fight another day.

With his icy, emotionless gaze fixed on Neil, the stranger again gestured to the trunk of the car with the barrel of his handgun.

Clawing past a pervasive sense of shame and humiliation, coupled with rampant paranoia, Neil lifted the trunk open with a trembling hand.

Do it for Destiny. For Erika. Because if you don't do what he wants, he'll find someone to take it out on. Better he's here threatening me than them.

His throat tightened at the thought of the two people he loved most in this world.

The flicker of black in the corner of his eye was the only warning he received before a hard, solid object cracked across his temple. Stars exploded outward from the site of the blow, and the tang of iron replaced the bitterness of bile on his tongue.

Neil began keeling forward into the trunk, but he was powerless to stop the movement.

Before he'd completed his slump into the car, another heavy blow came crashing down against the same site as the first.

Instead of stars, this time Neil was greeted with only blackness.

17

Scooting to the edge of her spot on the center couch cushion, Amelia stared down at the photo of Joseph Larson and Brian Kolthoff. Her apartment was quiet as she waited for Zane, who'd gone home after work to collect some of his things. Part of her was nervous and excited for what was to come when he arrived, but the other part of her couldn't shake the thoughts of Joseph Larson as Organized Crime's SSA.

After Spencer Corsaw's announcement that afternoon, the picture in front of her had taken on new importance. She trusted Alex Passarelli—at least when it came to the photo of Larson and Kolthoff—and when he said he'd received the image from a reliable source, she believed him.

If anyone could properly vet the source of their information, it was Alex. Even when he and Amelia had dated as teenagers, he'd been meticulous and precise at nearly every aspect of his life.

However, she couldn't very well waltz into SAC Keaton's office, plunk the picture down on her desk, and request that she fire Joseph Larson for gross misconduct.

She needed a date, a definitive location, and a piece of corroborating evidence. One or two photos by themselves wouldn't do the trick. Not if she couldn't provide context.

Amelia fell back against the plush cushions. From her fleece-lined bed beside the entertainment center, Hup lifted her head and turned her squinty gaze to her mistress.

"I don't know, Hup." Amelia pointed at the picture like the calico knew what she was talking about. "How the hell am I supposed to do this? Alex won't tell me who his photographer was. Even if he gave me the latitude and longitude and the atomic timestamp of when this was taken, it wouldn't really get me anywhere."

Hup blinked sleepily and rested her head back on her white paws.

Amelia huffed. "Of course you don't give a shit, but trust me, Hup. Larson's bad news for Organized Crime. Hell, he's bad news for the entire FBI. Remember when there was someone dirty in the office, someone funneling information to the Leónes?"

Stretching out her front legs, Hup yawned.

"I know. It's old news. Then after Kantowski tried to kidnap me and shoot me in the face so she could frame me for the Storey murder, we figured she must've been the leak. Right? Made sense, especially with everything we found in her storage locker. All the video feeds from the hidden cameras she planted in my apartment and those doctored pictures of me and Storey. But…what the hell did the Leónes want with Ben Storey? Or did they want anything with him? Are we really supposed to believe Glenn Kantowski was a lone wolf? I mean, it's possible, I guess."

The long-haired calico rolled over to expose her belly as her eyes drifted closed.

"Stop it." Amelia jabbed a finger in the cat's direction. "I know that's a trap. I still remember when Zane tried to rub your belly and you bit him." She blew out a long breath. "That's not what we're talking about anyway. We're talking about Joseph and about how he's bro-ing it up with Brian Kolthoff. How do we know Glenn was the only leak? If her motive was revenge, then why would we even think she *was* the leak?"

A whirlwind of what-ifs accompanied the hypothetical, making Amelia's head hurt as she tried to put together the puzzle.

There was a missing piece, and it had *some*thing to do with Brian Kolthoff and Joseph Larson.

Before she could spiral too far down into the mental abyss, a knock at the door jerked her out of the contemplation.

With a sharp inhale, she snatched up the picture, folded it, and rushed to her bedroom to stow it away in her underwear drawer.

Great. Now there's a picture of two perverts in the same drawer as my lingerie.

The thought was so ridiculous she laughed at herself. As she hurried back to the living area and then the foyer, she let the good humor find its way to her expression. After double-checking the peephole to make sure her visitor was indeed Zane and not another surprise visit by Alex, she threw the deadbolt and pulled open the door.

A new kind of anticipation pulsed through her veins as her gaze fell on the handsome face of Zane Palmer. "Hey. How was the drive?"

He shrugged and brushed the melting snowflakes from his shoulders before he stepped over the threshold. "Could've been worse, I guess."

Moving to the side, Amelia flushed as he shucked off his coat and shoes. They'd come a long way in the past month… from the secrecy and borderline mistrust they'd overcome during the Ben Storey investigation to Amelia accidentally spotting the nautical stars on his knees and shoulders.

Each of them had histories the other knew little about, but they'd come to a point of acceptance. It was okay for them both to have secret pasts, so long as they were honest about the present.

Though guilt still gnawed at her for keeping her history with the D'Amato family a secret, she wondered if the time was nearing to share that part of herself. Not just to assuage her conscience but to potentially give Zane a way to help her with the Joseph Larson situation.

Zane had all but confirmed his history with the CIA, and he undoubtedly still had contacts who were active in the Agency. She knew he wanted to do *something* to help, but so far, there hadn't been much he could do.

That was different now.

Could he help her verify the photo of Brian Kolthoff and Joseph Larson? Did the CIA have access to any information that would corroborate the relationship?

Her pulse sped up, and this time, it wasn't because of the butterflies in her stomach. Maybe the answer to the issue with Joseph had been in front of her the whole time.

As he straightened and turned to her, she offered him a grin. For the time being, she'd set Alex's photo on the backburner. "I'm glad the drive wasn't terrible. You ready for some cake?"

Desire replaced the pleasant expression he'd worn just seconds before. He took a step closer, his gaze lowering to her mouth. "Something like that."

A sultry smile took the place of her grin. Her heart hammered against her ribs, and her entire body was on fire. Years had passed since the last time she'd done this, and she only hoped to avoid making herself appear overly thirsty, as the younger generation would say.

All she wanted to do was grab him by the shirt collar, drag him to her room, and strip him, but this was their first time together, and she'd rather not come across like a cavewoman.

Nervous to her core, she turned toward her living room. "Well, what do you want to do, then?"

Before she could take more than a few steps, the warmth of his touch was on her waist. Sliding his hand beneath her shirt, he clasped her hip as he pulled her body flush with his. His heat was as intoxicating as any drug, and she was having a harder and harder time keeping her baser, caveman instincts at bay.

Maybe she didn't need to suppress the urge. Maybe she should just...

She didn't have to convince herself any further. As she took hold of his hand, she spun around to face him, circled her other arm around his shoulders, and leaned in for a drawn-out kiss. The instant she parted her lips for his tongue, she melted into him, matching his passion in kind.

Their moment the other night had been great, but she realized they'd both been holding back. Perhaps they'd each been afraid of rejection or of accidentally making the wrong move. Now, there were none of the usual first-date types of trepidation.

They both knew where this was headed.

Amelia bit down lightly on his bottom lip as they separated for the first time. Her breathing was hitched, and every nerve in her body was standing at attention.

The glimmer of unabashed desire in his gray eyes was all the confirmation she needed.

For tonight, at least, she could forget about the darkness that encroached on her world. Tonight, there was just her and Zane.

18

As I unlocked the basement door, my attention went straight to the bound, unconscious form of Neil Rosford. I'd gone through the extra trouble to hog-tie Neil with a length of sturdy nylon rope rather than the set of zip ties I normally used. Though the zip ties were faster and more convenient, a proper knot was typically more difficult to escape.

The wound in my arm still stung whenever I moved, and I'd learned my lesson from Lars Poteracki. Lars wasn't the first one to fight back, but the more I considered our brawl, the more certain I became he'd fought the hardest.

Was his resistance significant? Was God trying to send me a message through one of my sacrifices?

I eased the door closed and pressed my lips together as I considered the thought.

No. Lars had been selected by the Lord, and I'd been chosen to carry out this work. God didn't make mistakes. *Man* made mistakes.

The vicious battle between Lars and me had been a test. From time to time, the Lord had to throw a curveball at his followers to ensure their loyalty was steadfast. I'd bested Lars, and I'd shown God I could be counted on, even in difficult situations.

Renewed dedication to the mission flowed over me. Straightening my back, I descended the rickety steps to the basement. The golden glow of candlelight flickered along the walls, casting exaggerated shadows against the crags of the cinderblocks.

Even more than my previous three houses, the lower level of this place reminded me of the home where I'd grown up. I'd spent so much time in that basement, I was sure I could draw it from memory if I had a lick of artistic talent.

Especially the wardrobe.

A shudder crept down my spine at the thought. Not much light had made its way through those solid, oaken doors, but I'd memorized the feel of every nook and cranny. Aside from tracing my fingers over the splintery wood, there hadn't been much else to do when I was locked away for hours, even days at a time.

The punishments had been harsh, and I'd been resentful for much of my life. Only after my divine intervention did I see the events for what they really were.

Before that fateful day, I'd been set on joining the military and eventually becoming a police officer. My father had always been harsh, but he'd also been right. The world was a chaotic, sinful place that continued to devolve with each passing year. By becoming a law enforcement agent, I'd thought I could restore some semblance of sanity to this country.

So, when my mother died suddenly from a heart attack, my father requested I take over the family business, a small Italian restaurant in Terre Haute. I'd almost refused. But one of God's rules was to honor one's parents, so I'd bitten the bullet and helped my father run the restaurant.

My dear old dad passed a year later, and though I could have pursued my initial desire to join the police force, something had happened.

An angel, or maybe even God himself, had come to me one night. From then on, my purpose had been clear. Cleanse the sinners and spread the holy communion to the masses.

I'd known then I had to reach more people than just those in Terre Haute. After my first three sacrifices, I'd sold the restaurant, my parents' house, and any other remaining assets. The finances from the estate were enough to allow me to relocate frequently, but I'd still have to pick up jobs here and there if I wanted to make the savings last as long as possible.

Fortunately, working in a restaurant suited my design.

Blinking away the memories, I returned my focus to Neil as I descended the final steps into the basement. "Your sacrifice will do more good than you ever could have by yourself, Mr. Rosford."

I knew Neil couldn't hear me. I'd made sure he wouldn't come out of his slumber. I might have messed up the sedative dose on Lars, but I wouldn't make the same mistake twice. I never would again.

At the bottom of the stairs, I paused to gaze at the golden cross atop a rickety wooden bookshelf. The prop was nothing more than cheap plastic, but to me, it held a certain sentimental value. I didn't *need* anything to complete my ritual, but the sight of a holy icon seemed...fitting. It reminded me of my purpose.

As I snapped on a pair of vinyl gloves, I strode over until I towered over Neil's unconscious form. God had instructed me to cleanse a specific type of sinner. Though I was aware murderers lurked the streets of Washington Park—men and women who'd done more wrong than Neil or Lars—those sinners were too far gone for me to save. Their crimes were too egregious to be cleansed using my methods, and the Lord would sort them out when they met their end.

But men like Neil still had purpose. In death, I could save them, and I could use their life's essence, their blood, to save others.

I knelt at Neil's side. "Yours is a noble sacrifice, Mr. Rosford. I'm sure you'd understand the reason for all of this if you could see it from my perspective. I know you have a wife and a child. I saw their pictures in your wallet. You'd want the world to be a better place for both their sakes."

Other than the rhythmic cadence of Neil's breathing, I received no response. I wasn't sure why I sometimes felt compelled to explain myself to the subjects I acquired. Perhaps it reminded me why I was doing this.

Convincing Neil to give up his life for the betterment of perfect strangers wasn't a discussion I expected would go well if he'd been conscious. He might not have been an egregious offender like Ted Bundy or Dan Gifford, but he was still too far gone to be reasoned with.

He was the perfect middle ground. He was exactly what the Lord had described to me during His divine intervention. The fact that I was nearly certain that Neil was also a witness to my kidnapping of Lars Poteracki was merely a bonus. God's work, no doubt.

Glancing once more to Neil, I unrolled a blue tarp in front of my makeshift altar. I'd done this plenty of times in the past, but I still laid out a tarp in case of an accident. Though I knew how to clean blood off virtually any surface, rolling up and disposing of a sheet of plastic was far easier.

After the issues with Lars, I had rigged my preferred rope and pulley system, much like the types employed by slaughterhouses. The basement's floor joists were surely sturdy enough to support the *dead weight* of a full-grown man.

I chuckled at my gallows humor.

Hooking one hand beneath each of Neil's armpits, I hoisted him up onto his knees and dragged him over to the tarp. Aside from a quiet groan, he was as inanimate as the corpse he soon would be.

His chest rose and fell calmly, just as it would if he was at home asleep in his bed. Far be it from me to disturb his slumber.

I undid the binds around his ankles but left the rope tied around his wrists—another precaution. I was confident, but the stinging pain in my arm kept me wary.

After attaching Neil's ankles to the pulley system with practiced ease, I gave one forceful heave. With a hiss of rope, I pulled until my offering hung upside down from the rafters. I readjusted the location of my plastic bucket, pulled the hunting knife from its sheath on my belt, and knelt next to Neil's swaying form.

"Don't worry, Mr. Rosford. This might be the end for you, but so many others will know the grace and protection of God because of your sacrifice. I'll make sure you're properly put to rest."

I always tried to leave the bodies at a cemetery or near a church, but I'd had to send Lars to Lake Michigan. After the tooth-and-nail brawl, I'd figured a couple days in one of the Great Lakes would get rid of any trace evidence.

A cleansing. A baptism to complete his transformation.

Fortunately for Neil Rosford, he hadn't given me much in the way of resistance. He'd be provided a dignified final resting place. I'd pray over his spilled blood, perhaps even for hours, depending on how the Lord directed me. After adding a decanter of holy water to the blood, I'd be ready to funnel the liquid into my prepared IV bags.

Candlelight glinted off the silver blade as I turned the knife over in my hand. Years ago, I'd taken the six-inch hunting knife from my father's effects. He'd waved the thing in my face more times than I could count, threatening to cut out my tongue if I talked back to him. If my mother found the courage to try to step in to diffuse the situation, he'd do the same to her.

The man had been cursed with a hellish temper, and I assumed that was why he was never chosen for a divine task like I'd been. My work required a level head. Something my father never had.

A quiet moan drew me back to my task. Though the movement was slight, Neil shifted, and his body began to swing. Another utterance, this one more pronounced, followed. The sedative was wearing off.

It was time.

19

The sharp buzz of a ringtone blasted through Zane's dreams like a strong wind blowing away a cloud of dust. As he squeezed his eyes closed a little tighter, hoping the loud buzz was part of his imagination, the warm body at his side shifted.

Amelia.

Events of that night flooded back to him as the cobwebs of sleep fell away. Though his normal mode of operation was to crawl under a figurative rock to try to weather the storm of memories—recollections of Katya and his time in Okhotsk mainly, but there were plenty more buried in the depths of his psyche—he'd promised Amelia they would pick up their night where it had been interrupted by the call about Lars Poteracki.

Poteracki's body had turned up a little more than twenty-four hours earlier, but Zane could have sworn a lifetime had passed since then. He'd gone back in time to the start of his CIA career, and then he'd been ripped back to the present for the brutal murder of a seemingly innocent man.

Then, of course, there was his time with Amelia. The

warmth of her touch, her soft skin, the gentle curves of her body…

He hadn't let himself fall like this for a woman in what felt like an age. During his tenure with the CIA, romantic entanglements with the purpose of obtaining anything other than physical release were off the table. He'd tried to sustain a relationship with a woman named Natalia, but guilt had shrouded him for the duration of their time together.

Admittedly, his goal in getting together with Natalia had been to boost his undercover credibility. All the men around him were constantly in search of their next lay, and he hadn't wanted to draw unwanted attention his way.

In the end, guilt had won out in his mind. Natalia wasn't part of the Russian mob; she was innocent, and Zane had used her. Sure, he'd cared for her, but his primary intent was to cover his ass. The reality of their situation had weighed on him from day one, and before they'd been together a year, he'd ended the relationship.

From then on, he hadn't pursued another. His Russian cohorts had viewed him as something of a playboy, but for the most part, Mischa Bukov had been a lone wolf.

Maybe that was why he'd jumped at the opportunity for a supposed "real" relationship as soon as he'd left the CIA. It had crashed and burned before the two-year mark, but he'd learned a valuable lesson.

Or had he?

He wasn't sure anymore. He only hoped he wasn't repeating the same mistakes with Amelia. His heart told him he wasn't. The connection to Amelia was different from any other he'd experienced in the past.

His cell vibrated against the nightstand for the second time, and he realized with a start he'd almost drifted back to sleep.

He rested one hand on Amelia's shoulder as he pushed

himself to sit upright. She responded with a quiet groan, the sound muffled from where her face was buried in a pillow.

Zane scooped up his phone, and he noticed the caller was the same detective who'd gotten ahold of him on the night Poteracki was found. At three in the morning, a phone call from a homicide detective typically only meant one thing.

Wide awake now, he swiped a finger across the screen to answer. "This is Special Agent Palmer."

"Sorry to wake you, Agent." Detective Weldon Clark's voice was crisp and free of the thickness that tinged Zane's words. Clearly, the man was used to the third shift.

Zane had long ago become accustomed to late-night phone calls. As long as the reason was solid, he typically didn't mind the interruption. But tonight, with Amelia's body warm against his…

He cleared his throat. "It's all right. What can I help you with?"

"Homicide just caught a body in the Wood Grove Cemetery in Washington Park. We've been keeping an eye out for any scenes that match the MO of the Poteracki murder, in case they might be related." Still crisp and professional, Clark's tone changed little.

"Right." Though weariness still pulled on Zane's body, the mention of another murder scene with the same characteristics as Lars Poteracki's revived his mind's usual sharpness. "What'd you find?"

"Another bible verse. Vic's ID is Neil Rosford. License and cash still in his wallet. Throat was slit, and the wound's just about as deep as Poteracki's. We've already got CSU on the scene, but we're waiting to start bagging anything until you and your people get here."

As Amelia rolled over to her side, Zane could feel her gaze on him. "All right." He rubbed his eyes. "We'll be there as soon as we can. It's usually fifteen or twenty, but with the snow…" He sighed. His car had all-wheel-drive capability, and he hoped like hell it would be enough to get them to Wood Grove Cemetery. "I'll let my partner know. We'll get there as soon as we can."

"See you then." With the succinct farewell, the detective ended the call.

"What happened?" Amelia's voice was thick with sleep.

Memories of the garish wound along Lars Poteracki's throat resurfaced in Zane's mind. "The CPD found another body where a bible verse was carved in the vic's flesh."

From beneath his hand, the muscles of Amelia's shoulder tightened. "Shit. Okay. Let's go."

They each dressed in record time, and after Amelia refilled Hup's bowl, they were on their way out the door.

A deep layer of pristine snow covered almost every surface. The glow of the streetlights caught the white blanket, rendering the scene far brighter than a typical three a.m. sight. Plows had made their way through the street regularly, but the pavement was still invisible beneath the packed snow.

Clumps of snow clung to the skinny branches of trees and coated the boughs of the handful of evergreens around the apartment building. When Zane spotted the faint, colorful glow of Christmas lights beneath the snow that covered the nearest pine, he immediately jerked his attention away from the sight.

If he stared at the scene for much longer, he knew where his mind would take him.

Get up, Mischa.

His throat tightened.

Not now. He and Amelia needed to unearth his car, and they had to make their way to a crime scene.

Neil Rosford, potentially killed by the same lunatic who'd

slashed Lars Poteracki's throat and left a bible verse carved in the poor guy's chest.

Thoughts of murder and gruesome autopsies weren't usually Zane's go-to for grounding himself and chasing away the anxiety from his memories of Russia, but tonight, the mental imagery was exactly what he needed.

The excavation of his silver Acura went quickly with both of them shoveling. Amelia had even run back to her apartment to grab a broom to make the process easier. Zane had to admit, he wouldn't have thought of the technique. Literally sweeping snow off his car didn't *look* stylish, but it was efficient.

Zane assumed the plow trucks patrolling the neighborhoods throughout the day and night had made numerous passes, but the agents' trip to Washington Park was still slow-going. Despite his car's all-wheel-drive feature, they nearly got stuck on two different hills. Though the main streets were reasonably free of snow, the side streets were a different story. Chicago was a massive city, and Zane had no earthly idea how they handled two feet of snow.

Under normal circumstances, Amelia would have researched the name Neil Rosford as thoroughly as she could manage, and she'd have relayed the information to Zane. Due to the hazardous conditions, however, the entirety of their conversation revolved around getting there alive.

Finally, a full fifty minutes after he and Amelia had stepped out her front door, Zane pulled into a small lot and parked beside a black and white police cruiser. The flashing light bar cast an eerie red and blue glow on the blanket of snow that covered a postage-stamp-sized lawn. A sign at the start of the sidewalk was partially obscured and blowing snow had plastered half of the brick mausoleum with white.

With a quick glance at Amelia, Zane turned off the ignition, shoved open his door, and stepped out into the brutal weather. His typical attire, even for field work, was a tailored suit and dress shoes, but he was glad he'd altered his routine. Work boots, warm socks, and jeans were a far better fit for the snow-covered wasteland Chicago had become in the last twelve hours.

He and Amelia trudged through the parking lot in silence, only pausing to flash their badges to the pair of officers who stood at the gated entrance to the Wood Grove Cemetery.

True to its name, the place was home to more trees than most parks in Chicago. The interlocking branches overhead had blocked a portion of the snowfall, but as Zane and Amelia made their way to the law enforcement personnel who'd clustered around a granite statue of Saint Peter—their activity illuminated by a handful of battery-operated work lamps—Zane noted the faint *thunk* as a clump of snow fell to the ground.

Camera flashes briefly lit up the night as crime scene techs took photos of the area, dropping the occasional evidence marker as they worked. A pair of tables, each covered with a blue tarp awning, had already been set up not far from the statue. Apparently, the CSU had been given plenty of time to prepare while Zane had crawled through Chicago's snow-covered streets to get to the cemetery.

Not that he was complaining. The more work the CSU had already done, the more information they'd have.

The dark shape of a prone figure lay at the feet of Saint Peter. As the lone splotch of darkness in a sea of white, he was clearly visible, even at a distance. Keeping in mind what Detective Clark had said about the victim's throat being slit, Zane scanned the nearby area for any signs of blood.

He spotted none, and his curiosity deepened.

As Zane and Amelia neared the group of men and women, Detective Weldon Clark waved them over to where he stood beside another familiar face.

Zane was glad to be working with the same people and even more glad they were the same *competent* people. "Detective Clark, Dr. Francis."

The detective extended a gloved hand. "Evening, Agents. Or morning, I guess I should say. Sorry to wake you, but I thought you might want to have a look at the scene considering the similarities between this one and the Poteracki murder."

Zane accepted the detective's handshake. "No worries. You're right. I appreciate you letting us know."

Amelia nodded her agreement as she shook Detective Clark's hand. "We do appreciate it, thank you. Who called it in? It seems…desolate out here. Who was in the middle of a cemetery during a blizzard?"

Detective Clark shot her an appreciative glance. "I thought the same thing. But apparently, Wood Grove has had some issues with headstone vandalism lately." Clark gestured to a private security truck parked not far from the statue. "Curtis Osborne works security for the grounds, and he was doing his rounds through the cemetery when he saw someone lying in the snow by Saint Peter here."

If Rosford's body was the second corpse they'd found at a cemetery, then Zane's suspicion of the security guy would be piqued. However, considering Poteracki was thrown into Lake Michigan, miles away from Wood Grove Cemetery, his gut told him Curtis Osborne was merely a witness, not a suspect.

Zane lifted an eyebrow. "Is Osborne still here?"

"He is." Clark pointed to a couple uniformed officers who stood at the rear fender of a cruiser. "He's not a suspect right now, but he's in the back of the car. He seemed pretty shaken up by the whole thing. Said he's seen some weird shit working in security, but not a dead body with the throat slit from ear to ear."

Amelia tilted her chin in the direction of the statue. "Did he see anyone around? Anything suspicious?"

"Not that he noticed, no. He said his nightly schedule has him making rounds every three hours. There wasn't anything at the Saint Peter statue on his round before, so the body must've been dumped somewhere in that three-hour window."

Either the killer had monitored the security personnel before he'd dumped Rosford's body, or he'd simply gotten lucky. Zane hoped it was the latter, but from what they'd learned in the investigation so far, he wouldn't put his money on it. "Mind if we take a look?"

Dr. Francis produced a pair of blue vinyl gloves. "We documented the amount of snow accumulation before getting a reading on his liver temperature. He's still in the same spot we found him, which is partially covered by a concrete gazebo of sorts. That's why the body isn't completely covered with snow."

As Zane followed Dr. Francis, Amelia, and Detective Clark close on their heels, he glanced around, searching for any footprints that didn't belong. Though the crime scene techs had left their fair share of tracks, he knew they'd mark any footsteps that weren't theirs.

Again, there was more of nothing. "If someone hauled a body all the way to this statue to dump it, and in the middle of a snowstorm, shouldn't we have tire imprints or tracks somewhere?"

Though Zane expected Detective Clark to answer, Dr. Francis spoke up first. "You'd think, wouldn't you? It's tapering off now, but the vic would've been dumped right at the ending peak of the storm. Assuming he dumped the body right after Osborne had finished his rounds, his tracks would've been covered back up within the hour."

Zane swore. His first inclination had been they'd have an

easier time tracing a person who'd dragged a dead body through snow, but clearly, he was wrong. "The killer used the environment to his advantage."

"Sounds like a professional," Amelia said.

Why in the hell would a contract killer go out of their way to leave a body at the feet of a statue of Saint Peter? The only viable explanation Zane could come up with at that moment was the individual who'd hired the hitman had specified the corpse be left in the cemetery.

Was the body's placement some kind of message? A warning to a rival crime boss?

Or was it all the twisted ritual of a serial killer?

Zane's palms grew clammy at the notion. His gut told him the religious symbolism and the detailed similarities from each body were more akin to the ritualistic methods of a serial murderer and less emblematic of a hitman. Unless it was a hitman trying to make them think a serial killer was responsible.

The possibilities whirled through his mind as he and Dr. Francis approached the victim's feet, and Zane mentally filed the questions away for later consideration.

Rosford's skin was tinged blue, his complexion nearly the same white shade as the snow. Just beneath his chin, the pale skin gave way to reddish-purple tissue. Not torn and shredded like a wound from an animal attack, but neatly severed, the same way a butcher cut the meat for a steak from a cow.

The lighter shade of cartilage of Rosford's esophagus was just barely visible from Zane's vantage point. Though he'd been curious how Dr. Francis and Detective Clark had spotted the bible verse carved on the body without disturbing the scene, the sight at Saint Peter's feet answered the query.

Unlike Poteracki, Rosford's shirt had been cut away to expose the macabre message.

Zane gestured to the body. "Did you do that?" He knew the answer but felt compelled to confirm.

As expected, Dr. Francis shook his head. "No. Seems to me the killer wanted us to see this."

Stepping to stand beside Zane, Amelia pressed her lips together, appearing thoughtful. "Why the difference between this guy and Poteracki? Poteracki's shirt wasn't cut open."

Picturing the scene of Lars Poteracki's still body, a lightbulb flashed in Zane's mind. "Maybe he didn't cut it to make sure we saw it. Maybe he cut the shirt so he could carve it in the first place. Poteracki was wearing a button-down, remember?"

Understanding dawned on Amelia's expression. "Right. So, he cut this guy's shirt because he couldn't unbutton it."

Dr. Francis gingerly picked his way forward and knelt at Rosford's side. "Based on the status of rigor mortis and the vic's liver temp when I got here, I'd put his time of death somewhere between nineteen-hundred and twenty-three-hundred. Or seven p.m. and eleven p.m., for you civilians. That's taking into account the air temperature out here."

Now that they'd closed the distance to Rosford's body, Zane tilted his head to read the message on the man's chest. "Romans 12:1-2. That's really specific."

Clark fished his phone from the pocket of his peacoat. "I looked it up before you got here. According to the English Standard Version, the verse says, *'I appeal to you therefore, brothers, by the mercies of God, to present your bodies as a living sacrifice, holy and acceptable to God, which is your spiritual worship. Do not be conformed to this world, but be transformed by the renewal of your mind, that by testing you may discern what is the will of God, what is good and acceptable and perfect.'*"

The hairs on the back of Zane's neck prickled to attention. "The verse on Poteracki's chest was almost uplifting. This one sounds...well, preachy. No pun intended."

Amelia crossed both arms over her chest. "It sounds like something you'd hear at a baptism. Now, how about the obvious question." Her green eyes shifted between the three of them. "Where's all the blood? Even if the body was dumped, there should be *something* here, right? There's nothing on his face, and there's hardly any on his shirt."

Dr. Francis's expression turned stony. "Normally, I'd say it depends on how long the body sat before it was moved, but the lack of spatter on the vic's face or clothes is peculiar. We can assume he bled out where he was killed, but that doesn't explain the lack of blood on *him*." Pulling up the victim's shirt, the doctor gestured for a tech to assist him, and together, they rolled the man to his side.

"Very little livor mortis." Amelia's breath was barely above a whisper.

Dr. Francis nodded. "You win the prize. When I get him on the table, I'll be better able to ascertain how much blood volume remains in his system."

The invisible spider legs were back on Zane's skin. Ensuring a lack of blood evidence *did* seem like a valid tactic for a contract killer to employ. Plenty of cases had been steered in the right direction or solved completely based on patterns of blood spatter.

But when the body wasn't even at the scene of the crime, why go through the trouble to keep the victim's body clean? Or worse, why remove the majority of blood at all?

Dracula.

The lack of blood was another marker indicating Lars and Neil had been killed by the same person.

Making sure to steer clear of the ground close to the body, Zane knelt across from Dr. Francis as he forced, once again, the mental image of the fanged demon from his mind.

As he peered down at the gaping wound in Neil Rosford's throat, the dark shape of a tattoo caught his attention.

A scorpion.

Zane sucked in a sharp breath as his stomach clenched. "Shit." He glanced up to Amelia and gestured to the tattoo. "Did you see the tat on his neck? It's a scorpion. This is…was our witness. The dealer who sold the heroin to Poteracki."

For a beat, Amelia's eyes flew open wide, but she nodded her agreement a second later. "Scorpion. We'll need to contact his next of kin to get a positive ID, but the tattoo goes a long way to confirming this was our witness. We'll run prints too."

Zane was grateful the lunatic who killed Neil had left his license on his corpse. That would make life a little less complicated. It also meant he wouldn't need to ask for an identification of Scorpion by the young prostitute with the strawberry blonde curls. Her appearance stabbed Zane's conscience, reminding him of his failure in Okhotsk.

He gritted his teeth, hoping the expression would be attributed to the scene in front of them and not the ghosts in his head. "Let's pay a visit to Rosford's next of kin. They might have information we can use."

They either knew something, or they were next.

20

Erika was just about asleep when the rap of knuckles against the front door woke her. She'd been lying on the couch for hours, trying in vain to get some rest. Neil hadn't replied to any of her text messages that night, and though the lack of communication wasn't unusual, she was still worried.

She was always worried.

After she'd placed the bowl from her late-night cereal in the dishwasher, she'd stretched out on the small sectional to wrap up the week's reading assignment for her economics class. Her hope had been to either focus on the text or for the content to bore her to sleep. Unfortunately, she'd managed neither. Her thoughts had continued to drift back to Neil.

She rubbed her face and took in a long breath through her nose. The blue glow of the digital clock on the entertainment stand read 5:03. What time had she started to drift off? Four, maybe four-thirty?

And better yet, who in the hell was knocking on her door at five in the morning? Or had the knock been part of her dream?

The cobwebs of sleep still shrouded her brain as she rose to stand. Was her mind playing tricks on her?

Better check the door just in case. Maybe Neil forgot his keys.

A pang of hope swelled in her chest, but the optimism was short-lived. She was spacey and had a tendency to forget an important item when she went out, but Neil's memory was sharp. In the unlikely event he'd forgotten his keys at home, he'd have noticed shortly after he left the house, and he'd have sent her a text or called her.

Is he hurt? Did he get robbed? Oh my god, please let him be okay.

Tiptoeing as quickly as possible, she rushed to the front door. As she squinted through the peephole, a mixture of sadness and fear curdled in her stomach.

Something bad had happened. She could tell.

Instead of Neil, she spotted a man and a woman she'd never seen before. Based on the pair's coats and neat hairstyles, they weren't from around here.

They were cops.

She didn't pause to let the dread settle in her chest.

Five a.m.

Destiny was sound asleep in her room. Though the girl's door was closed, Erika didn't want the pair of detectives to repeatedly beat on the door with their infamous "cop knock." Law enforcement had a particular way of knocking that could wake the dead.

Without undoing the chain lock, Erika flicked the deadbolt and opened the door a crack. She'd never had a personal vendetta with cops until she'd worked as a prostitute.

Back then, she'd just been a scared teenager trying to escape an abysmal home life, but the CPD had never viewed her that way. Even though Erika and the girls she worked with had been sexually assaulted on multiple occasions, they never dared report the crimes to the police. Some of the older women had tried, but they'd each been laughed out of the precinct. Or worse, arrested.

Glancing from the man to the woman and back, Erika let every ounce of suspicion show through in her face. She'd taken a few classes on criminal justice, and she knew a few things about the way the law worked in this country.

"Can I help you?" Her tone bordered on haughty and didn't betray the uneasiness that roiled in her stomach.

The man reached into the pocket of his frock coat, and Erika reflexively flinched backward. She expected him to double down and glower, but his gray eyes softened.

Slowly, he held up his other hand. "It's all right. I'm just reaching for my badge."

Embarrassment heated Erika's cheeks, and she wanted to slam the door in their faces so she could go hide under the blankets of her bed, but she resisted.

Gritting her teeth, she nodded for him to continue.

"I'm Special Agent Zane Palmer, and this is my partner, Special Agent Amelia Storm." He flipped open a small leather case to reveal an identification card that read "FBI" in bold, block letters. "Are you Erika Brabyn?"

"Yes." Erika's knees had suddenly turned to rubber, and she clutched the door handle in a death grip to keep herself upright. She repeatedly swallowed before she was confident she could speak. "F...FBI? What...why?" Licking her dry lips, she pulled herself up a little straighter. "What do you want?"

The female agent tucked away her badge and inclined her chin toward Erika's apartment. "Could we come in, Ms. Brabyn?"

Go away! Get the hell out of here! I don't want anything to do with you people. I don't want my neighbors to see me talking to you, and I don't want you to wake up my daughter. I don't want to hear what you have to say. Neither of you belong here. Go back home to your nice houses and your fancy cars, and get the hell out of my life.

None of the vitriol made it to Erika's tongue. She already knew something terrible had happened. These were *Feds*, not city cops.

She swallowed past the tightness in her throat, managed a weak nod, and unhooked the brass chain. "Please be quiet. My daughter is still sleeping."

A hint of something resembling sympathy flashed in the man's face as Erika flipped a light switch. Wordlessly, she gestured to the sectional couch. Perhaps a woman with better manners would have offered the two agents a beverage, but etiquette wasn't high on her list of priorities right now.

The two agents took their seats, and Erika positioned herself at the edge of the chaise. She wanted to tell them to spit it out, to rip off the band-aid, as the saying went. But once again, words failed to reach her tongue.

Clearing her throat, Agent Storm straightened her back as Agent Palmer produced a small notepad from his pocket.

Expression gentle, Agent Storm turned to Erika. "Ms. Brabyn, I'm afraid we have some bad news. Your…partner, Neil Rosford, he's dead."

Tears stung the corners of Erika's eyes before the woman had even finished the sentence. As much as she wanted to put on a brave exterior and show no weakness in front of two emissaries of the justice system that had failed her over and over again, she couldn't find the strength to fake it.

For more than a year, ever since Neil had begun to dabble in selling anything harder than weed, Erika had lived in constant dread of a visit like this. Any night he came home a little later than normal, her mind always took her to the darkest possibility.

She'd imagined cops showing up at the door to arrest her,

leaving Destiny as a ward of the state. She'd imagined Neil being beaten and robbed and then left for dead. No matter how many mental health remedies she'd tried, none had ever worked.

And now, here she was.

Seated across from two agents from the FBI who'd just told her the love of her life, the father of her young daughter, the man who'd helped her climb out of the figurative gutter...

Was dead.

Erika wanted to cry—not just sniffle as she tried to wade through the remainder of the agents' visit, but truly cry. Bury her face in a pillow and sob until she passed out.

How was she supposed to break the news to Destiny? The sweet girl adored both her parents, but she was most definitely a daddy's girl. How did Erika explain death to a child who wasn't even five years old?

Stop it, Erika. Not while they're here. Pull yourself together. Get this interview, or whatever the hell it is, over with. They want something. Otherwise, the man wouldn't have pulled out a notepad.

Even though Neil was dead, Erika wouldn't betray his memory. She wouldn't rat him out now or ever. The people around him were a different story.

When she finally summoned up the fortitude to square her shoulders, she had no idea how long she'd been silent. As she returned her focus to the two agents, she spotted no indication of irritability or impatience, so either the pair was adept at handling grieving spouses, or Erika's sense of time had briefly become warped.

She reached for the glass of water she'd left on the coffee table and took a sip. Her mouth was as dry as a desert, and her tongue felt like sandpaper.

But she had to speak.

"What happened?" Her voice was hoarse but not meek. She could live with that.

Sympathy returned to Agent Storm's face. "He was murdered."

Though the single word was like an ice pick tearing through Erika's heart, and though the earth's gravity seemed to have just quadrupled, she fought to hold herself together. She balled both hands into fists until her nails dug into the sensitive skin of her palms.

She'd fall apart later. Not now. Not in front of these people.

Information, Erika. Get information. Learn as much from these two as you can. That's what they're here to do to you, right?

As she glanced to her clenched fists, she recalled her and Neil's conversation from the night before. One of Neil's clients, Lars, had been knocked unconscious and then abducted. Neil had memorized the license plate number of the vehicle, but he'd not told the details to Erika. Either he'd simply forgotten, or he'd wanted to protect her in case she received a visit just like this one.

Seeing Lars Poteracki's murder in the local news had sent shockwaves through Erika, and she'd almost begged Neil to stay home for a few nights. At least until things in Washington Park cooled down.

He couldn't, though. Bills loomed over their heads, and if they didn't maintain a steady source of income, they'd default on the payments. Living paycheck to paycheck was a never-ending battle.

Guilt settled in on Erika's shoulders like a cape made of lead.

She should have begged.

Should have pleaded. Should have done anything to keep him from leaving the house.

Focus, Erika.

"How…how did it happen? Did you find the guy…the person who did it?"

"Not yet." Agent Storm tucked a piece of dark, blonde-tipped hair behind one ear. "We have a few questions we'd like to ask, if that's okay? Anything that might help point us in the right direction."

There was an honor code among outlaws, especially drug dealers. No matter what, you never talked to the cops.

Fuck them. If they killed Neil, then they can rot in a prison cell for the rest of their lives. I'm not keeping this shit to myself just because some pricks slinging dope in Washington Park might not want me to talk.

Erika took in a deep, steadying breath and nodded. "Okay. What do you want to know?"

Agent Storm scooted forward in her seat, her focus shifting exclusively to Erika. "Had Neil mentioned anyone following him lately? Or anything that might've stuck out from the usual, such as someone who'd become angry with him?"

Here it was. If Neil had been killed in part of a drug-related dispute in Washington Park, Erika was about to become a rat.

She didn't care. She wanted Neil's killer to pay.

"He…kind of." She interlocked her fingers to keep herself from wringing her hands. "He told me about something weird he saw. Something that happened a few nights ago. On Sunday."

The female agent's eyebrow quirked up. "What happened on Sunday?"

From Neil's strange behavior on the night Lars Poteracki was abducted all the way to the moral debate Neil had experienced when considering whether to report the incident, Erika told them everything. She spared no detail. As long as the information didn't incriminate her personally, she answered each of the agents' follow-up questions.

The discussion didn't leave her feeling any better, but at least she could eventually rest assured she'd done everything in her power to help find Neil's killer.

21

Leaning forward in his chair, Zane propped both elbows atop the polished table as he stared at the writing on the whiteboard. To his side, fat snowflakes drifted past the room's expansive window. Fortunately, the snow predicted to fall into the early evening was only supposed to accumulate to two inches. Compared to the near two feet of snow Chicago had gotten the day before, a couple inches seemed like chump change.

For the past few hours, he and Amelia had pored over the backgrounds of Neil Rosford and Lars Poteracki. They'd run through everything from the men's high school years to the dates of their deaths but had found virtually nothing to link the two together.

According to Poteracki's statements from the Ersfeld case, he and Rosford hadn't interacted with one another beyond an occasional score back when Poteracki still used. During Kevin Ersfeld's reign of terror, Rosford had laid low. In fact, he was one of the few dealers in the area to slide under Ersfeld's radar altogether.

When the prostitute from Washington Park had told

Zane that Rosford kept a low profile, she hadn't been exaggerating. For a drug dealer, Rosford was squeaky clean. The guy had no rap sheet, no juvenile record, and no record of ever cooperating with law enforcement. Hell, he'd barely even crossed paths with law enforcement.

If there was no common thread between Rosford and Poteracki, then they were left with one viable scenario.

"Rosford was killed because he was a witness." Zane straightened his back and stretched his arms in front of himself.

Tapping a dry-erase marker in the palm of one hand, Amelia shot the whiteboard an inquisitive glance as she nodded her agreement. "It's the only thing that really makes sense at this point. Unless we're missing something else that connects these two."

"I doubt it." Zane skimmed the information Amelia had written. She'd included summaries of Rosford and Poteracki's respective histories—what they could find in the FBI's databases, at least. Still, with all the information side by side, an obvious, meaningful connection eluded them.

With a sigh, Amelia crossed her arms. "So, Poteracki was killed because he was a federal informant, and then Rosford was killed because he was a witness. Sure seems like the sort of thing a contract killer would be used for, doesn't it?"

"And considering all the old cases we found in ViCAP, it's a contract killer who's been active for a long time." Zane left the remainder of his observation unsaid. They both knew hitmen who operated for lengthy periods were often so ingratiated into the world of organized crime that they were nearly impossible to identify.

Amelia arched an eyebrow at him. "Or a serial killer. It doesn't seem very in character for a hitman to carve bible verses into his victims' chests, you know? That's the part that's tripping me up. And if he killed Rosford because he was a witness, why'd he wait so long?"

Zane had considered the gap in time between the men's deaths, but he didn't have an answer to Amelia's question. "You're right. Poteracki was killed on Sunday, and Rosford was killed last night. He'd been out to Washington Park each night in-between. Plus, the bible verse carved on his body didn't have any relevance to him *being* a witness in the first place. Maybe the killer tried to intimidate him first and then decided that wouldn't be enough?"

Rubbing her temple, Amelia returned the marker to its magnetic holder. "I don't know. If we include the murders from Terre Haute and Milwaukee, then our guy has racked up quite a body count. I can't imagine someone who's killed that many people would hesitate to take out a witness." She pressed her lips together as she pulled out her phone.

He and Amelia had been poised to go through the cold cases from Indiana and Wisconsin today, but Neil Rosford's murder had forced that plan to the backburner. They'd both hoped for a fresh lead from the newest scene, but they'd been stymied. Unlike Poteracki, Rosford either knew his killer or was taken by surprise. There weren't any defensive wounds, indicating the man had put up a fight. The battle was over before it even began.

Zane was so absorbed in his mental walkthrough of Rosford's murder that he didn't notice the excitement on Amelia's face until she was waving her phone in the air.

"We just got a message from the lab." She circled the table and took a seat at his side. A whiff of her strawberry and coconut shampoo followed the movement. "They finished the analysis on that piece of skin found between Poteracki's teeth."

A hopeful rush spread through Zane's chest. "Did we get a match?"

"Sort of. Not a match to an individual, but a match to some old cases." Amelia opened her laptop, typed in the password, and navigated to her email inbox.

"From one of the murders in Terre Haute?" He scratched his unshaven cheek. Until now, they hadn't had a chance to go through the cases to learn whether DNA had been collected from any of the old scenes.

"Yeah…one of the Terre Haute cases from three years ago, and then another from Detroit. In both cases, the DNA was found under the victims' fingernails." As she pulled up the message from the lab, she scooted a little closer.

"It's confirmation." A glimmer of hope sparked in Zane, pushing back the cobwebs of exhaustion. "Confirmation the same guy has been killing people like this for…what? Four years, at least."

Amelia tilted her head. "The four-year-old cases from Terre Haute don't have any DNA evidence on file, but the MO is exactly the same. Throat slit, massive blood loss, bible verse carved on the body."

Zane's hope was abruptly overshadowed by the thought of the time-consuming task in front of them. Turning to Amelia, he rolled his chair away from the table. "We've got all these cases to go through, then. Looks like we're going to be here for a while."

A twinge of weariness accompanied the determination on Amelia's face. "Yeah, looks like. If he's got a body count this high already, then we need to get through these cases sooner rather than later to see if we can find a pattern, learn more about his motivation."

"Right. Because we *know* he's going to kill again. We just need to figure out who the target will be." Zane pushed to his feet and stretched both arms above his head. "I think that calls for some more coffee."

Amelia rubbed her eyes. "I think so too. With a double-shot of espresso."

He shot her a grin as he plucked his coat off the back of the office chair. Though he felt guilty they hadn't had a chance to talk about the status of their relationship since they'd slept together the night before, he knew Amelia shared his focus. Neither of them was going anywhere, and they'd have plenty of time to talk about their future once they'd found the person who'd slit Lars Poteracki and Neil Rosford's throats.

After confirming Amelia's coffee order, Zane took off to the parking garage. His car handled well in the inclement weather, but he was still grateful the newest front wasn't more lake-effect snow.

Memories blanketed him with each falling snowflake, and he'd had his fill of both when he and Amelia had been at Washington Park the day before.

Even in warmer weather, the recollections were never far away. But when heavy snow blotted out the horizon and Christmas carols blared from speakers in stores and restaurants, the shadow of his past towered over him like a giant.

Sliding into the driver's seat of his Acura, he pulled the door shut and took in a long breath. "Coffee, Zane. You're going to go get coffee, and then you're going to work a case. A case for the FBI, which is where you work. In Chicago, which is where you live. Not the CIA. Not Okhotsk. *Chicago*."

But what about the girl who looked just like Katya? The prostitute he'd talked to in Washington Park. What about her?

He clenched his jaw, glaring at the windshield to keep the memory at bay. "*Chicago*. There're hot dogs every two blocks, it's always windy, and traffic absolutely blows."

When the voice of doubt in the back of his head didn't answer, he took the silence as his cue to continue. Despite what he'd just told himself, there were few drivers on the road for his short trip to his and Amelia's favored coffee shop.

By the time he stepped out of his car, the snowfall had increased to a near-whiteout. He turned to look back in the direction of the FBI office—the ten-story glass building was difficult to miss on a normal day—but he could hardly make out the gas station at the end of the block. The forecast had predicted only an additional two to three inches of snow, but he wondered how accurate their guess was.

Weather forecasting was the only job where a person could be wrong frequently and still have job security.

He rubbed his tired eyes and trudged toward the two-story café. Warm light glowed in the wide glass windows at the front of the building, promising warmth, and more importantly, caffeine.

As he pushed his way in through the double doors, he stopped abruptly.

In the corner of his eye, he caught the glimmer of colorful lights adorning a tall pine. The glow reflected off the shiny ornaments and tinsel, and a golden star sat proudly atop the tree.

It's just a damn Christmas tree. It's December. They're everywhere. You need to get used to this.

Gritting his teeth, Zane let the door close behind him, swallowed the bitter taste in his mouth, and started for the counter. A young man with neatly styled jet-black hair greeted him with a wide smile. The barista was a full-time shift manager at the café, and Zane regularly saw him when he came to pick up coffee.

See. It's fine.

To emphasize the fact to himself, he forced a smile to his face. "Hey, Aaron. How're things going around here with the..." he glanced over his shoulder and waved a hand at the wintry scene outside, "the weather?"

Aaron lifted a shoulder and let it fall. "Slow. Boring. Half the staff called in because they didn't think they'd be able to get here. If I didn't live so close, I don't think I'd have made it in, either."

Zane sometimes wished he had a job where he could call into work on excessively difficult days. "Yeah, I don't doubt that. I spent forever helping my..." He paused. His what? What was Amelia Storm to him right now? They hadn't been given a chance to talk about it the night before, but he didn't think they'd revert back to business as usual after they'd had sex.

When he noted the curiosity on Aaron's youthful face, he knew he needed to say something.

Rubbing his temples, Zane buried his embarrassment. "Sorry, I just lost my train of thought mid-sentence. Which is exactly why I'm here."

Aaron's face brightened with a grin. "That's a mood. What can I get you?"

Zane recited his and Amelia's orders, chitchatted with Aaron while he prepared the drinks, and then headed back out into the frozen tundra to his car.

The interaction with Aaron had returned some normalcy to Zane's mind, and he was cautiously optimistic he'd avoided another flashback incident.

Until he turned on the radio in the middle of an advertisement for a holiday concert.

He avoided Christmas songs like the plague. Though his chosen station rarely, if ever, played Christmas music, he couldn't entirely avoid the festive music this time of year. It was every-damn-where. In television shows, grocery stores, dentist's offices, and now, apparently, radio commercials.

During his time in Okhotsk, the only music he'd had

access to was three CDs packed with holiday tunes. Most were in Russian, and Zane ran little risk of running into them here in the States.

One disc, however, had been comprised of the most popular Christmas songs from around the world. "Silent Night" had been a favorite of the men at the docks, though Zane still had no earthly idea why.

He snapped out a hand to switch off the radio, but not before the eerie melody seeped into the air around him like a noxious gas.

His heart hammered against his chest. The music was gone, replaced with silence and the quiet hum of the Acura's engine.

Still, he heard it. He heard that damn song, and then, something else.

Get up, Mischa.

Rurik was long dead, but the man's words were just as clear as if he was sitting in the passenger's seat. Squeezing his eyes closed, Zane clamped both hands around the steering wheel and bowed his head. The memory was already here, and he knew there was no point in trying to stuff it back down into the depths of his psyche.

"Get up, Mischa!" Rurik barked. It was the second time he'd given the order, and if Zane didn't comply, he wouldn't enjoy the third request. Zane knew that Rurik's biggest pet peeve was repeating himself. He'd seen the man brandish a weapon for less.

The tang of iron filled Zane's mouth, and the cold, splintery wood of the dock dug into his face like the world's most uncomfortable pillow. Zane wished he was resting in a cold, hard bed. He wished the sight of Katya's thin form on a dock at Okhotsk Bay was a figment of his imagination and that the hulking figure at her side was a dream person.

But Katya was really here. So was Sergei Isayev, and the burly

Russian had shoved Katya face-first into the ground right before Rurik had hit Zane with a hefty right hook.

Pain lanced deep within Zane's jaw from the site of the blow, leaving him wondering if his cheekbone had been fractured. Spitting blood onto the weathered wood, he gritted his teeth and pushed himself up to a kneeling position.

Rurik's hateful blue eyes were already on him. Though Zane had been confident he could best the man in a one-on-one brawl, right then, he didn't want to test his luck. The sheer malevolence radiating from those pale blue orbs was almost enough to knock him right back on his ass.

A quiet groan jerked Zane's attention to the prone figure at Sergei's booted feet.

Katya.

As panic swelled in Zane's chest, he turned back to Rurik. "Why is she here? She didn't do anything. Does the boss know that you're messing with the merchandise?" He hated referring to human beings as product, but he was here to blend. Not to change the vernacular of Russian mobsters.

Rurik jabbed a finger at Zane. "This isn't about her. It's about you, Mischa. Who in the hell told you to waste our *medical supplies on this little bitch?" For a beat, he paused as if he expected an answer. But when Zane opened his mouth to reply, Rurik cut him off. "No one! That's who! You made that decision yourself, without consulting your superior."*

Though Zane wanted to rise to his full height to tower over the shorter man, he forced himself to remain still. He'd planned a rebuttal on the same day he'd brought the antibiotic ointment to Katya—one he'd thought *his boss would understand.*

"She was hurt. Her wound was infected. She would have died!" Before Rurik could catch on to any sliver of emotion in Zane's voice, he forged ahead. "She's young, and she's pretty. She's worth a hell of a lot more than antibiotic ointment and a couple pills!"

Muscles rippled with tension in Rurik's jaw. "That wasn't your decision to make, Mischa. You're not in charge here. You understand that, right?"

Swallowing his knee-jerk retort, Zane lowered his chin and glared at the wooden dock. He'd figured common sense would overshadow the chain of command, but apparently, he'd figured wrong. At the same time, he was certain that Sergei and Rurik wouldn't have dragged Katya out of the girls' house and all the way down to the dock just to shove her over once as a message to Zane.

He wanted the altercation to end with another punch to his face, but he knew better.

Rurik had something far more insidious up his sleeve.

If Zane wanted to change the outcome, all he could do was try to reason with the man. Licking his salty lips, Zane looked back up to Rurik. "I was looking out for the business. For the bottom line. I didn't...I shouldn't have done anything without your approval. I just thought..." He trailed off as he glanced at Katya.

The poor girl had curled into the fetal position, but her eyes were obscured by matted curls.

"You thought what?" Rurik crossed his arms and let out a derisive snort. "Thought you'd clean her wound, and she'd fall in love with you? Is that what you wanted, Mischa? Did you want her to like you? Why? So she'd spread her legs for you?"

I helped her because I'm not a piece of shit like you.

Zane gritted his teeth so hard he thought they might break.

Rurik gestured to Sergei, and the taller man retrieved a length of rope from inside his puffy coat.

Heart pounding a relentless cadence against his ribs, Zane forced himself to maintain as calm an exterior as he could manage. Was the rope for him, or was it for Katya? Surely, the boss wouldn't authorize Rurik to kill a loyal soldier just because he'd brought cheap medical supplies to one of the girls. Right?

Time moved at a fraction of its normal pace as Sergei planted one booted foot to either side of Katya's prone body. The big man knelt, shoving her none too gently onto her stomach as he did. He jerked one of her thin arms behind her back and then the other.

Zane's pulse pounded so loudly in his ears that he hardly registered Katya's muffled pleas for mercy.

Why was Sergei binding Katya's hands? Wasn't Zane the offender? Shouldn't he be punished?

Strawberry blonde curls blocked out her bright green eyes, but Zane could tell she'd shifted her focus to him. "Mischa, what's happening? What are they doing?"

His blood had gone cold, and his muscles felt as if they'd been wrapped in barbed wire. He wanted to speak, to ask Rurik and Sergei what they were doing or what he could do to make them stop. But any time he tried, he knew he had to remain silent.

I'm a covert operative for the Central Intelligence Agency of the United States of America. I'm here in Okhotsk to infiltrate the Russian mafia and to find and prevent threats to American national security. My work could—no, my work will save lives. Tens. Hundreds. Maybe even thousands.

But it'll all be worth nothing if I give myself away, or if I die.

In the midst of Zane's panicked attempt to remind himself who he was and why his role was too important to sabotage, Sergei had fastened a knot to bind Katya's wrists to her ankles.

The poor girl had been hog-tied while Zane had let his mind wander to the CIA.

Fighting his instinctive urge to right this wrong, Zane managed to turn his head toward Rurik. "What's he doing? W-why is he tying her up?"

The fires of hatred in Rurik's eyes had died down, and in their place was the cold, empty ash of nothingness. "The boss likes you, Mischa. I do not know why, but he does." He gestured to the bound Katya. "This is a lesson. This is what happens when you don't obey the chain of command and when you let your dick lead you around out here."

Zane's automatic response was to reiterate the fact he hadn't been interested in sleeping with Katya. Hell, she was barely seventeen, and he was twenty-two. There were only five years between them, but they were an important five years. She was a damn child.

He bit his tongue until he tasted a renewed tang of iron.

Don't give yourself away. You're one of them.

Face expressionless, Sergei rose to his full height and produced a six-inch, partly serrated knife. Zane had seen the blade before, usually when Sergei was trying to impress the others by stabbing the table between his fingers.

Zane held onto the inane thought as a flurry of snowflakes whipped past his head. Better he hole up in his mind's eye and watch Sergei's drunken stunts than pay attention to how the hulking man towered over Katya.

"Pay attention, Mischa." *Rurik's sharp voice cracked through Zane's half-hearted attempt to dissociate.* "We're doing this for you, remember?"

How could he forget?

Blinking away the tears that had formed from the wind's cold bite, Zane reluctantly shifted his focus to Katya and Sergei. Whatever violence was about to befall the poor girl, Zane shouldered the responsibility for it.

Sergei hunched over and grabbed a fist full of Katya's curls, pulling her pale face away from the dingy wooden dock.

Bile churned in Zane's stomach as he watched. He fully expected the brutal Russian to slit her throat and then toss her body into the sea.

Instead, Sergei dragged the blade along her pale cheek, leaving a trail of crimson in its wake. Though Katya's bottom lip trembled, she remained silent. Her fair skin had taken on a bluish hue, and Zane wondered how much longer she could even survive out here without proper clothing.

As Sergei moved the knife back toward Katya's arm, a rush of naïve hope, warm and welcoming in its falseness, surged in Zane's chest. He was like a dying man in the desert who'd stumbled upon a mirage.

Realistically, why would Sergei sever the binds he'd only just finished? Why would he make one superficial cut to Katya's face and then let her loose?

Almost like an answer to Zane's unasked questions, Sergei jabbed the tip of the knife into Katya's exposed forearm. Though her silence so far was admirable, maybe even courageous, the façade ended as soon as Sergei ripped the blade all the way back to her elbow.

Tears streamed down her face, mixing with the bright blood that dribbled from the cut on her cheek. "Please. You don't have to do this. I'll do anything, anything you want. I swear I didn't ask him for anything. He just...brought me the supplies. I didn't want any of it. If...if I'd known, I'd have turned them down."

Was she trying to throw him under the bus? He might have felt a flicker of anger, but he couldn't find it within himself to fault her. To her, he was just another Russian goon. Another pervert who'd eagerly take his turn raping her if he was given a chance.

If their roles were reversed, he'd sure as hell throw Mischa under the bus.

"Shut up, bitch!" Rurik snapped. "This isn't about you." His dead eyes drifted to Zane, and he let the unfinished sentence linger in the air.

This was about him. About Mischa.

Katya let out another visceral cry as Sergei made a matching cut on her other arm. The big man lifted a shoulder and glanced to Rurik, then to Zane. "The bottom-feeders like a little blood. It's like an appetizer for them, I think."

Zane's brain struggled to piece together the words that had just come from Sergei's mouth. *Bottom-feeders? Appetizers? What in the hell was he talking about?*

Without another word of explanation, Sergei bent down and

hoisted Katya off the ground like she was a paper mâché doll and not a living, breathing, bleeding human.

"What...where?" Zane's words were cut short as Sergei strode to the edge of the dock.

The burly man hardly made a sound as he heaved the girl into the gray, choppy water of the Sea of Okhotsk. Her scream tore through the mournful howl of the wind, but only for a moment.

Only until she went underwater.

Zane jerked back to reality—to his warm car, his hot coffee, his expensive coat. All things Katya had likely never experienced in her short life. A life cut short by his mistakes.

He pulled in a shaky breath, leaned back, and rubbed his eyes. The damned commercial, the one that had pulled him into the flashback in the first place, was over, and the NPR segment had resumed.

On the outside, everything was as it should be. The normalcy was a façade Zane had to maintain for...how long?

"Shit." He slumped down in his seat.

The DNA results. The cases from Terre Haute, Detroit, and Milwaukee, on top of the two from Chicago.

Draping an arm over his face, he clenched his jaw. Could he even *pretend* to be normal right now? Christ, he could still hear Katya's scream echoing in his head. Rurik was gone, but Zane could swear the Russian sergeant's intense stare was cutting through him.

"No." Though he was alone, he still didn't want to add the second part out loud.

I killed him. Just like he killed Katya. I cut him up and threw him in the ocean.

It wasn't Zane's proudest moment, but he didn't regret that the prick was dead. Sergei eventually met his untimely end as well, and though Zane played a part, he wasn't the one to deal the lethal blow. That honor had been given to Maksim Dragunov.

As it so happened, Sergei and Rurik had been part of a years-long plot to overthrow their location's commander. The men were tough as nails, and they were as brutal as they were ruthless. However, they'd lacked a key component required for a successful mutiny…intelligence…chicanery. Their machinations were so basic, they could've been crafted by a teenager.

Shaking off the memories, Zane reached in his coat for his cell. He hated omitting information from Amelia, but he didn't feel the time was quite right for him to give her a full explanation of what was occurring in his brain. Though he wanted to throw himself at the case in an effort to keep the memories at bay, he also didn't want to half-ass his work. If he missed an important detail that resulted in someone else being hurt…

Stop it!

He was too distracted. He just needed to…sleep? Recharge? He wasn't sure. But he needed to do it alone.

Hey, I got our coffees. I'm going to bring them back to the office, but I'm not feeling so hot. I think I'll have to call it an early one, but I can drop you off at home if you want?

Three dots appeared at the bottom of the screen, indicating she'd begun typing a response almost immediately.

Sure, that's fine. This is all case research, so I can do it at home. Let me get my stuff, and I'll just meet you in the parking garage.

His muscles were still tight from the surge of adrenaline that had accompanied the vivid flashback, but he breathed a sigh of relief at her message. Though he doubted Amelia had ever stood by and watched the Russian mob murder an innocent girl, he knew she harbored her fair share of battle scars.

He wasn't sure he'd ever tell her about what had happened in Okhotsk, and he doubted she'd pry.

For now, however, he just needed to get the hell out of…here.

Just hide. Let it pass. Deal with it a different time. In the future, after this case is over.

He snorted at himself.

The future. Sure.

What kind of future could he even have? That was the real question.

22

Cassandra shrugged on her black peacoat, snatched up her messenger bag, and wrapped a red scarf around her neck. As glad as she was to be done with her workday, she wasn't particularly thrilled having to return home to face her personal life.

After saying goodbye to the administrative assistant who sat at the front desk to the U.S. Attorney's Office, Cassandra made her way to the adjacent parking garage. Fortunately, not much snow had blown in to reach her car. Though she appreciated the efficient gas mileage of her compact hybrid, days like today made her wish she'd bought the biggest damn truck on the lot.

She snorted to herself at the mental imagery. Her, a five-foot-four woman who was usually dressed in a pencil skirt and a pair of Louboutins, climbing down from a massive rig that she'd need a stepstool to climb into.

No, the hybrid definitely suited her better. She'd just have to suffer through the winter.

Fortunately, despite her car almost getting stuck two different times, the forty-five-minute drive wasn't much worse than a normal trip in Chicago's godawful rush-hour traffic.

During the trip, she'd caught a handful of muffled text message pings from her handbag in the passenger seat. As she parked and then entered her building, she found herself hoping none of the texts were from Joseph. With any luck, the snow-covered roads would dissuade him from making the arduous journey to Cassandra's condo.

Once the door was closed and locked behind her, she released the sigh she didn't realize she'd been holding since she'd left the office.

Her brief discussion with Amelia Storm the day before had left her with more questions than answers. Though she was neck-deep in the Yuri Antonov case, her mind wouldn't stop drifting to the mystery of Joseph's ex-girlfriend, Michelle Timmer.

As curious as Cassandra was about Timmer's relationship with Joseph, she still knew absolutely nothing about the woman. An online search for her name had turned up a handful of social media accounts located in the Chicago area, but Cassandra didn't even know which one was the *right* Michelle Timmer.

Eventually, by process of elimination, Cassandra had narrowed down the search to two viable options. One of the women hadn't updated her timeline in months, and the other was newly engaged...to a woman. Her posts, which were public, confirmed she had no interest in men.

Which left Cassandra with the one who hadn't made a post in more than four months. Not that the woman had been particularly active on social media beforehand. Aside from sharing the occasional humorous meme or inspirational post, Michelle had hardly used her online accounts.

However, one major aspect of Michelle Timmer had leapt off the screen.

Her appearance.

Long, wavy red hair, fair skin, and a flawless hourglass figure.

Apparently, Joseph has a type. The thought left a sour taste on Cassandra's tongue.

Her first idea had been to research Timmer using the resources available to her at the U.S. Attorney's office. But such a search had the potential to show up on the radar of her bosses, and she didn't want to try to explain her way out of using government resources to dig into her boyfriend's ex.

Plus, Joseph was an FBI agent. More than likely, he had a friend or two in the U.S. Attorney's office, and Cassandra sure as hell didn't want word to make it back to *him*.

Rather than risk the fallout if she was caught researching Timmer at work, Cassandra had reached out to a detective friend of hers. The grizzled veteran of the CPD's homicide department was one of the first acquaintances Cassandra had made in the city, and as luck would have it, the woman owed her a small favor.

Considering Detective Campbell's nearly twenty years on the force, Cassandra trusted the veteran investigator knew how to procure useful information without raising eyebrows. Besides, Cassandra was well-aware of Joseph's less-than-favorable opinion of city cops, and the likelihood of word getting back to him was slim to none.

Even after all the safeguards, a pit of unease remained in Cassandra's stomach. She could rationalize her actions all she wanted, but the twinge of guilt and shame wouldn't leave her alone.

Shucking off her coat, hat, and boots, she flipped on the lights and deposited her laptop and purse next to the comfortable sofa in the living room. A change of clothing came next, followed by a can of sparkling water. Bubbly water, as she preferred to call it.

Only when she was situated in her usual lounge spot did she dig out her phone. Noting there were no missed calls, she allowed herself a fleeting moment of relief.

A spark of excitement burned as she spotted her newest email. "Speak of the devil. That didn't take Campbell very long."

Cassandra ignored the handful of unread texts—all from Joseph, of course—and opened the message from Detective Campbell.

Evening, Halcott. Here's everything I was able to dig up on Michelle Timmer. Turns out she's been missing since sometime in July.

Cassandra halted on the word "missing," and for a moment, she swore her heart stopped beating. Dragging in a deep breath, she pushed past the miasma of anxiety to read the rest of Campbell's message.

This is everything the CPD has on her and her case. It isn't much. Just a statement from a boyfriend and a couple neighbors. She worked in the FBI's forensics lab, and her boyfriend was an FBI agent. He came in and gave us a statement before the CPD had a chance to go to him.

"Shit." Cassandra spat the word as much as she said it.

Joseph's ex-girlfriend—with whom he had an allegedly non-serious relationship—had been missing since July?

A search of her apartment found her toiletries were missing as well as two of what appeared to be a matching three-piece set of luggage. Drawers were left open, and a few dresses were on her bed. A neighbor spotted her leaving with a rolling suitcase and a carry-on bag over her shoulder. It appears as if she left of her own accord, though neither her phone nor her credit cards have been used since she was reported missing.

With a shaky hand, Cassandra set aside her phone and pulled her laptop from the messenger bag. She didn't give a shit what Joseph's texts said. She wanted to know why in the hell he'd neglected to mention the fact that his ex was *missing*.

For that matter, why hadn't Agent Storm said anything? Did Storm even know Michelle was missing? Was that what Storm was going to say before Cassandra cut her off?

"There's nothing creepy about this. Not at all. Nothing unnerving about the FBI agent you're dating having an ex who's been missing for five months."

In moments like this, Cassandra wished she had a pet. Preferably a large German shepherd, but she'd settle for a moody cat who hissed at visitors in an attempt to scare them away.

Fresh paranoia knotted in her gut as she scanned through Michelle's personal information and then navigated to Joseph's statement.

According to Joseph, Michelle seemed out of sorts the last couple times they were together. He claimed she'd often glance over her shoulder and that she was especially jumpy. Since their relationship wasn't serious, Joseph hadn't felt it was his place to ask about her obvious paranoia. Though in retrospect, he'd realized what a mistake he'd made.

Otherwise, as Detective Campbell had noted in the body of the email, the CPD had collected a whole lot of nothing. Michelle had no local family and no close friends in the city. She'd only been reported missing after she'd failed to show up for work for the third day in a row. Her boss had tried to call her, but her cell was dead.

The CPD was called in for a welfare check, and that's when they discovered Michelle was nowhere to be found. Her phone, car, and two pieces of luggage were the only items missing from the household.

No signs of foul play. No evidence of a struggle. No witnesses who'd overheard an altercation.

Goose bumps rose on Cassandra's forearms.

Not long before landing her spot in the U.S. Attorney's office, she'd prosecuted a homicide case where a husband had murdered his wife. Initially, he'd told authorities his wife had simply up and left him and their two children. He'd claimed he'd returned home from work to find her personal effects gone, as well as her vehicle.

The man had been thorough. He'd even gone as far as making social media posts from her account about how she was seeking a "fresh start." Never mind that she'd been a devoted mother, and she hadn't so much as said goodbye to her children.

In cases like hers, the spouse was always the prime suspect. Statistically speaking, when a woman was murdered, a male lover or acquaintance was most likely to have committed the crime.

Six months after the man had reported his wife missing, her car was dredged up from a nearby lake. Inside were all the items the husband alleged she'd taken—her cell, a suitcase of clothes, a laptop, and even a handful of paperbacks.

When the forensics team had popped the trunk, they'd found the wife dismembered and stuffed into five black garbage bags.

During the trial, Cassandra hadn't held any punches. She hadn't been able to throw the death penalty at him, but she had secured a conviction and a sentence of life without parole.

Biting down on her lip, she forced aside the memories.

Maybe her years as a prosecutor had left her paranoid. Maybe Michelle truly had packed up her things and taken off for greener pastures. Maybe someone else had spooked her like Joseph had told the police.

Joseph could've cheated on her. He could've broken her heart, and that's why she decided to leave. Michelle might have wanted more from their relationship, and when he didn't...

Cassandra massaged her temples.

Somehow, she doubted a woman who'd graduated from Yale at the top of her class to become a well-regarded forensics analyst would throw away her promising career just because some asshole had cheated on her.

Trust your instincts.

She'd been operating on little more than gut feelings so far, so she didn't see why that ought to change now.

There was no way Michelle had simply vanished into thin air.

Something here was very, very wrong.

A sharp knock at the front door sent a jolt of adrenaline laced with fear through Cassandra's veins. Jerking bolt-upright in her seat, her gaze reflexively went to the shadowy hall that led to her bedroom. She kept a loaded handgun hidden in a clever false-bottom drawer beside her bed, but otherwise, her only option for self-defense was the rack of knives in the kitchen.

Get ahold of yourself. It's not even six in the evening. No one's showing up to try to kill you at dinner time on a weekday. And they certainly wouldn't knock. Someone's delivery driver probably got the wrong address, or the neighbor locked themselves out.

She pulled in a deep breath and rolled her shoulders. "Who is it?"

"It's me."

At Joseph's muffled voice, Cassandra's stomach lurched.

What in the hell was he doing here? Shouldn't he be at Montanelli's Steakhouse with whatever unwitting woman he'd convinced to warm his bed while Cassandra was busy?

Her scowl was involuntary. As much as she wanted to shout back to tell him to piss off, her eyes were drawn to the digital files of the Michelle Timmer case. "Just a second."

If Joseph had something to do with Michelle's disappearance, then he was dangerous and potentially unhinged. The absolute last thing Cassandra needed to add to her list of stressors was a violent ex-boyfriend who happened to be a federal agent.

Quickly, she closed out of the documents Detective Campbell had sent, cleared her browser history just in case, and locked the computer. Chances were, all Joseph wanted was to get off.

She snorted to herself. That's all he *ever* wanted.

Brushing off the front of her fleece sweatshirt, Cassandra reluctantly rose to her feet. The sooner she got this over with, the sooner he'd leave, and the sooner she could look at Michelle Timmer in more depth.

She was walking a dangerous line, but she'd gotten herself into this mess by letting a suave smile and a chiseled body override her basic common sense.

One way or another, she'd get out of this.

23

As Amelia stepped back to glance over the length of the whiteboard, she blew on her newest cup of black coffee. She'd arrived at the FBI office bright and early that morning, and she'd had her pick of conference rooms. With the connected cases they'd discovered over the last twenty-four hours, Amelia figured she was more than justified in procuring a larger incident room for their growing investigation. She'd wheeled the murder board from the previous space down the hall to the upgraded room.

Scanning the list of names, dates, and locations, she wondered if they'd need another agent or two in addition to the extra space.

She'd tried to organize the victims based on the time and place of their murders, and she'd come away with four separate groups.

The oldest cluster of homicides committed in Terre Haute was also the largest. A total of six victims matched the current killer's modus operandi, with three murders occurring four years ago and a second batch of three murders taking place the following year.

Next came a trio of matching crimes in Detroit, Michigan, all of which were dated approximately two years ago. After Detroit was Milwaukee, and once again, there were three victims with bible verses carved into their flesh. The Milwaukee murders were almost exactly one year old, and Amelia suspected the timing wasn't a coincidence.

The more she stared at the whiteboard, and the more she thought about the specific MO of each crime, the more convinced she was they were not dealing with a contract killer at all.

After Dan Gifford, she had to admit she'd been struck with a renewed interest in the inner workings of serial killers. So much so that she'd considered transferring to the Violent Crimes Division of the FBI.

Well, that and the fact Joseph Larson was likely pursuing the position of SSA of Organized Crime.

Anger bubbled at the thought of her former case partner. For a beat, the bitter taste on her tongue wasn't the result of the godawful coffee she'd gotten from the breakroom.

She also remembered her promise to herself to follow up on Michelle Timmer's case. Opening her laptop, she sent a quick message to one of the detectives she knew, asking for an update.

She sent up a prayer as she hit the send button, hoping the young woman had been found safe and sound. Maybe the forensics work had gotten to her, and she simply needed some time away.

Tightening her grip on the mug, she took a quick sip and recentered her focus on the whiteboard and her current case. The problem with Joseph would still be there tomorrow, unfortunately. And there was nothing she could do about Michelle until she heard back from the detective. Today, she had to focus on narrowing down the details of the bible verse murders before the killer struck again.

It wasn't just Joseph she had to purge from her anxious brain. She and Zane still hadn't talked about sleeping together, and his abrupt departure from the office the night before had her worried. Her concern wasn't necessarily about their relationship but about his mental wellbeing overall.

Though she'd not prodded him about the specifics, she'd gathered his thirty-four years were marked with more than their fair share of hardship. Not just from whatever work he'd done for the government—the CIA—but also from his upbringing.

His younger sister had died in a car accident when she was still in grade school, and though Zane's recollection of the event hadn't been all that detailed, Amelia had gathered the memory was still fresh and painful.

Amelia knew a thing or two about loss. Most importantly, she knew how grief could affect each individual in a different way. The holidays were purported to be the most joyous time of year, but for too many people, the season was a pointed reminder of what they'd lost.

Was that what was bothering Zane? Amelia wasn't so self-absorbed to think their night together was the source of his distress, was she?

As sweat began to bead at her temples, she rubbed the bridge of her nose. Her mind was wandering again. She needed her wits to stay in this damn room, not take off to parts unknown.

Setting her mug on the edge of the table, she shrugged off her cardigan. "Why in the hell is this place as cold as a meat locker during the summer, but it feels like a sauna as soon as October rolls around?"

With a huff of indignation, she gave herself a mental shake, determined to pick up where she'd left off before her brain went on its scenic vacation.

"These patterns are too specific for a contract killer. Why would a hitman only kill three people and then take a year off?" Mind whirling through all the possibilities, she tapped her foot as she scanned the dry-erase board for the five-hundredth time. "Three victims, each spaced out by around a year, and each in a different city. Well, except for the six victims in Terre Haute."

Unless a hitman was offering a three-for-one deal, she doubted a contract killer's work would line up quite so neatly.

Asking for help in her personal life had never been an easy feat for Amelia, but fortunately, she didn't hesitate to seek out guidance when it came to her work. And right now, she needed a fresh set of eyes from someone who didn't deal with mafiosos for a living.

Thanks to her last case, she knew just the people to consult. Dean Steelman and Sherry Cowen, the two Violent Crimes agents who Amelia and Zane had been teamed with in Cedarwood, were located a mere one floor below the Organized Crime Division.

Cowen was in Florida for her wedding, but Amelia had learned during her bizarre run-in with Cassandra Halcott the day before that Dean Steelman was preparing for the upcoming Antonov trial. Whether or not he'd be here today, so shortly after two feet of snow had been dumped on the city, Amelia wasn't sure.

She pulled up his contact information. "He was here yesterday, wasn't he? Why wouldn't he be here today?"

Hopefully, he hadn't decided to take the day off for a three-day weekend. She knew the names of a couple agents in VC, but she couldn't say she was on text-messaging terms with any of them. A brief consultation with an agent she already knew would be far less time-consuming than having to go through the SSA of VC or through SAC Keaton.

Amelia kept her message succinct, mentally crossing her fingers that Steelman was already in the office at quarter 'til eight. If she didn't have someone to bounce ideas off soon, she'd have to draw a face on the whiteboard to pretend she had a conversational partner.

Midway through pacing the carpeted floor in front of the whiteboard, her phone buzzed in her hand. As she unlocked the device and opened the message, she finally let go of the tension in her shoulders.

Like Amelia's initial text, Steelman's response was short and to the point. *All I've got on my plate today is more trial prep, and honestly, it can wait. I could use a break to look at an actual case right now.*

Amelia silently pumped a fist in the air before she sent Steelman the room number of the conference space she'd overtaken. While she waited, she powered on her laptop and opened any remaining case-related files, including the list of bible verses carved on the victims' bodies.

When her phone vibrated against the table beside the laptop, she half-expected to discover Steelman had remembered an urgent errand he had to attend, and he wouldn't be a sounding board after all.

Her chest tightened with anxiety when she noticed the newest message was from Zane. *I am so sorry. I just woke up. It took me a while to get to sleep last night. I'm going to hurry up and get ready, and I'll be on my way to the office. Do you want me to grab you anything on my way in? Coffee or food or something?*

Slumping down in her chair, Amelia heaved a relieved sigh. He'd been acting weird, sure, but the offer to pick up food or coffee was normal Zane behavior. And right now, witnessing Zane behaving normally was like a physical weight lifted off her shoulders.

Only if you're going to swing by that place that makes those miniature chocolate croissants. Otherwise, I'm good. Don't worry about oversleeping. You're always here an hour before me anyway. It's about time I get here first for a change.

As she hit send, a polite knock drew her gaze to the door. "It's unlocked."

The closed blinds clattered as Dean Steelman eased open the door and stepped over the threshold. At thirty-seven, his whiskey brown hair wasn't yet streaked with gray, nor was the slight shade of trendy stubble he allowed to darken his cheeks.

A couple strands had fallen over his eyebrow, but Amelia was almost certain the stray hairs were an intentional part of his aesthetic. Along with his neatly pressed navy suit and pastel blue dress shirt, he looked every bit the part of a detective from a noir crime film. Hell, even his *name*, Dean Steelman, sounded like it was made for a criminal investigator.

His vivid sapphire eyes went first to Amelia and then to the whiteboard. "Morning, Agent Storm. I heard you might have caught a serial case?" Though Steelman had been at the Chicago field office for years, his voice was still laden with his native Southern drawl. Amelia found it curious how Zane's Jersey accent had faded so much, but Steelman sounded as if he was fresh off a plane from his home state of West Virginia.

Her first thought was to get up to shake Steelman's hand, but she quickly reminded herself they were in the height of flu season. Offices spread germs like petri dishes, and she had far too much on her plate to risk getting sick, even if it was just a temporary ailment.

Stretching both legs in front of herself, she gestured to the list of names she'd spent the morning curating. "We thought it could've been a contract killer, and I suppose it still could be. Make yourself comfy, and I'll run you through what we've got so far."

With a half-smile, he pulled out a chair on the other side

of the circular table. "Sounds good. This a new case you and Palmer caught, or...?"

Amelia glanced to her phone, scanning the newest message from Zane. He'd started the text with a laughing emoji and had advised that no, unfortunately, he was not planning to drive twenty minutes out of his way to pick up miniature chocolate croissants.

As she returned her attention to Steelman, she noted a curious glint in his eyes. Before a flush could creep up her neck, she cleared her throat and waved a dismissive hand. "That was Palmer. He's running a little late, and I asked him to get us some mini croissants."

A smirk tugged at Steelman's mouth. "And?"

She sighed dramatically. "No dice. I guess the place is too far out of his way, and he already feels bad for being late."

Steelman chuckled, a good-natured grin on his face. "I wonder if he and Sherry are related. She's always here an hour or two before me, and when she gets here at the same time as me, she'll apologize for being late."

"They might be." The moment of humor was like a sliver of sunshine after a week of overcast skies. Between Steelman's observation and the breakfast pastry banter, Amelia felt some semblance of normalcy return. "Okay, well, anyway."

Resting his elbows on the table, Steelman turned to the whiteboard. "Right. How'd this fall in Organized Crime's lap, for starters?"

Amelia pushed to her feet. As she approached the whiteboard, she felt like a teacher preparing to present a lecture.

"This guy." She tapped a knuckle beside where she'd written Lars's details on the righthand side of the board. "Lars Poteracki. His body was pulled from Lake Michigan late on Tuesday night. He was a federal informant for a big bust earlier this year. The guy he put away, Kevin Ersfeld, pled out, so there wasn't a trial, and his likeness was kept out of the media. Plus, Ersfeld was killed in a fight a couple months after he was sent to prison."

Steelman whistled through his teeth. "That didn't take long."

"No, it sure didn't. Ersfeld didn't have a lot of friends when he was put away. Most of the people that worked under him were more than happy to roll over on him for a more lenient sentence."

Amelia went on to describe how Ersfeld had terrorized Washington Park during his heyday. She also included a synopsis of the research she and Zane had done on Ersfeld's family—namely, there was no one who would have thought to avenge the man by going after the informant who'd put him away in the first place.

Next came Lars Poteracki's background, including the car accident that had killed his sister shortly before his own murder. Steelman agreed that losing his twin might have spurred Poteracki toward a relapse, which explained why he was in Washington Park buying heroin.

Once she'd covered the most recent victim, Neil Rosford, she stepped away from the whiteboard and dropped both hands to her hips. "The only description we've got of the alleged kidnapper is a vague physical description, and then the information about his car."

Steelman drummed his fingers against the table, his gaze fixed on the whiteboard. "There's definitely a pattern here, and I think you're right to consider that you might be chasing a serial instead of a hitman."

I was afraid you'd say that.

Amelia kept the bleak thought to herself. "I suppose that's where you come in. From what I can tell, he's been killing in threes. All the victims whose files I've dug up were found with bible verses carved in their skin. Usually their chest, unless they were women. Then the verses were on their backs."

The gruesome detail might have caused distress in the average person, but Steelman's intent stare didn't waver. "Lookin' at these names, there's only one woman in each group of victims. Why do you think that is?"

"I've got no idea." Amelia held both hands out at her sides. "All I know is that it's consistent. Too consistent for the average contract killer. Hitmen accept contracts where they get paid well, and most of them don't care much about who they're supposed to kill. As long as they can pull it off and get paid, that's all that matters. For a hitman to accept only specific contracts, I don't know. It doesn't make sense."

Scratching his temple, Steelman leaned back in his chair. "All right, so let's set aside the hitman theory for just a second. Let's look at this like we're thinkin' it's a serial killer."

The request was easier said than done, but Amelia was desperate for a new approach that would yield real answers. She swept her gaze over the list of names, dates, and locations. "Okay. Three victims in each…batch of murders. Two batches in Terre Haute, then one in each of the other cities. How common is that with serial killers? Are they usually mobile?"

Steelman crossed his arms, his appearance thoughtful. "Plenty of 'em are. You've heard of the serials who work as long-haul truckers and whatnot, haven't you? They'll work a job where they travel the country and kill people along their route. Usually prostitutes or transients, folks that the authorities gloss over."

A lightbulb flickered to life in Amelia's mind at the mention of working girls. "All the women I found in ViCAP were prostitutes. Three of them had prior solicitation charges, and the fourth hadn't ever been picked up, but the case notes were pretty clear she was a sex worker."

"That's one common thread." Steelman lifted an index finger. "In VC, one way we get a better idea of who and what we're dealing with is by figuring out a pattern of behavior. By definition, serial killers are ritualistic. They don't go off willy-nilly and start killing random strangers. There's always a reason for what they're doing."

As Amelia mulled over the agent's words, a knock was followed by the faint *whoosh* as the door swung inward to reveal Zane.

Though he claimed to have overslept, the shadows beneath his gray eyes were indicative of little to no rest. Otherwise, aside from his jeans, hooded sweatshirt, and leather jacket being much less formal than his typical Tom Ford suit, he was as put-together as always.

His attention fell on her as the door latched closed, and she mentally cursed the stupid pitter-patter in her chest. They were at *work* and in front of a colleague.

Biting the inside of her cheek, Amelia gestured to Zane's stainless-steel thermos. "No mini croissants, I see."

He shot her and Steelman one of his patented grins. "I told you I wasn't going to drive twenty minutes out of my way. I didn't even stop to get myself a coffee, *and* I'm taking advantage of casual Friday."

Amelia laughed, allowing the bit of humor to temporarily push aside her anxiety over Zane's recent demeanor. "I guess you really were in a hurry, huh?"

Stifling a yawn with the back of his hand, he plopped down in the seat next to Dean Steelman. "I was. I was thinking about this case, hoping we'd make some headway today." He shot Steelman an appreciative glance. "Which I'm guessing is why you're here, right, Steelman? We're taking a closer look at the serial killer angle?"

"Yes, sir. We sure are." Steelman tilted his chin at the whiteboard. "The first kills we're aware of took place in

Terre Haute about four years ago. And that's the only city where this person killed a second group of people...that we're aware of. It's more than likely he's from Terre Haute or at least familiar with the area. Maybe he was born there, moved away, and returned with a vendetta. You'll have to check out the Terre Haute cases carefully. But let's put a pin in that for now."

Amelia stared at the whiteboard, marveling at the benefit a fresh perspective provided.

"Lookin' at the victims all lined up here, there's definitely a pattern. See the dates? All of 'em were killed in December, sometime before Christmas. There's a little variance, but not much. Seems a little weird for a hitman, doesn't it?"

Though Amelia had noticed the similar dates, she hadn't put a tremendous amount of thought into them before now. "They're all killed within the span of a week too." She looked from one list of names to the next, confirming her spur-of-the-moment observation. "Poteracki was killed on Sunday, and today's Friday." She let the significance of the statement hang in the silence between her and the two men in the room.

Steelman laced his fingers together to prop up his chin as his eyes flitted back and forth along the whiteboard. "Right. Doesn't look like there're any specific days he kills on. Some of the vics have four days between their TODs, and some only have one. But he *does* kill them all within a week."

Zane cocked an eyebrow. "Do you suppose it might have something to do with lunar cycles?"

Amelia hadn't considered the option before, but it would explain the discrepancy in the dates themselves. "All the religious symbolism so far points to some form of Christianity. Lunar cycles would fall more into the pagan side of things, wouldn't they?"

Leaning back in his chair, Zane shrugged. "Sure, but look

at Easter. The date for Easter is based on lunar cycles. And the pine trees we see every Christmas? Those are from pagan holidays too. Winter Solstice, if I remember right. Plenty of pagan symbolism made its way into Christianity. It's what happens when Roman emperors start making a bunch of nonbelievers convert, I guess. They converted but still held onto some of their old symbols."

"Good catch." The observation struck Amelia as something of a breakthrough, but there wasn't much they could do with the information yet.

She wanted to catch this guy before he killed the final person in his twisted ritual, and she sure as hell didn't want to wait for him to strike again next year. Not that he'd even be in Chicago when he did. Clearly, the killer knew better than to drop too many bodies in one location. Chances were good he'd relocate after claiming his third and final victim.

If he relocated, the odds of finding him before he killed again would fall significantly. They'd be playing a guessing game, trying to figure out which city he'd absconded to before it was too late.

Zane turned to Amelia and Steelman, his expression quizzical. "And we're sure he always kills three people in the span of a week, right? We're predicting he's going to go for someone else before this is all said and done?"

Steelman nodded. "If we're looking at it from a serial angle, then yes. Without a doubt, he's going to kill someone else before Monday. If you throw the contract killer angle in, then it gets a little messier."

A twinge of uncertainty tugged at Amelia's chest. Just because she'd dealt with one serial killer in Cedarwood, Illinois didn't mean she was used to the psychopaths. "Then we stay on the serial killer track. It's the worst-case scenario, if that makes sense. So, we plan for the worst."

Zane bobbed his head in understanding before taking a

drink from his thermos. "We plan for him to kill someone else so we can stop him."

"We just have to figure out who his next target is." Steelman scratched his cheek and glanced at Amelia's laptop. "Normally, I'd say that's one hell of a task, but from what I can tell so far, this guy's MO is *really* specific. He left a bible verse on every vic, didn't he?"

Amelia rapped her knuckles on the whiteboard. "Every single one. I wrote the book, chapter, and verses up here and copied the text of them all into that document you're looking at."

Zane held up a finger. "For starters, we've got him killing at the same time every year. Possibly connected by a pattern we haven't noticed yet." He raised a second digit. "He always kills his victims within the span of a week, and there are always three of them. Last but not least, he always leaves a bible verse carved in their skin. What about the causes of death? Throats slit in all cases?"

Finally, Amelia thought they were getting somewhere. "Yeah, every single one. They were all cut down to the spine, just like Rosford and Poteracki. Massive blood loss in each case, but none of the blood was at the scene."

Zane's determined gaze was fixed on the whiteboard. Even though he'd seemed out of it the night before, Amelia knew what that expression meant—he wouldn't let this case go until he had answers. "Each vic was killed elsewhere, then. Bodies dumped. How many of them had defensive wounds like Poteracki? That guy had to have fought like hell."

A renewed surge of energy powered Amelia as she snatched up a dry-erase marker and pointed to one of the victims' names. "I marked the ones with defensive wounds with an X beside their name."

"What about the asterisks?" Steelman asked.

"Rap sheets."

His forehead creased. "What kind of rap sheets?"

"Nothing major. Poteracki had a record, and even though Rosford was clean, he was a known drug dealer, so I figured I'd look at the other vics too." Amelia scanned the whiteboard. More than three-quarters of the names had asterisks beside them. "Mostly possession, solicitation for the women, and a few charges of minor trafficking. There wasn't any pattern to whether the charges were local or federal, though. Poteracki's drug charge was federal, but this guy, Mark Pennington from Detroit, was charged locally."

Zane's expression turned grim. "Are we thinking the killer could be in law enforcement?"

Drawing in a long breath, Steelman linked his fingers behind his head. "I don't know. You've got DNA evidence, don't you? What kind of cop would leave something like that behind?"

"True." Zane tapped an index finger against his thermos. "And the varying locations don't make a lot of sense for a cop, either. It could be someone who goes on a holiday vacation every year, but that seems…unlikely, you know?"

"More unlikely than you think." Steelman crossed his arms as he scrutinized Amelia's laptop. "Aside from the fact these cities aren't exactly on the TripAdvisor list of desired hotspots." Amelia snorted and wiped the dribbling coffee from her chin as the VC agent smiled before continuing.

"We have to remember Dan Gifford was the exception to the rule. There aren't many serials out there like him. That guy was smart. Maybe not Ted Kaczynski smart, but he had to be close. And he was a chameleon. He arguably blended in with 'normal' society better than BTK. But one thing Gifford did that Rader couldn't was hunt outside his comfort zone. This…" he pointed to the whiteboard, "this is on a whole different level. If we want some more specific answers, we'll need to reach out to BAU."

Amelia perked up at the mention of the Bureau's Behavioral Analysis Unit. The men and women who picked apart and dissected the motive behind some of the country's most heinous murderers fascinated her. It wasn't a job she particularly desired, but the work itself was intriguing. She certainly wouldn't turn down a chance to interact with one of the men or women in the BAU.

Zane held up a hand before either Amelia or Dean could go on. "I think that's a good idea. But first, can we look at the one weird part of this guy's pattern? Most of the vics are male, but there's one woman's name in each location."

Smacking the marker against her palm, Amelia scrutinized the list of names. "I noticed that too. I also noticed that in every 'cycle,' the woman is the last one to die."

As Amelia and Zane both turned to Dean, the VC agent tilted his head, appearing thoughtful. "It's part of the pattern. He's killing two men and one woman. You said all the women are prostitutes, right, Storm?"

"Right."

"And they're all killed about a week or so after the first male victim."

Amelia took a quick look at the calendar hanging beside the dry-erase board. "Poteracki was killed on Sunday the sixth."

Steelman laid his hands flat against the table. "So, if his pattern continues, he's going to kill another woman within the next couple days. Probably another working girl."

Understanding dawned on Amelia. They really were working against a ticking clock. "Both his victims so far have been poached from Washington Park. Does that mean he'll go there to hunt for the woman?"

"I don't know." Steelman reached into the pocket of his suit jacket and produced his cell. "But I know someone who might be able to get us a better idea of what we're dealin' with. Someone in BAU. I think we're dealin' with someone on a moral crusade since the majority of our vics have rap sheets, and he's carving bible verses into them. But I'll let BAU have the final word there."

Amelia and Zane exchanged fervent glances. Her gut told her the person who'd slit Lars Poteracki's throat down to the spine would most definitely strike again. Once he'd claimed his third victim, he'd disappear to another city. They'd be completely in the dark until another body dropped.

There was no other option. They had to strike first.

24

With a cardboard drink carrier of coffees in one hand and a paper bag of baked goods in the other, Zane used his elbow to press down on the lever handle of the conference room door. After poring over Poteracki, Rosford, and all the old victims' cases for a solid three hours, they'd decided to take a breather to refresh their minds.

Zane had volunteered to go pick up an order from the café down the street, but he was fairly sure Amelia and Steelman had worked through their so-called break. When Zane had left, Amelia had been in the middle of a phone call with a detective in the homicide department of the Terre Haute police department.

During the short trip to the café, Zane had half-expected the snowy streets and blowing wind to trigger another meltdown. However, he'd kept the radio in the car turned off, and the café had been too noisy to hear the song playing on the overhead speakers.

Unlike the overcast gloom from the day before, the sky was bright and sunny. In all the time he'd spent around the Sea of Okhotsk, he could count on one hand the number of times he'd seen the sun. The constant dismal weather was appropriate for what went on in that hellhole.

He shook off the glum thoughts. He had a bag full of treats and a drink carrier loaded with three seasonal lattes. This was as far from Okhotsk as any human being could ever hope to get.

As he stepped into the conference room, his attention shot straight to Amelia. Her forest green eyes met his, and other than offer him a half-smile, she didn't move from where she was slumped down in an office chair, her cell pressed to one ear. Steelman was nowhere to be found, likely still off on his own for their small, late-morning break.

Setting down the lattes, Zane unrolled the top of the bag, careful to make as little noise as possible. He usually liked to wait for everyone to arrive before he started eating, but he'd skipped breakfast. His stomach had been grumbling for the last hour, and he was eager to silence it.

Though Amelia hadn't spoken since he'd stepped into the room, the tinny voice on the other end of the line was still going strong. Whoever she'd called, they were in the middle of talking off her ear.

Motioning to the paper bag, Amelia straightened in her chair. "Okay. That makes sense. I appreciate your insight, Detective."

As the tinny voice replied, Zane took his cue and retrieved a chocolate croissant and a napkin. Amelia insisted she hadn't *actually* expected him to stop by the little bakery while he was on his way to the office that morning, but part of him still felt he'd disappointed her.

In an effort to make up for the failure, he'd ordered a handful of the regular-sized pastries from the café down the street. The mini croissants were Amelia's favorite breakfast-time treat, but the normal croissants were a close second.

Zane pushed the napkin toward her, and she offered him

a wide smile in response. "All right, Detective. You have a good weekend too. Thanks again. Bye."

Focusing on his pastry, Zane forced his way past the rush of warmth that had struck him at the sight of her smile. With as glum as the past twenty-four hours had been for his mental health, he was surprised by the sudden flood of endorphins. "Who was that? Same guy you were on a call with when I left?"

She took a bite and shook her head. "No. Different detective. He and his partner worked one of the murders in Milwaukee. A small-time dealer named Thomas Maddox was found washed up from Lake Michigan just like Poteracki. I wanted to hear from the source and see if there were any similarities, you know? Any reason why Maddox and Poteracki would be the ones the killer chose to dump in the lake."

With as specific as the murders had been so far, Zane wouldn't have been surprised to learn there was yet another pattern in this madman's modus operandi. "And?"

She lifted a shoulder and let it fall. "Not much in terms of their backgrounds. But Maddox had extensive defensive wounds, just like Poteracki. The Milwaukee PD even collected some DNA evidence from underneath his fingernails, which is impressive considering they estimated he'd been in Lake Michigan for three days."

"And that DNA matches the DNA found on Poteracki, right?"

"It does. So whoever killed Maddox is likely the same person who killed Poteracki. And that same DNA was found on another victim from three years ago in Terre Haute, Krystal Avila. In Avila's case, the DNA was found in a small blood stain on her shirt. They thought it was her blood at first, but fortunately, someone tested the blood types of all the different stains, and that one was different. Avila was O positive, but one spot was A negative."

"Good move on their part." Although he and Amelia were discussing multiple brutal murders, the headway on the case had pushed aside much of the despondency he'd suffered earlier that morning.

He could never undo what had happened to Katya, but any time he had the opportunity to do a little good in the world, he liked to think he was making amends. The line of thought was silly and probably naïve, but he clung to it like a life raft in an Atlantic storm.

As Zane plucked his latte from the drink holder, Amelia glanced to the closed door, lowered her head, and scooted closer.

Oh, shit. Did I do something wrong? Did I forget something? I've been so preoccupied lately, I wouldn't be surprised.

Her expression was a cross between concerned and anxious, which only added fuel to the inferno of doubt in his mind. The few milliseconds before she spoke seemed to drag on for an eternity as he ran through every worst-case scenario fifteen different times.

"Are you feeling better? You know, after last night. You just…you looked like…" She paused, chewing at her bottom lip before continuing. "You looked like something was bothering you. More than just a physical thing. Is there…anything I can do? To help?"

Relief threatened to wash over him, but he held the sentiment at bay with his wall of self-doubt. Should he tell her?

Tell her what? What can I even tell her?

He twisted the cardboard sleeve around the red and green cup. "It's…hard to explain." It wasn't, but he wasn't prepared to broach the subject in any depth while they were still in the FBI office. "The holidays are just." He sighed. "They're not my best time of year, you know what I mean?"

Her mouth twitched in a sympathetic smile. "I definitely know what you mean. This time of year can be difficult for some people, myself included." She reached out to rest her hand on his forearm, squeezing lightly. "I get it if you don't want to talk about it. Especially, well...*here*. But you're not alone, and if you do want to talk about it, I'll be here."

If they hadn't been in a conference room in the middle of the FBI field office, he'd have leaned in and kissed her. As he settled for a smile instead, he hoped it conveyed even a fraction of the affection he felt for her in that moment. "Thank you, Amelia. That means a lot. And not to ride in on your coattails, but the same goes for you. I'm here if you need me."

The light that came to life on her face was almost enough for him to forget about the memories that had haunted him the past few days.

Before either of them could add to the moment, the door swung inward as Dean Steelman entered the room. In a flash, Amelia's hand was back on her coffee. His attention shifted from Amelia to Zane, but his expression was calm and level. If he realized he'd just interrupted a heart-to-heart conversation, he didn't show it.

Zane gestured to the drink carrier in the center of the table. "There's your peppermint mocha, Steelman. I grabbed us some pastries too."

The man's face brightened. "You are a lifesaver, Palmer." He pulled out a seat across from Zane and scooped up his coffee. "You know, for the longest time, I just drank black coffee. Sometimes with a little sugar or milk, but mostly just black. It's all we had in the Army, and my old military buddies would've given me hell for ordering a peppermint mocha."

Amelia snickered. "You and me both."

"Not that I give a shit. They can drink that nasty ass black, breakroom coffee if they want." He grinned and held up the paper cup. "When I moved to Chicago and got partnered with Sherry for the first time, she brought me one of these on accident. Haven't looked back since."

Zane made a show of swishing his own cup. "There's about a million calories and six-thousand grams of sugar in these, but it's not much worse than a twenty-ounce bottle of non-diet soda, honestly."

"True." Steelman reached for the bag of pastries, his face turning stern. "Agent Redker from BAU ought to be up here in ten minutes or so. I sent everything we had over to him a little while ago, so he'll have an idea of what we're dealing with. It might not be the most in-depth profile, but we've got to work with what we've got."

Sipping his latte, Zane held up a finger. "Speaking of, while I was waiting for our food, I looked up where we're at in terms of lunar cycles right now. The moon is waning, and we'll have a new moon in three days."

Steelman and Amelia exchanged curious glances as she wiped her fingers and set aside the half-finished croissant. "We've got a few minutes while we're waiting for Redker, so let me look up the dates of some of the old murders and see what I can find."

As Amelia powered on her laptop, Zane figured there was no time like the present to rehash the details they'd uncovered so far. "And there's still no pattern with the bible verses, is there?"

Sifting through the scripture had been Steelman's pet project. According to him, he'd been raised in an extremely strict, religious household, and the Bible was drilled into his head at a young age.

Steelman shook his head as he swallowed a bite of croissant. "No. Some are weirdly uplifting, like the verse on Poteracki's chest. And some sound vengeful, and some are preachy. Redker will probably be able to make more sense out of them than I can."

Zane probed further. "Forget the messages for a minute. What about the chapters and verse numbers? Is there a pattern there?"

"Unfortunately, no. At least not that I can see. It appears his focus is on the text of the message and not buried in a numeric pattern or code. We're running it through software, though, in case the system sees something we don't."

Amelia's fingers *tap-tapped* along the keyboard. "I think you might be onto something with the lunar cycles, Palmer. Check this out." She turned the computer so the screen faced Zane and Steelman. "This is from Terre Haute, four years ago. May Clements, a prostitute with a couple priors for solicitation. Killed on the twenty-seventh of December. Two days before a new moon. She was the last victim in that cycle."

A combination of unease and curiosity settled in Zane's stomach. "What about the next one from Terre Haute?"

Lips pursed, Amelia made a few clicks and key presses. "Krystal Avila. Another working girl. Her body was found," she paused, her eyes narrowing as she leaned in closer to the screen, "in a cemetery. Beneath a statue of the Virgin Mary."

The hairs on the back of Zane's neck rose like quills on a porcupine. "That symbolism is…a little on the nose, don't you think?"

"A little." Amelia waved at the computer. "But she was killed on December twenty-second. Three days before a new moon."

"Shit." Steelman ran a hand through his caramel brown hair. "Two is a coincidence, three is a pattern. And we've got a new moon coming up in three days."

Silence descended on them as the implication hung in the air. Zane had been confident that they'd be facing the potential for another murder before the killer went underground again, but the new moon pattern was a bizarre sort of confirmation that made the possibility feel that much more real.

"Just to make sure." The keys clicked as Amelia punched in another date. "From Detroit, two years ago. Jenny Donovan, the last victim in that cycle. Her time of death was estimated to be on the fifth of December. New moon was on the seventh."

Steelman lifted a brow. "Where was her body found?"

The corner of Amelia's mouth turned down in a distasteful expression. "Another cemetery. This time next to Saint Christopher."

Zane was so absorbed in the most recent discovery he almost leapt out of his chair when a knock sounded at the door. Quickly, he grabbed his coffee to take a drink in hopes that the motion would disguise his obvious jumpiness.

"It's open," Steelman called. To Zane's relief, the agent's focus was far away from him.

Laptop beneath one arm, BAU Agent Layton Redker stepped into the room, easing the door closed behind him. His salt and pepper black hair was styled in its usual faux mohawk, and his brown eyes were as shrewd as they'd been the first time Zane had met the man. With his well-pressed suit and slick blue tie, he was the closest the FBI had to offer to the types of agents depicted in Hollywood. Well, the faux hawk might be a little extreme, but everything else about him checked all the boxes.

Until a couple months ago, Redker had been a tenured agent in the Bureau's Cyber Crimes Division. Unbeknownst to Zane—then again, there was no reason he'd have known anyway—Redker had been in the process of finishing up a Ph.D. in psychology. When the time had come for a seasoned BAU agent, Bill Dumke, to retire, Redker had been chosen to take his place. If Zane remembered right, Dumke's retirement had come right after the end of the Gifford investigation. Zane didn't blame the man for leaving a few months ahead of schedule after that case.

"Afternoon, Agents." Redker set his laptop on the table as he took the only remaining seat. "Long time, no see."

Though Redker's demeanor was no-nonsense most of the time, Zane appreciated the slight, underlying sarcasm that never quite went away. "Yeah, it's been too long."

With a slight smile, Redker powered on his laptop. "Not too often I get to work with Organized Crime these days. Although, based on what I've seen, it doesn't exactly look like you're dealing with a hitman or a mob boss here, are you?"

Zane's laugh was part snort. "No, it sure doesn't. Usually, we'd hand this over to our friends in VC." He gestured to Steelman for emphasis, and the other man nodded. "But the more we dig into this thing, the more it looks like we're fighting against the clock."

Like the flip of a switch, Redker was all business, any hint of sarcastic good humor gone. "I'd have to agree with that deduction, Agent Palmer. Usually, we in the BAU take a little longer to develop profiles, but your guy..." he scratched his temple, "has a really distinct pattern of activity. Doesn't necessarily make him any easier to find, unfortunately, but it does make his next victim easier to find."

"We'll take that. If we can figure out who his next target is or where he's going to poach them from, then we can try to get ahead of it." Zane reviewed the list of names scrawled on the dry-erase board. Four cycles over a period of four years, and now the killer was on his fifth. The body count was at fourteen, and it would only continue to rise.

Redker's determined expression matched the rest of the room. "All right. I'll run you through what I've got so far." He cleared his throat and tapped a couple keys. "First, there's the religious symbolism. Now, I wasn't raised in a religious household, but chances are good that our killer was. This isn't something he picked up overnight or after his friend dragged him to mass one day. These values of his, they've been ingrained in him since his early development."

Zane's childhood hadn't been all sunshine and rainbows, but he couldn't imagine what sorts of events could damage a person so thoroughly that they wound up like *this*.

"One thing is for sure, though." Redker scratched his temple, his attention fixed on the laptop. "This guy operates based on his own strict set of values. Not every serial killer does that. Guys like Ted Bundy or Richard Ramirez, they didn't even have a set of morals. I doubt they ever even stopped to think about it."

The concept wasn't all that foreign to Zane. Mafiosos often operated within their own warped set of ideals as well.

Amelia's forehead creased. "How does that work, exactly? Their pseudo-morality, I mean."

"It's complicated, but most of the human psyche is." Redker leaned back in his chair, looking from one of them to the next. "They're still driven by the need to kill. It's not something they'll just forget about. But there's some mechanism in their head that feels the need to rationalize it or to put reason behind it. It could be based on cognitive dissonance, especially in this case."

Steelman rubbed his chin, his expression thoughtful. "Cognitive dissonance? That's what my dad would've called a ten-dollar word."

A hint of amusement passed over Redker's face. "In layman's terms, it's what your brain does when it's trying to make you feel better about something you've done that runs counter to your morals. For our guy here, that'd be murder. Whether he consciously realizes it or not, he's coming up with ways to rationalize it. All the religious symbolism makes me think he's on some sort of moral crusade."

Steelman made a sound in his throat akin to a cough. "That's what we usually wind up with when we see killers combining murder and religion. In my experience, anyway."

Redker lifted his hands again. "Now, it's still possible he's experienced a break from reality, but I don't think that's the most likely scenario. The first murders were in Terre Haute four years ago, and every year since, he's killed another three people in the same way. That tells me he passes himself off as 'normal' in between his cycles."

To Zane, the ability to blend in was the most unsettling aspect of serial killers. The way they could commit the most heinous murder, only to shower off the blood and return home to their spouse. "What about the locations? Isn't it uncommon for a serial killer to hunt outside their comfort zone?"

Redker shot Zane an appreciative glance. "It is, but I don't think this guy is hunting outside his comfort zone at all. I think he's relocating."

Icy barbs of unease stabbed at Zane's chest. "He kills three people, then moves?"

"Something like that. The first two cycles were both in Terre Haute. Could be he was afraid of being caught, and that's when he decided to start moving around."

Amelia visibly perked up. "The DNA on Krystal Avila's shirt. If the Terre Haute PD included that in their press releases, then he'd have known they'd found DNA. Maybe that's why he left Terre Haute, and his next cycle occurred in Detroit."

"Exactly." Redker scanned his laptop. "It looks like most of the bodies were found in cemeteries. My guess is he was trying to give them a suitable resting place, except for those who had defensive wounds. I think the reason for that is a combination of his desire to get rid of trace evidence and his indignation that they dared to fight back in the first place."

Amelia frowned. "So, our vics either go along with this guy's moral crusade, or they get tossed in Lake Michigan?"

"Maybe he views it as a form of baptism." Steelman drummed his fingers on the table. "That's a long shot, but it's the first thing that came to my mind."

"That'd be his way of rationalizing it," Redker said. "Based on where he's dumping the bodies, it's likely the killer lives near Washington Park. Near enough for the area to be familiar to him."

The BAU agent gave his mouse a couple clicks. "I checked on the ZIP codes of all the previous victims. Each trio, excluding the bodies found in Lake Michigan, were all found in the same part of their respective cities."

"You mean in a cemetery." Zane's observation was a statement more than a question.

"Yes, all except the people he dumped in the lake. They weren't always at the same one, but they *were* always found at a cemetery."

Now, they'd arrived at the one piece of information Zane genuinely wanted to know. "Do you think he'll hunt for his next victim near where the other victims were taken?"

"More than likely." Redker cleared his throat. "I looked through the case files for all the cities, and this killer's pattern is to troll for his trio of victims in the same general area. The first vic here was an FBI informant who had recently been to Washington Park to buy drugs. The second vic's girlfriend, Erika Brabyn, said in her statement that Neil Rosford told her about seeing Lars Poteracki abducted from Washington Park. She also told us where Neil typically posted up to sell drugs to his regulars. Again, this was Washington Park. It's reasonable to assume this killer will complete his triad by using Washington Park's less reputable areas as his hunting ground."

Steelman straightened in his seat. "Now we have a fairly

good idea where he's going to hunt for his next victim *and* that his timeline is within the next three days."

Which left them with only one option, as far as Zane was concerned. "We need to set up surveillance around the area. We can use the description Erika Brabyn gave us and keep an eye out for a car that matches it."

"Undercover." Amelia crossed her arms. "We can't exactly post up in an FBI surveillance van and just hope everyone will continue business as normal. We're going to have to blend in so we don't spook him."

As much as Zane hated the way she'd said *we*, he knew better than to try to come between Amelia and her duty as a federal investigator. They'd gone undercover together once before, and she'd held her own. Staking out Washington Park was arguably lower risk than their trip to a mafia-affiliated nightclub had been, anyway.

He swallowed to return the moisture to his mouth. "Undercover sounds like the play."

Steelman dropped both hands palm-first onto the table. "Then let's figure out the details and get this show on the road."

25

Zane's familiar Acura moving toward her brought much-needed relief to Amelia's freezing body. She'd been positioned at a corner in Washington Park for hours, mingling with the group of working girls who'd claimed the area for the night. Though she'd alternated between this intersection and another less busy corner a couple blocks north, both locations had been relatively quiet so far.

Without pausing to gauge the reactions of the other girls, Amelia strode to the curb, the clack of her high-heeled boots muffled by what snow remained on the sidewalk. The Acura slowed to a stop, and even though Zane had given her a heads-up to expect him and the car, she was jolted by a split-second of panic.

What if she accidentally got into the wrong vehicle? What if the man behind the wheel of *this* Acura was here for a prostitute to get him off?

She swallowed the irrational thoughts and stepped onto the street.

Her reflection in the Acura's passenger side window was a sight to behold. The cheap, knockoff Sherpa coat barely reached past her waist, and a black miniskirt didn't cover much more. With ripped fishnets and knee-high boots to complete the ensemble, she either resembled a working girl or a member of an eighties hair band. She couldn't decide which was more apt.

As the window inched down a crack, she caught a whiff of mint and cedar—the scent she'd come to associate with Zane's car.

Leaning toward the Acura, she met his gray eyes and offered him a sultry smile. "You looking for a date, honey?"

He returned her expression with one of his trademarked grins. "As a matter of fact, I am."

A light *click* told her the locks were disengaged, and she wasted no time prying open the door and sliding into the passenger's seat. The heat from the seat warmer, as well as the temperature of the air itself, were welcome reprieves.

As soon as they pulled away from the group of prostitutes, Amelia slumped down into the warmth of the seat.

Chuckling, Zane glanced at her. "How's the past half hour been? Anything new?"

She reached to the cupholder for the coffee she was sure had become tepid. In order to avoid suspicion, both Layton Redker and Zane had driven by to pick up Amelia, making it seem like she'd gone off with a john. They'd driven different cars each time, and she hoped they wouldn't run out of options. The FBI had plenty of vehicles on-site at the field office that were reserved specifically for undercover work. Tonight wasn't the first time an agent had posed as a working girl.

"Nothing new, not really." Sure enough, as she took the first sip, the bitter, black brew was about as warm as the cup in which it was served. But in her position, beggars couldn't be choosers. "What about Steelman? He's a couple blocks south of me still, isn't he?"

"Yeah, he's still there." Zane pulled the car into the dim parking lot of a closed liquor store and killed the headlights. "He hasn't heard or seen anything useful yet either. Just the same that you've been noticing. Everyone's on edge, even the homeless community."

Amelia swirled the lukewarm coffee before she took another reluctant sip. She and Dean Steelman had both been outfitted with low-profile earpieces and hidden mics. Plenty of hair concealed Amelia's, and Steelman had donned a wig to do the same. Though Steelman was dressed far more warmly than Amelia, Amelia had the advantage of thawing out in a car periodically.

They made sure to keep visits from her "johns" spaced out sporadically so she wouldn't appear to be on any kind of schedule. In addition, Amelia had suggested they limit the number of visits to match the flow of clientele received by the other women. Since Amelia was the new girl on the block, she wanted to make sure her number of johns reflected that status. She was here to hunt for a serial killer, not pick a fight with a prostitute or her pimp.

On cue, Steelman's voice crackled to life in Amelia's ear. "On edge is one way to put it. Apparently, damn near everyone's heard about Scorpion turning up dead at the feet of Saint Peter. Some of the guys around here are talking about demons and shit."

"The girls are too," Amelia said. "A couple of them have even mentioned Feds looking around, asking about Poteracki. Obviously, the visit Palmer and I made the other day left an impression."

Their appearance in Washington Park was the reason Dean Steelman had gone undercover instead of Zane. Since Amelia hadn't actually interacted with any of the working girls, she figured her odds of being made were relatively low.

Zane drummed his fingers against the steering wheel, his

expression focused. He and Redker both sported their own earpieces, though they didn't have to worry much about concealing theirs. "That almost fits our guy's narrative. He probably wants them to think he's an avenging angel or some such nonsense. I wonder if he knows how much the neighborhood is spooked right now. You think he might avoid it and go somewhere else if he does?"

"Doubt it." Even through radio waves, Layton Redker's certainty was clear. "All the previous vics were from the same area. He picks a place where the dealers and prostitutes hang out, and he sticks with it. This is a ritual for him, and I doubt he knows we're onto him. He won't break that ritual unless he's got a damn good reason, which he doesn't. And guys like this, they love that sense of control. He'll stick around here to enjoy it, if nothing else."

With all the mystery that still surrounded serial killers for Amelia, she was amazed that someone could be so confident about their insight. Not that she distrusted or doubted Layton Redker—quite the opposite. The man was a wealth of knowledge, and it was damn impressive.

She returned the coffee and rubbed her exposed thighs. "All right, so the plan's still the same. Keep an eye out for the car, and if we see it, we follow it."

Based on Zane's concerned glint, he wanted to add more, but not while they were on comms with their fellow agents.

Offering him a reassuring smile, Amelia reached for his hand. As their fingers interlocked, she did her best to convey reassurance and confidence. She knew he was worried about her position on the street, and she'd be lying if she said she wasn't a little nervous. However, the worn tote handbag she carried held not only her service weapon but handcuffs and her badge. With Dean Steelman fewer than two blocks away, she was confident in her safety net.

She and Zane didn't speak much on the return journey,

but truthfully, there wasn't much to say. The chatter in Washington Park so far that night was consistent with a killer being on the prowl in the area, but no one had a single clue of the perpetrator's identity.

Cold night air whipped past her as she stepped back into the open. As much as she wanted to turn around to give Zane one last reassuring smile, she had a role to play.

Tugging on the collar of her cheap coat, she mentally cursed the unspoken rule of dress for prostitutes. Couldn't men who wanted to pay for sex just be satisfied with seeing a woman in a pair of coveralls and earmuffs? Why in the hell did the girls out here have to advertise themselves with low-cut tops and short skirts when the temperature was close to twenty degrees?

Amidst her silent complaints, she shuffled back toward the edge of the decrepit apartment building that took up most of the corner lot. The structure loomed above the handful of young women, throwing them into even more shadow than the night itself. When Amelia considered how many of these girls were here of their own volition and how many were trafficking victims, or runaways with nowhere else to turn, the gloomy setting seemed appropriate.

Her throat tightened as she pretended to be interested in her nails while scanning the four young women who occupied the street corner. And they were *young* women. Girls, even.

As two more girls approached the lot across the street, Amelia kept their figures in her periphery. One sported long hair as black and sleek as a raven's feathers, and the other had teased her curly, strawberry blonde locks to add volume. A brunette from Amelia's corner waved, then made her way to the two newcomers.

Must have the same pimp or something.

The thought left a bad taste in her mouth, but there

wasn't much she could do about it. Even if she paraded over to the three girls and proclaimed her position as an agent with the Federal Bureau of Investigation, her presence wouldn't make a bit of difference in their lives.

Arresting them would only cause more harm than good. If anyone wanted to truly better their situation, they'd have to cut the head off the snake, so to speak. At least if the pimps and traffickers were gone, the girls would get more of a cut from their work—potentially even enough to pull themselves out of the life.

Amelia hated the sense of powerlessness she felt as she watched the black-haired girl saunter over to a silver SUV.

She bit the inside of her cheek.

Focus. You're here to be on the lookout for a serial killer. For once, you're not after the damn traffickers.

She snorted quietly.

Time dragged on at an agonizingly slow pace. Aside from keeping a watchful eye on the visible area, Amelia had little to occupy herself in the downtime. She didn't want to interact with the women too much in case she gave herself away. Their undercover op was last-minute, and Amelia didn't have much in the way of a cover story.

Surveillance. Not even real undercover work, is it?

Amelia had stood around in relative silence for so long that when Dean's voice came to life over the earpiece, she jolted in place.

"Heads up. A black Mazda matching the description just pulled up to a stop sign. One of you ready for the plate number?"

"Go ahead." Zane's eager response matched the sudden flood of anticipation rushing through Amelia's veins.

Steelman rattled off the series of letters and numbers. "It's headed your way, Storm."

Blood pounded in her ears as she stepped away from the

side of the building. Keeping her stride measured and nonchalant was a Herculean feat. She wanted to sprint to the corner, to shove aside any of the working girls who thought to get into the Mazda. There was no guarantee the car belonged to their suspect, as the make and model of the vehicle was fairly common.

If Amelia leapt in front of the rest of the prostitutes and hopped in the passenger's seat of the Mazda, and if the driver *wasn't* the killer for whom they were hunting, they'd be up shit creek without a paddle. In the best-case scenario, Amelia would reveal her badge, and they'd be forced to take the man into custody.

She had the option to use her discretion and to not bring him in, but then they risked him opening his mouth and blowing their undercover op.

Either way, they'd lose precious time. Amelia couldn't get in that car.

Surveillance.

She clenched her jaw as the word whispered through her mind.

Harsh, white light fell over the intersection as the black Mazda rounded a corner. The engine was almost silent in the distance, the vehicle's pace sluggish as it approached. Amelia had hoped the passenger's side of the vehicle would face her so she could get a glimpse of the man behind the wheel, but she had no such luck.

The pair of girls, the strawberry blonde and her brunette companion, both strolled to the curb.

"Found him." Zane's proclamation cut through Amelia's onslaught of worry for the pair of women across the street. "Name's James Amsdell, age twenty-nine. White male, about six-foot. According to public records, he moved to Chicago in January. Before then, he lived in Milwaukee."

"Shit," Steelman spat. "Don't tell me. Before that, he was in Detroit?"

"Yes." Zane's tone had become grave. "And Terre Haute before that. He was born in Indiana, lived in Terre Haute for most of his life until about three years ago."

Either the world's biggest coincidence had just pulled up beside the vacant lot across the street, or a serial killer was about to lure his third victim of the week.

From her vantage point, most of the blonde's body was obscured as she approached the Mazda. To Amelia's chagrin, the windows of the car were tinted as dark as the city of Chicago allowed. Between the tint and the low light, she couldn't make out a damn bit of the driver's features.

She should have gone over there as soon as Steelman had notified her the car was headed her way. Based on the direction—the fact the Mazda was headed north—she should have realized the passenger's door would face the other side of the street.

Adrenaline thrummed as she took the first step onto the packed snow. If she hurried, could she still make it?

The frizzy blonde curls disappeared from view, answering her question.

"Shit, we need to follow them. Where are you, Palmer? Redker?" Amelia didn't let her intent stare leave the car as it began to pull away.

"I'm right around the corner. Hold on, I'll pick you up." Zane's assurance calmed the worst of Amelia's panic, leaving only determination in its place.

They'd found their prime suspect. Now, all they had to do was catch him before he killed his young passenger.

26

As I pulled to a stop at a red light, the girl with the strawberry blonde curls shifted in her place in the passenger's seat. I could tell my silence unnerved her. She'd no doubt become accustomed to men making their lewd demands right off the bat, and she had to have noticed I wasn't her typical clientele.

With one hand on the wheel, I rearranged the syringe in the pocket of my coat. She and I still had a bit of a drive to make, and it was only a matter of time before her curiosity got the better of her. I'd already activated the child safety lock on her door, but as soon as she realized we weren't headed to some dark alley for sex, she'd cause a ruckus. They always did.

For the time being, I'd enjoy the uneasy silence. No conversation, no radio, just the sounds of the engine and the road.

And the smell of her damned perfume.

A pair of headlights glinted in the rearview mirror as the traffic signal turned green.

Glaring at the other vehicle, I pressed my foot down on

the accelerator to zip past the intersection. I'd intended to turn and begin to head toward my house, but I hadn't stuck around this long without my fair share of paranoia.

Traffic in this part of Washington Park was slow-going so late at night. For another car to pull up behind me as I was just about to exit the neighborhood was…bizarre.

Was it the girl's pimp? Had they sent a goon to ensure the safety of their merchandise?

Or was it the cops?

Ice water trickled into my veins at the notion. I was still confident law enforcement had no idea who I was, but could I have just fallen prey to a sting operation?

My gaze shifted back and forth between the road and the rearview mirror. Through the bright glow of the car's headlights, I recognized the vehicle as a late-model Acura.

Since when did city cops conduct sting operations in sleek sedans?

An image of the site where Lars Poteracki's body was pulled from Lake Michigan flashed across my mind. The well-dressed man and woman I'd previously determined were Feds.

I ground my teeth together, my grasp tightening around the steering wheel. An Acura seemed like the type of car a Fed would drive.

The theory was a longshot, but I'd rather not take my chances. My pretty passenger and I would be taking a roundabout route to my house, or perhaps to an alternate location altogether. First, I needed to determine whether or not the Acura was following me, and then, if they were, I'd find a way to lose the tail.

"Um, dude, where the hell are we going?"

The girl's voice was the manifested reminder my situation was markedly more complicated than simply ditching my stalker.

Waving my hand in a casual dismissal, I offered her a smile. "Just somewhere I like to go. Don't worry, we'll be there in no time."

Her suspicious green eyes told me she hadn't bought a single word. She might have been a whore, but she was a keen observer. "Why don't you just drop me off up here at this gas station? I…don't think this is going to work. You'd better just find another girl."

I widened the phony grin. "Why do that when you're already right here?"

Charming women hadn't always been my strongest trait. After the hard lessons my father had drilled into me while I was growing up, dealing with the opposite gender was more a chore than anything. Not that prostitutes were vulnerable to the same type of charm as other women.

That's why I had the syringe.

A twinge of panic settled in beside her skepticism. "No. I need to go."

As the upcoming traffic light switched to yellow, I mentally cursed my luck. If I hadn't been tailed by a car that may or may not have been a cop, I'd have seriously considered blowing through the intersection. An on-ramp to the freeway wasn't far ahead. Once I hit the interstate, I'd have a better shot of ditching the Acura, and the girl would have nowhere to go.

But she'd become suspicious. The last thing I wanted was to be pulled over for running a red light and for her to insist to the cop I was kidnapping her.

Forcing my expression to remain neutral, I reluctantly slowed the car to a halt. As much as I didn't *want* to come to a complete stop, I'd make the most of the situation.

I flattened both palms against the wheel and heaved a sigh of feigned resignation. "Okay. Fine. I'm sorry. I don't do… this very often, and I just wanted to make sure I was out of the neighborhood in case there were, I don't know." I waved a hand in the air as I pretended to be tongue-tied. "Any cops around, or something. If I got a citation or went to jail, I could lose my job."

Her stony expression didn't change in the slightest, and I began to inch my hand back toward my pocket.

"That's fine. Just take me back, and we'll call it even." As she clutched her purse on her lap, I realized for the first time that one of her hands was obscured by the patterned fabric.

What did she have in there? Pepper spray? A handgun?

I'd rather not find out.

Still grasping the steering wheel, I popped the cap off the hypodermic needle in my coat pocket. My strike had to be swift and decisive—more importantly, I had to take her by surprise.

I needed to increase my charm. "Okay. Do, uh, you want to listen to anything on the radio? I have satellite stations. What kind of music do you like?"

She pressed her lips together, but as the traffic light flicked to green, her attention briefly left me.

That split-second was all I needed.

In one fluid motion, I jammed the syringe into the muscle of her upper thigh, all while pulling away from the intersection. Her mouth had barely opened by the time I pressed down on the plunger, injecting the fast-acting sedative into her system.

Yelping in surprise, she frantically dug deeper into her handbag. Before she could find whatever she sought, I clamped my hand down on her forearm to hold her in place. Though she resisted, her waning strength was no match for mine.

"Wh-what the hell? What did…you…do?" Her wide eyes began to glaze over, her posture becoming slumped and listless.

As I clicked on my turn signal for the interstate, tension left the muscles of her forearm. Her shoulders sagged, eyelids drooping. I relinquished my grip and returned my focus to the rearview mirror.

To the headlights of the damned Acura.

I couldn't take her back to my basement, that much was abundantly clear. Even if I lost the tail, I couldn't be sure how much they'd learned about me. For all I knew, a whole precinct was waiting back at my house. I'd return to the place, but not with this unconscious prostitute in my company.

No, I had just the place for her. If I couldn't use her to help cleanse the masses, then the least I could do was give her a final baptism before she died—a last-ditch effort to save her soul.

After that, I'd deal with the damn Feds.

27

Having just passed the northern limit of the city of Chicago, Zane was confident he'd outplayed James Amsdell. Covertly following suspects was a trick he'd learned before his twenty-second birthday, and it was one he'd employed countless times throughout his CIA *and* FBI careers. Amsdell was still in his sights, but Zane had hung back at a comfortable distance and flicked off his headlights.

Fortunately, they'd left the interstate and now drove along a stretch of road bordering Lake Michigan. Houses and businesses had thinned, leaving them cloaked in darkness relative to Chicago. The lack of a streetlight every fifteen feet was conducive to Zane staying hidden behind Amsdell, but the gloom went both ways.

Any time the Mazda turned, Zane was certain he was about to lose him. The drive had been a tense one, and Zane wished like hell they had some idea where Amsdell was headed.

As if she could read his mind, Amelia glanced out the passenger's side window and shook her head. "Where in the hell is this guy going? We've been on the road for, what, a half hour now?"

"Thirty-three minutes. How far back are Steelman and Redker?" Zane didn't take his eyes off the Mazda. The taillights were glowing red pinpricks at this distance, and if his attention slipped for even a moment, he'd risk losing the vehicle.

"They're about five minutes behind us. They're closing the gap slowly but should pick up the pace once they're outside the city limits."

The two agents had wound up stuck behind a train not far outside of Washington Park, and despite Redker's self-proclaimed lead foot, they still hadn't recovered. To add to the complication, they'd drifted outside the effective range of their earpieces. Now, other than their cells, they had to rely on an old-school police radio to communicate quickly.

If they had a single damn clue where Amsdell was headed, they could have requested the assistance of the Cook County Sheriff's Office. Or the CPD. Or the night shift agents back at the damn field office.

After quickly changing into a pair of warm sweatpants, long sleeve t-shirt, hoodie, and winter coat Zane had stowed in his car for her, Amelia had been researching their suspect. She checked for alternate addresses, vacation properties, relatives, or any other location north of the city that could be relevant to Amsdell. However, he was an only child, and both his parents were long dead. They'd owned a restaurant in Terre Haute, which Amsdell had sold four years ago—the same time as the first cycle of murders.

"What do you think he did to the girl with him?" Amelia's question sank a stone in Zane's stomach.

Though Zane hadn't witnessed Amsdell pick up the young woman in question, Amelia had given him a rough description.

Slender, fair skin, average height. Strawberry blonde curls.

Just like the girl he'd spoken to when they'd visited Washington Park a couple days earlier. Just like Katya.

He swallowed, his mouth suddenly dry. "I don't know. He must've done something, though. Otherwise, she'd be raising hell, and he'd have pulled over to deal with her by now."

"Could've knocked her out." The hopeful tinge to Amelia's words was undeniable.

They both knew what types of atrocities Amsdell was capable of enacting on another person and how mentally unstable people like him could be. If she'd grated on his nerves a little too hard, Zane had no doubt he'd do more than just knock her out.

He shook off the glum thoughts and refocused on the taillights. Several long minutes passed in nearly complete silence.

In one moment, the pinpricks of light glowed brighter, and then they disappeared.

"Shit." Zane's heart knocked against his chest as he eased his foot down on the gas pedal.

"He turned. I didn't see any headlights, though. Either there's a building there, or he's driving in the dark too." White light flashed in his periphery as she unlocked her phone to pull up satellite imagery of the area. Amelia's diligence had saved their asses once at the beginning of their pursuit. Zane only hoped it would be enough to point them the right way a second time.

Flexing his fingers against the steering wheel, Zane leaned in toward the windshield. He strained his eyes, searching the darkness for any sign of an upcoming turn. Tall, snow-covered trees loomed to either side of the road, partly obscuring the backs of houses on their left. Hard as he looked, he could find no driveways that gave access to the residential community.

On the righthand side of the highway was Lake Michigan. The water wasn't visible from this far inland, but they'd passed a number of right turns that led to the various marinas dotting the shore.

"There's a right turn up ahead." Amelia pointed at the windshield with her free hand. "That's got to be where he went. There isn't anything else for a ways after that."

Finally, he had a damn direction. "What's at the end of that road? A house, or…?"

"A marina. It's private, not commercial. Pretty small from what I can tell based on the satellite image." She tapped the screen a couple more times. "I don't see any roads that head out of there aside from the one that leads *in*. I wonder if he knows that? It looks like a dead end."

Why in the hell would Amsdell go through all the trouble of driving more than thirty minutes outside of Washington Park just to pull into a dead end? "Does he own a boat?"

"I can check again, but no, I don't think so. Just the Mazda. He rents the house where he lives. Maybe he's renting a boat? And he's going to use it to get away from the city? If he noticed he was being followed, he might be spooked. He might be trying to make a break or something."

Or he might be in the middle of dumping the body of his most recent victim.

Zane silenced the negative voice in his head. One way or another, they'd catch him, and they'd get him *tonight*.

Though Zane was cruising down the road at fifteen over the speed limit, he felt like they'd taken a full hour to reach the damn turn.

A reflective sign partly obscured with snow advised they were about to enter Schulz Marina—a privately owned and operated space for boat enthusiasts to dock their vessels.

Or a concealed location for a serial killer to dispose of his latest victim.

Silence blanketed Amelia and him as he steered the Acura down the snow-covered road. Gradually, the copse of leafless trees thinned, providing an unobstructed view of the marina. A picnic area, including several scattered tables, a fire pit, and a handful of grills, took up the clearing to the right. On the left was a squat building with only a few dark windows facing their direction.

The empty parking lot appeared to have been plowed at least once or twice, though the snow from yesterday was still undisturbed. Aside from the tire tracks leading to a familiar black Mazda.

Amsdell had taken the parking stall closest to the boardwalk entrance.

"Shit!" Amelia exclaimed.

A cold hand of dread closed around Zane's throat. If they could see Amsdell's car, then he could see them.

Zane veered the Acura behind the building, his pulse pounding in his ears. He could only hope the split-second maneuver had put them out of Amsdell's line of vision in time.

Killing the engine, Zane held his breath and strained his hearing. His senses were on high alert, his eyes flicking from one window to the next, searching for the slightest movement to indicate Amsdell's approach.

But the night was quiet. The snow-covered marina was still. All he could hear was the low whine of the winter wind.

Amelia's voice finally broke the strained silence. "Do you think he saw us?"

Licking his lips, Zane forced himself to relax his death grip on the steering wheel. "I don't know. There was still some distance between us, and it's dark as hell out here. The engine on this thing is really quiet, so maybe it was drowned out by the wind."

Or maybe he's preoccupied with his passenger.

They needed a plan, stat. "How far out are Steelman and Redker?"

Amelia's cell lit her face with an eerie white glow. "Six or seven minutes now, and the cavalry is right behind them. I'll send a message to let them know where Amsdell stopped."

"Okay." Goose bumps prickled the back of Zane's forearms.

His instincts told him they had to do more than just wait. They needed to see what in the hell Amsdell was doing. Was he sitting in his car listening to "American Pie" on repeat, or was he about to hijack a damn boat and sail off into Lake Michigan with his captive?

Zane wanted a closer look at that car.

Pulling his service weapon from his leather jacket, he turned to Amelia. "We're hidden from him here, but we need to keep an eye on what he's doing. In case he tries to escape somehow."

Jaw tight, Amelia nodded. "Agreed. A lot can happen in seven minutes."

"Exactly." Turning off the inside lights, he reached for the door handle. "We can hide around the corner of the building. The parking lot isn't much bigger than an average apartment building's lot. We'll be close enough to see what he's doing but should be far enough that it'll be easy to stay out of sight. Especially since there're all of two functioning streetlights in this parking lot."

"I saw cameras on them." She lifted a shoulder, and he could tell her hopeful expression was forced.

"Whether or not they actually work is the real question. Something tells me there's a reason Amsdell came here instead of one of the eight-billion marinas we passed on our trip north."

Amelia tossed him a wide-eyed stare. "You think this is where he dumped Poteracki's body?"

"I'd put money on it. There's no way he just drove out to a random marina to do his dirty work. Plus, we're north of the city, so it makes sense with the direction of the lake's currents." He tilted his chin in the direction of Amsdell's car. "Come on. Let's get a better look at what this prick is up to."

"All right. Let's go." She slowly pushed open the car door and reached for her service weapon.

Zane followed suit, careful to make as little sound as possible. The wind provided a white noise backdrop, but the cold night was eerily quiet. Even the soft crunch of his footsteps seemed like enough to wake the dead.

As he and Amelia neared the edge of the building, the back half of Amsdell's Mazda came into view. An enclosed trash area jutted out about ten feet in front of them, and fortunately, the wooden structure was large enough to conceal them both.

He gestured to the fenced-in dumpster, nonverbally suggesting to her they move closer.

Their short trip was made in absolute silence. No matter how hard Zane strained his hearing in an effort to discern what Amsdell was doing, he repeatedly came away with nothing. Not even the car's engine was humming.

Why in the hell is he sitting in his car with the damn thing turned off? What is he doing? Is he waiting for us? Is he waiting for someone else?

A hint of adrenaline crept into Zane's veins as they hunkered down to conceal themselves behind the six-foot-tall fence. He glanced over his shoulder to ensure no surprise visitors were creeping up on their location.

Did Amsdell plan to commit suicide by cop? Had he known they were on his tail all along?

Or worse still, did he intend to make a final stand to take as many law enforcement agents with him as he could when he died?

Zane's stomach knotted as an unsettling realization dawned on him. Sure, they'd uncovered his pattern. They knew he killed in threes, and he tended to target prostitutes and drug users.

But they had no idea what type of defense mechanisms were in his back pocket.

Aside from a forty-five-caliber handgun registered in his name, Amsdell owned no other firearms about which they knew.

Had he secretly stockpiled an arsenal? Had he done business with a morally vacuous arms dealer? The kind of people he sought to eliminate?

Clamping his teeth together, Zane let the biting cold of the night air recenter him for a moment. With Amelia at his back behind the dumpster, he finally forced himself to peek around the corner.

The Mazda was quiet. No exhaust, no hum of the engine. Just nothing.

Zane focused on the vehicle's tinted windows. The glass was dark, but thanks to the meager glow of a streetlight beside the car, he could just barely make out movement through the rear windshield.

A figure from the driver's side leaned over to the passenger's seat, and the driver was busy working on…something.

Killing her? Raping her? Doing god only knew what else?

He hated the doubtful voice as soon as it started to speak. At the same time, he knew it might very well be accurate. They could already be too late, or worse, they could be sitting back here hashing out a plan while Amsdell was busy killing that poor girl.

More than the moment of pessimism, he hated the quieter voice insisting their jobs would be easier if the girl was already dead. Then, they could charge in, arrest Amsdell, and end this damn chase.

Stop. Focus. Figure out a plan. You're a federal agent, dammit.

He inhaled a deep, steadying breath.

Ducking back behind the fence, he turned to Amelia. "He's in the car. Or someone is. I can't see much through the tinted windows, but there's movement from the driver's side. We need to get in closer, but we also need to know what we're dealing with."

She pressed her lips together, her face a mask of determination. "Binoculars won't help in the dark. Not even night vision helps with tinted windows."

He flashed her a mirthless smile. "We don't have any night vision anyway."

"True." She exhaled a small fog of condensation and shook her head. "And the last thing we want is for him to know we're coming. If he sees us, then he'll almost definitely kill that girl."

Amelia's candid observation tugged at his heart, but he knew she was right. "How do we get to him without him seeing us?"

She craned her head to peek at the picnic area. "There aren't too many cover spots between us and them. Over in the picnic area, there are plenty, but we'd have to get over there first. Then we might be able to stay hidden while we get closer to the car to get a better idea of what exactly Amsdell's doing before backup gets here. Make sure he doesn't do anything…*else*."

Zane scanned the picnic benches and large trees. Even with the white backdrop of the snow, Amelia was right.

Plenty of props could provide adequate cover for a couple spies.

Problem was, they had to run across a parking lot to get there. As occupied as Amsdell was, there was no way he'd miss two people darting out in the open. Even if they kept low to the ground, the snow had put them between a rock and a hard place. Neither he nor Amelia were wearing white, and they'd stick out like a couple beacons.

The dull *thud* of a car door pierced through the moment of contemplation like a needle popping a balloon. The receding adrenaline returned in full force as Zane and Amelia exchanged fervent glances.

Amsdell was on the move.

Forcing his breaths to be steady, Zane leaned forward, each motion measured and diligent as if he were traversing a minefield.

A black, hooded sweatshirt shrouded Amsdell's face in shadow as he strode around the back of the Mazda. Coupled with his black cargo pants, gloves, and leather coat, the guy sure as hell *looked* the part of a dangerous killer.

Zane's lungs burned, but he still couldn't permit himself to take a breath.

When Amsdell paused at the passenger's side door and looked over his shoulder, Zane felt his heart stop.

Shit! Did he see me?

He eased back behind the relative cover of the fence to prevent any sudden movement from drawing attention to their location.

"What the hell happened?" Amelia's voice was barely a whisper.

Slowly, Zane drew in a lungful of precious oxygen. "I don't know. He got out and walked around to the…"

Before he could finish the explanation, a car door opened, followed by the quiet crunch of footsteps. As he and Amelia stood rooted to the spot, Amsdell grunted like he was power lifting at a gym.

The soft whimper that came next was most definitely not a sound emitted by a twenty-nine-year-old man.

Amelia's mouth drooped open as Zane met her incredulous stare.

"She's alive," Amelia breathed.

Relief, as warm and welcoming as a shot of morphine, bloomed in Zane's heart. They *weren't* too late. Katya was still alive.

His stomach lurched.

She's not Katya. She's not Katya. She's not *Katya, dammit.*

Good lord, he was losing it. He needed a vacation. Ten vacations, back-to-back. But first…

Swallowing the bile inching its way up his throat, he pressed his shoulder against the fence and leaned forward ever so slightly.

Amsdell had a person draped over his shoulder and kicked the door closed.

As Amsdell started for the docks, the girl's bound wrists bounced against his back. "We're almost done here, tramp. You'll be at peace soon enough."

The words were like shards of ice, even colder than the frigid lake in the distance or the snow on the ground. His tone was calm, as if he was speaking to a cashier or a coworker.

For a beat, Zane genuinely missed dealing with contract killers. Truly, there was more humanity left in a person who accepted payments to eliminate rival mafiosos than there was in someone like James Amsdell.

Amsdell's voice grew fainter as he walked. "It's too bad I won't be able to use you to cleanse others. You won't get to serve your full purpose, but I can save you from your life of sin."

The man went on, but by then, the wind obscured every other word. He was taking the girl out along a dock, but why?

Zane had a bad feeling he knew exactly why.

Several vessels were moored to the pier, but Amsdell walked past the first as if it didn't exist. When he neared the next boat but made no move to board it, the scene changed in front of Zane's eyes.

In place of Lake Michigan, he saw the Sea of Okhotsk. In Amsdell's place was Sergei and Rurik, and in the girl's place...

Katya.

Adrenaline jolted through him like a living thing. "Shit, he's going to throw her into the fucking lake!"

He barely heard Amelia's confused response, hardly even registered her presence at all.

James Amsdell was about to throw the girl into Lake Michigan, her hands and legs bound, just like Sergei had done to Katya all those years ago.

Back then, Zane had been powerless to stop the two Russian men.

Today was different.

Without another word, Zane bolted from the cover of the fenced-in dumpster. His sights were set on a large pine at the edge of the picnic area. From there, he'd hustle to conceal himself behind Amsdell's car and then a stack of wooden crates at the start of the dock.

He wouldn't let down another innocent girl like he'd done to Katya. Either he'd save her, or he'd die trying.

28

Amelia's head reeled as if her brain had been tossed into one of the old-school lottery machines, spun around for a couple hours, and then plopped out onto the floor.

One hand grasping her service weapon, she rested the other against the splintery wooden fence to maintain her balance.

After proclaiming that Amsdell intended to throw his victim into Lake Michigan, Zane had taken off. He'd ignored a handful of smaller structures—such as a line of shrubs, a grill, and a picnic table—that would have provided a stealthier approach.

Instead, he'd gone straight for the pine tree, and now he was crouched in the shadow of the Mazda.

She cursed under her breath as he sprinted out from behind Amsdell's car.

Situations like this were precisely the reason the Bureau didn't permit couples to work together in the field. Amelia was sure the whirlwind of thoughts would be far more manageable if she'd just watched Dean Steelman run toward what may well be his death.

Come on. Keep your head in the game. There has to be something you can do. We've still got a few minutes before backup gets here. We just have to hold out until then.

At the rate Zane was going, he'd alert Amsdell of his presence long before Steelman or Redker arrived.

What in the hell was he planning?

He had to have seen the handgun tucked behind Amsdell's back, right?

They both knew the man had a forty-five registered in his name, and neither of them was wearing Kevlar. Not that a bullet suppression vest would have mattered much for a close-range shot from a forty-five. The bullet might not pierce the material, but its impact could definitely cause internal damage.

Amelia was confident Zane could handle himself in a fight, but she wouldn't stand by and watch him throw himself at Amsdell.

"Shit!" Right now, *she* was his only backup.

Sweeping her gaze over the snowy parking lot one more time, she noted the distance Amsdell had made along the dock. His back was still facing her, but there was no telling how long that would last.

Rather than bounce from the pine to Amsdell's car, Amelia made a beeline for the Mazda. She was playing catch-up, and that didn't allow her the luxury of stealth. She had to rely on luck and speed.

If Zane had the slightest idea Amelia was tailing him, he gave no indication. He'd snuck from behind the crates to a trash receptacle and then to another more distant stack of crates.

Zane was fast. Too damn fast. There couldn't be much more than fifteen feet separating him from Amsdell.

After a few seconds to catch her breath, Amelia poked her head around the rear fender of Amsdell's car to make note of his and Zane's positions. Zane was still kneeling behind the same crates, his tall frame barely concealed.

Without permitting her vision to leave Amsdell and the bundle over his shoulder, Amelia darted to the stack of crates at the start of the dock. She kept her steps light, confident he couldn't hear her over the wind and water from twenty-five or so feet away.

When he stopped walking and turned to face the water, Amelia was sure he'd seen them. Holding her breath, she hunched lower, peeked around the crates, and waited.

For several grueling moments, he stood still. The murmur of his voice drifted over to her on the wind, but she couldn't make out what he was saying.

Her pulse began to slow. He hadn't seen her.

What in the hell is he doing out there? The girl is alive. We heard her. Is he really going to throw her into the lake like Zane said?

Amelia's heart dropped through her stomach as Amsdell eased the girl off his shoulder and into his arms. Stepping toward the railing that lined the dock, he paused.

In that moment of cold silence, his stance turned almost reverent, as if he was cradling his hostage to his chest like a daughter.

Naïve optimism stabbed at Amelia's brain.

Maybe this was part of the ritual. Maybe he always took his victims out to the lake before he brought them home and slit their throats.

Could they have caught him early in the routine? Would they be able to intercept him when backup arrived, safely acquiring the young girl before he could harm her further?

Before she could even finish forming the question, Amsdell leaned forward and extended his arms over the railing. Without a pause or even a moment of hesitation, the blonde fell into the shifting black water.

The entire scene was surreal. For a split second, she viewed the scenario as if she was floating outside her body.

Surely, this wasn't happening, right?

There was still so much of the girl's life ahead of her. So many experiences, so much joy. Obviously, as a prostitute on the streets of Washington Park, she hadn't had an easy start to life. No one worked the streets because their years had been filled with sunshine and puppies.

But staring down the barrel of one's own mortality tended to make a person reevaluate their lot in life.

For this individual, that opportunity might never come. Whether she drowned first or succumbed to hypothermia, her story would stop before it had even truly started.

Amelia forced the grim thoughts from her head. This wasn't a dream. This was reality, and she needed to act fast.

As Zane rose to his full height behind the crates, Amsdell's head jerked around like it was on a swivel. To Amelia's horror, both Zane's hands were empty.

What had he done with his service weapon?

Amsdell snapped one hand behind his back, no doubt reaching for his forty-five.

Before he could take aim with the powerful handgun, Zane disappeared over the edge of the pier. In the twenty-degree night, the splash as he dove into Lake Michigan was barely audible.

Shouting a series of expletives, Amsdell rushed over to the crates, took aim at the approximate location Zane had gone underwater and fired three shots in rapid succession.

The raucous retort of the forty-five clamored through Amelia's head like someone had smashed together a pair of cymbals beside her ear. After the concussive blast of the gunshots, Amsdell would be temporarily rendered deaf.

God, I hope these crates are solid.

She'd have preferred to be behind a tree, but she'd have to

take what she could get. Because she was about to become Amsdell's new obsession. If she didn't, the man would merely wait for Zane to resurface.

"James Amsdell!" She put as much force into the shout as she could manage. Though dull compared to the gunshots, the echo of her voice off the nearest boat was satisfying. "This is the Federal Bureau of Investigation. You've just fired your weapon at a federal agent, and deadly force *is* authorized! I'm going to give you one chance to set down your weapon and get your hands up!"

Amsdell whirled around to face her, the forty-five at the ready, and ducked behind his own stack of crates.

So much for his one chance.

Amelia contemplated her angles just as Amsdell took a step back. It wasn't center mass, but it would stop him just the same.

"Gotcha, you son of a bitch."

The crack of her nine-mil wasn't as cacophonous as the forty-five, but her ears rang just the same.

Despite the distance, she noted the fine mist of crimson as the bullet ripped through Amsdell's right knee. A howl of pain followed as Amsdell crumpled behind the crates where Zane had only just hidden.

Zane, who might already be dead, and who would *definitely* be dead if he didn't get out of the water within the next minute and a half.

The fires of rage stirred in her heart. Who in the hell was Amsdell to think he was another human being's judge, jury, and executioner? The justice system was flawed, sure, but it existed for a reason. This wasn't the Wild West.

She suddenly regretted firing a warning shot at Amsdell's knee.

I should have hit him in the head and ended this.

But even a psychopath like Amsdell deserved their day in

court. More importantly, the families of Amsdell's victims deserved the closure a trial and conviction could bring them.

Just as Amelia opened her mouth to issue another, harsher warning, a fifth gunshot cracked the night air. Splintered wood exploded from the corner of a crate near Amelia's shoulder, forcing her to crouch down to make herself a smaller target.

Two more blasts followed the first, one going wide and the other slamming into the boardwalk.

Amsdell had fired a total of six shots. Between the force of the slugs so far and her knowledge of the single firearm registered in his name, she was certain he was sporting a forty-five. The capacity of his weapon's magazine was seven, according to the digital records filed after his purchase.

He had one more shot, and she needed to bait it out of him so she could get to him before he had a chance to reload.

Heart thundering, Amelia inched closer to the edge of the ruined crates. With a jolt, she realized the boxes were indeed empty, and their construction was lackluster, to say the least.

Good thing Amsdell's a lousy shot when he's got a bullet in his knee.

"Amsdell, this place will be swarming with FBI agents in three minutes or less. They know where we are, and they know where *you* are. If you don't put down your weapon and surrender now, then a sniper *will* take you out when they get here."

Never mind that Zane and the bound girl would already be dead by then.

Her stomach twisted.

Why was he so quick to dive into freezing water after a girl he didn't even know? Why couldn't he have…have what? Let her die?

Stop it, Amelia. You're in the middle of a damn shootout. Focus.

Get rid of Amsdell, and do it fast. Bait the last shot out of him and take him down.

He seemed to enjoy returning her shots, and he *didn't* seem to want to listen to her orders.

Snapping up the sights of her Glock, she quickly spotted Amsdell's faint shadow. He was crouched behind the cover of the crates, but the white fluorescence from the parking lot lights betrayed him.

Amelia settled her aim on the second stack from the top —the crates that would be closest to Amsdell's head. She didn't think the nine-mil would pierce the box to actually hit him, but the splintering wood would be jarring, just as it had been for her.

She squeezed the trigger, then immediately ducked back down out of sight.

Through the ringing in her ears, she barely heard Amsdell's surprised exclamation.

However, she sure as hell heard the retort of the forty-five.

Then, nothing.

He was out…she hoped. She had to move.

Like it was Amelia Storm's rite of passage, Amelia leapt to her feet and sprinted down the dock, her footsteps leaving *thunks* against the wood.

Like she'd hoped, Amsdell hadn't expected the abrupt advance. Amelia bore down on his hiding spot in a matter of moments. Grasping at the crates, he hoisted himself to his feet as he began to raise the forty-five.

Unfortunately for him, the slide had already popped backward, a sure-fire indicator the weapon was out of ammunition.

Amelia swatted the handgun out of his grasp like he was a toddler with a pair of scissors. With a clatter, the forty-five skidded across the worn dock and *plunked* into Lake

Michigan. Disarmed and without the full use of one of his legs, Amsdell was finished. He was a cornered animal, and Amelia was the hunter who'd put him there.

Whether Amsdell was cornered or not, she couldn't let herself slide into a sense of complacency.

Cornered animals were the most dangerous, especially when their freedom and even their life was on the line.

She took a step back from his kneeling form and started to bring the Glock to bear. "James Amsdell, you're under arrest. You—"

The sentence was cut short as a furious roar ripped free from Amsdell's throat.

Springing from behind the crates like a coiled snake striking at its prey, the man launched himself at Amelia. The instant she caught his first minuscule movement, she swiveled to the side, hoping to avoid the brunt of the head-on tackle.

Amsdell's shoulder clipped Amelia's left side, and she had to move her body with the sudden momentum to keep from falling over. A dull pain rippled out from her rib cage, and she found herself hoping she'd only sustained a nasty bruise and not a broken bone.

With quick reflexes, Amelia spun in a semi-circle, almost like the ballerina she'd never been graceful enough to be. All the while, her right hand never loosened around her service weapon.

The fury of failure and adrenaline had fueled Amsdell's movement, and though the blow was powerful, it was devoid of the same grace that had kept Amelia on her feet.

With a heavy *thud*, Amsdell's chin slammed into the wooden dock before he could brace himself. Amelia expected him to realize his folly and surrender, but to her continued surprise, he planted both hands on the ground and shoved himself partially upright. His hateful gaze snapped to her, and as their eyes met, she realized he was making his last stand.

Did he think himself a martyr? Layton Redker had ascertained Amsdell was on some fucked up moral crusade. Most saints in the Christian religion had been martyred, so the idea would play perfectly into Amsdell's twisted thought process.

He thinks he's going to become a martyr? He might have just killed a federal agent!

Renewed fury bubbled in Amelia's veins. Planting both feet solidly, she waited for Amsdell to stand before she exploded into action. With a swift step forward, she arced her arm back and swung.

Her knuckles collided with Amsdell's cheek, the force of the blow reverberating through Amelia's shoulder. Like a ragdoll, he flopped to the side, barely managing to catch himself on the railing to prevent a fall into Lake Michigan.

Amelia clamped down on the Glock with an iron grasp. Before he could regroup from her punch, she cracked the grip of her service weapon across his temple with so much force, she worried she might have killed him.

As he crumpled to the ground, she pulled a pair of cuffs from her coat. After checking Amsdell's pulse to confirm he was alive, she rolled him onto his stomach and wrenched both arms behind his back.

She cinched the silver bracelets closed with a metallic snap and conducted a quick pat down to check for additional weapons. There weren't any.

Breathing ragged, her mind a chaotic storm of dread and anger, she rose to her full height. Trepidation clamped its icy hand down around her throat as she scanned the dark waters of the lake, searching desperately for movement that might be Zane or the young girl.

All she saw was the seemingly endless shifting darkness.

The glow of white light crept into the corner of her eye, and she glanced to the source. Headlights. Steelman and Redker were here.

Despite the surge of relief at knowing their backup had finally arrived, the lead weight on her heart remained.

How long had passed since Zane dove over the edge? Two minutes? Maybe three?

Could he still be alive? Hypothermia set in quickly, but she couldn't be sure *how* quickly. Dr. Francis had mentioned the lake temperature when they'd sat in on Lars Poteracki's autopsy.

What had it been then? Forty-something? That wasn't bad, was it?

Sliding her service weapon into the waistband of her sweatpants, Amelia clenched her fists and turned toward the newly arrived vehicle. Just as she was about to flag down Redker and Steelman, her attention snapped to a scarcely illuminated figure on the rocky shore.

Another car pulled in beside the first, and as the new set of headlights swept over the area, Amelia's knees suddenly went wobbly. It was Zane. He was hunched over the still form of the blonde, rhythmically pressing his hands against her chest.

Her relief at seeing Zane alive and moving was quickly replaced by a sickening sense of dread and failure. They'd tried so hard and put themselves through so much risk to try to rescue the girl. As Amelia peered at her still form in the distance, the entire effort seemed to be for naught.

Clenching and unclenching her hands, she chewed on her bottom lip as she watched Zane perform another series of compressions. He pinched the blonde's nose and leaned down to breathe into her mouth.

Oh no.

The autopsy photos of Willow Nowland's bruised, lifeless

face flashed inside her head. They always put forth their best effort to save the victims of the maniacal killers they chased, but failure was a part of life, including Amelia's job as a federal agent.

As Zane jerked upright, the girl flopped to her side. Bracing herself against the rocky shore with her still bound hands, her body shook as she coughed.

She was alive.

Amelia bit the inside of her cheek to stave off tears of relief. If she hadn't had an unconscious, trigger-happy serial killer at her feet, she'd have sprinted down the dock to check on the drenched pair.

Flashes of red and blue melded with the harsh white of the headlights, reflecting off the lake's surface like some sort of magician's fire.

The cavalry had arrived.

29

Zane blinked to clear his vision as the haze of sleep finally loosened its hold. A single slat of sunlight pierced through the gap in the curtains of the hospital room's only window. Yawning, he rubbed his eyes and picked up his phone to check the time.

Almost four in the afternoon.

"Jesus, how much did I sleep?" However long it had been, it didn't feel like enough. With a sigh, he let his head fall back onto the pillow.

He and Paige, who he'd just barely saved from the freezing waters of Lake Michigan, had both been loaded into ambulances and rushed to the hospital.

Paige. That was her name. Not Candy like she'd used on the streets. Paige Milling. Barely eighteen years old and working the streets to escape an awful home life. Maybe this could be her fresh start. Her reset.

At the time of their transport to the hospital, he'd been confident he'd avoided a nasty case of hypothermia. He hadn't been in the water for that long. From the time he'd gone over the railing to the time he hauled her to the shore was…what? Two minutes? Maybe three?

When Zane had pulled himself and Paige onto land, she hadn't been breathing. Amidst enough gunshots to constitute a war zone, Zane had knelt over the girl and performed CPR until she came to.

He hadn't *thought* he'd succumbed to severe hypothermia, but he'd been far closer than he assumed. If an ambulance hadn't arrived when it did, their situation would have become much more dire.

It hadn't, though. They were both taken to the same hospital, provided with a million-and-a-half heated blankets, warm IV fluids, and even humidified oxygen. Once his body temperature had risen, the staff had finally let him sleep. Amelia had been in the room when he'd drifted off, but he was alone now.

Someone has to deal with Amsdell, don't they?

He sank a little deeper into the pillow. Even though most of what was left of the case was paperwork and court prep—provided Amsdell didn't plead out—he'd rather be at the office working than stuck in a hospital room by himself.

By himself…and his thoughts.

The memories of Katya and Rurik, of Sergei and Maksim. Of Okhotsk and all the terrible shit that happened there.

Though he was prepared for a tidal wave of crushing guilt and shame, the sensation seemed…dull. Distant. All the negative feelings were still there, but they were *muted*.

Maybe the shock of the sudden heavy snow had left his system? Maybe he'd finally gotten used to Christmas decorations?

Or had he finally done something to redeem himself in his mind?

Diving into the lake after Paige had been suicidal. With the combination of a madman firing shots blindly into the water, the darkness, and the deadly cold temperatures, one wrong move would have resulted in disaster. If Amelia hadn't caught Amsdell's attention, Zane would have been a sitting duck when he came up for air the first time.

Perhaps he should have handled the situation differently. He knew for certain his past experiences had propelled him toward reckless action, but he'd be damned if he shared the knowledge with anyone else. As far as they were all concerned, he was a hero.

In reality, he was just some fool chasing ghosts for redemption.

If he hadn't dived into the lake when he did, Paige would have died. As he'd suspected, her hands and feet were bound, and she'd still been in the haze of whatever sedative Amsdell had dosed her with.

His guilt had saved her life.

He snorted to himself. At least it had finally done someone a little good.

Maybe that's why the memories didn't sting quite so much. After all these years, the weight of his guilt had finally led to something good.

A light knock at the door pulled him from the reverie.

"Come in." He stifled a yawn and pushed himself to sit upright.

As the door creaked open, he half-expected to see one of the nurses or even a doctor. Instead, Dean Steelman stepped over the threshold and offered him a grin. Steelman's typical suit was gone, replaced with what Zane assumed was the man's casual attire. Dark jeans, boots, a hooded sweatshirt, and a black peacoat draped over one arm.

"Hey, Palmer. How you feelin'?" Steelman let the door fall closed before he made his way to a chair beside the bed.

Zane offered an exaggerated shrug. "I'm not dead, so

that's a plus. I'm still tired as hell, but I don't feel like I'm going to keel over or anything."

Turning in his seat, Steelman hung his coat on the back of the chair. "Nothin' quite like not dying, is there?"

"I…guess?" Zane had definitely felt better, but Steelman had a point. Even being drained of all energy, both mental and physical, was a step up from being six feet under.

"Amsdell's in holding, stuck there until arraignment on Monday. A doc checked him to make sure he doesn't die while in custody. You know…lawsuits." Steelman didn't even crack a smile. He was always right down to business, and Zane appreciated that quality in a person. "Storm and the Assistant U.S. Attorney are dealing with him. Statements and interrogation and whatnot. Redker and I have been pitching in, but it's mostly been their show."

"He going to plead out, or…?" Part of Zane hoped Amsdell would go to trial so his despicable acts could be illuminated, but part of him knew such a dog-and-pony show would be a waste of taxpayer money.

Steelman stretched and leaned back in his seat. "It's looking that way. He doesn't have much of a leg to stand on. CSU is still at his place, and they've already found multiple blood stains in the basement. We've got a list of his old addresses, and we'll see about going through those next. The folks who live there might not appreciate it, and I doubt they'll be happy when they find out they're living somewhere a person was murdered."

Zane rubbed the back of his neck, noting his muscles were still sore. "I sure as hell wouldn't be. We were right, then? It was all some religious, moral crusade?"

The other agent hesitated before he replied, piquing Zane's curiosity. "Yeah. He's, uh…delusional, I think is the technical term. He told Halcott and Storm he was on some kinda divine mission. God had come to him in a dream four and a half years ago and told him to start killing the sinners and…" Steelman scratched the side of his nose and sighed, "using them to keep the innocents pure of heart, or some such shit."

Clearly, there was more to the succinct explanation. "How exactly did he think he was doing that?"

"Remember he worked at a restaurant, right? And his parents owned a restaurant?"

Oh shit. He'd seen enough horror films to know where this was headed. "Yeah, I remember."

Steelman rested his hands on his knees, palms up. "He didn't cut 'em up and put 'em in the soup, but all that blood loss we noticed? All the slit throats? He took that blood and 'distributed' it to the masses to free them from sin."

Zane's stomach did an uncomfortable flip-flop. "He put the blood in the food at the restaurant? That's what you're saying?"

Steelman raised his hands in a gesture of surrender. "I'm telling you what I heard on the other side of the two-way mirror. The Bureau shut the place down after collecting all the evidence and then called in the CDC to contact and contain anyone who may have consumed the tainted food. Amsdell was trying to explain his whole process to Storm and Halcott, but he wouldn't talk to Redker or me. Guess he doesn't like us all that much."

Dragging a hand over his face, Zane slid back down to his pillow. "Wow. That's something else. How's Paige?"

The smile was back on Steelman's clean-shaven face. "The kid you pulled from Lake Michigan, yeah. She's good. I stopped by her room before I came here. The nurse said she was awake for a little while earlier, ate some food. Vitals stable, all that good stuff."

"Good. Poor kid's been through enough without having to deal with lasting damage from some psychopath trying to *baptize* her, or whatever the hell." Never mind that she was going to be stuck paying hospital bills for the rest of her life. Zane doubted Paige was insured.

While trying to keep her awake and conscious after pulling her from the lake, he'd learned she'd just had her eighteenth birthday. Her mother had died when she was younger, leaving her and an older brother in the care of their abusive father. When her brother had started to creep into her room at night to grope and eventually assault her, her father had refused to punish him because "men have needs, and she ought to learn how to satisfy them if she ever wanted to be a wife."

Zane's heart had broken for the girl as she'd regaled her story. He had no idea why she was comfortable giving him all the information, but he assumed it had something to do with her desire to be heard and seen by a person in a position of authority.

He made a mental note to circle back to Paige's brother and father. If they were sick enough to abuse their family like they'd abused Paige, then they likely had an entire closet packed with skeletons. Since Paige was a key witness against James Amsdell, Zane would have time to discuss the situation with her.

Amsdell might have been the first john who tried to kill her, but Zane doubted he'd be the last. She'd barely been on the street for a year, and she'd already had one near-death experience.

He hadn't seen any track marks on her body, nor had she exhibited any signs of being high aside from whatever Amsdell had given her. Drugs were a huge pull for women who worked the streets, but if she could pull herself out before an addiction started, she'd stand a much better chance.

If there was anything he could do to help her get out of

the lifestyle, he would make his best effort, starting with her hospital bills.

Steelman's voice cut through his contemplation, and Zane wondered how long he'd been staring into space. "Well, I just wanted to see how you were doing. Make sure you're all right. But you look like you haven't slept in a week, so I should probably hit the road, huh?"

As if to emphasize Steelman's point, Zane yawned. "Yeah, that might be a good idea. I think I've still got a lot of sleep to catch up on."

Grinning, Steelman rose and grabbed his coat. "You and me both, buddy. Oh, I don't know if she told you, but Storm should be stopping by later. She said something about bringing you food, and I told her about that sandwich shop by work. Herman's. It just opened a few weeks ago." He patted his belly. "That place is great. You should tell her to stop there."

Zane chuckled. "I'll mention it. Thanks for the recommendation."

The other agent touched a hand to his head in an informal salute, a mannerism that reminded him keenly of Amelia. "I'll see you soon. Get some rest and feel better, all right?"

"I'll do my best." Though Steelman had never seemed standoffish, his warm demeanor was more reminiscent of a friend than an occasional coworker. Zane hoped they'd have another chance to combine forces.

As the door swung shut behind Steelman, Zane pulled the blankets up to his chin and let his eyelids droop.

For the first time since before the holidays had started, he was confident his sleep would be free of nightmares.

It might have taken him more than a decade, but finally, he saw closure on the horizon.

30

Taking the final sip of her caramel latte, Cassandra set the empty cup to the side of her laptop. Across from her in their little corner booth, Amelia Storm stared intently at the screen of her tablet. The two of them had been working in close proximity for the last few days, ever since the showdown at Schulz Marina. In order to get a little fresh air and to get the hell away from the FBI office for a change, they'd come to a café not far from the field office.

The same café she and Joseph had gone to the day they'd met.

Cassandra mentally sighed. Joseph was still a problem she needed to fix, but James Amsdell and Yuri Antonov were higher priorities. Antonov's lawyers had tossed yet another bullshit motion at Cassandra and the U.S. Attorney's office, so his trial was delayed for the eight-hundredth time.

Meanwhile, he sat in his high-rise condo with an ankle monitor to keep him company. If he'd been remanded, the trial would have been over weeks ago. Funny how that worked.

Her hectic schedule hadn't allotted for much free time,

but in what little she could set aside, she'd done more research on Michelle Timmer. Short of physically speaking to the woman's friends and colleagues, Cassandra had dug up every tidbit of information she could find.

To her chagrin, none of it had changed a damn thing. Cassandra still had the same questions she'd had when she first asked Detective Campbell for the case files.

Rubbing the bridge of her nose, she tried to force her focus back to the laptop. She needed to shove Michelle Timmer to the back burner until at least one of the other two cases was off her plate.

But the nagging sense that something was very, very wrong persisted, like an itch she couldn't scratch.

Had Amelia Storm known Michelle? Michelle had worked in forensics, so maybe the two had crossed paths on a case. Cassandra still wasn't sure about Storm. She couldn't be sure everything she said to the woman wouldn't make it back to Joseph. Though Storm claimed she and Joseph weren't close friends, Cassandra knew how easy it was to lie.

She was a lawyer, after all.

Clearing her throat, Cassandra met the agent's curious glance. "Hey, this isn't really related to the case. Well, it's not related at all, but it's something that's been bugging me."

Storm straightened in her seat, genuine curiosity in her eyes.

"Remember when I asked you about Joseph last week?" She held the agent's gaze, studying her for the slightest sign of deception.

"About how he was doing? Yeah, I remember. What's...wrong?" Her hesitancy struck a pang of guilt in Cassandra's heart. Clearly, Amelia Storm didn't enjoy the topic of Joseph Larson.

Who would, honestly? He's a jackass.

If Storm disliked *talking* about Joseph this much, then what were the odds she'd be acting as a spy for him?

Slim to none, but Cassandra wasn't willing to take her chances. She'd broach this discussion as carefully as she'd handle nitroglycerine. "I was curious about his ex, Michelle, so I looked into her. Now, I know that sounds like crazy girlfriend shit, but hear me out. Michelle Timmer has been missing since July."

When Amelia Storm's expression remained unchanged, Cassandra realized the woman had known all along.

Amelia shoved a hand through her hair. "Yes, I knew about that, and when you brought up Michelle's name, I realized I hadn't followed up with the Chicago PD for an update. I'm ashamed so much time has passed, and I've been too busy to even think about that poor woman."

The spark of fury that had first ignited in Cassandra lessened. "Have you learned anything new since our talk?"

Amelia shook her head. "No. I sent an email to a detective I know, asking for an update, but I haven't heard back from him yet."

The spark went out completely. Cassandra held Amelia's gaze. "Any insights on what happened to Michelle?"

The two women stared at each other for a very long time before Amelia leaned forward and lowered her voice several octaves. "Look, Cassandra. We don't know one another very well, but I *do* know Joseph. I know what he's capable of. I can't go into any details, but he's got friends in low places, okay? He's dangerous, and you need to get the hell away from him."

Of course she couldn't go into any details. Did she even *have* the damn details? Or was she just fucking with Cassandra's head? Was she one of those women who felt she needed to knock all her female peers down a peg just to feel good about herself?

So many responses, most of which were saltier than the Dead Sea, whipped through Cassandra's head at the warning.

After a moment of silence, she settled on the least hostile. "Why did you wait until now to warn me about him?"

Storm raised her shoulders and held the stance before letting them fall. "I didn't know you. And after the whole thing with the Storey case, I didn't figure you'd want to hear anything from me about your dating life, you know?"

Through her anger, Cassandra could make out a portion of the agent's logic. It was true they hadn't been on the best terms before the Gifford investigation, and working closely together on the Amsdell case had indeed bridged a gap.

"Okay." Cassandra swallowed a sigh. "I'm not saying I don't believe you. Honestly, I'm pretty sure he's been cheating on me, so I've been planning to dump his ass anyway."

Storm sipped her coffee and offered an approving nod. "That's good."

"But what do you mean he's got friends in low places?" Cassandra blurted out the question without thinking. She didn't want to push Agent Storm's buttons. Not until she knew more about the woman and her background. "And how do you suppose I'm in danger? Does it have anything to do with Michelle? Did you *see* him do something when you worked together?"

Apparently, she couldn't keep the lawyer part of herself in check, no matter how hard she tried.

When she wanted answers, she couldn't get herself to shut the hell up.

One day, that mouth is gonna get you killed. Her foster father's voice echoed in her head, only adding fuel to the flames of her simmering anger.

Agent Storm rotated the paper sleeve around her cup and

slowly shook her head. "I'm sorry. I can't say. You know how it is in this line of work, right?"

Cassandra bit down on her tongue. Hard.

She had too much on her plate already. She didn't need to deal with this shit right now.

"Right." Cassandra picked up her laptop and none-too-gently shoved it into her messenger bag.

Agent Storm must have forgotten Cassandra was in this line of work to bring the truth to light, not bury it under the rug.

That was the whole reason she'd wanted to work at the U.S. Attorney's office. Simone Julliard, the U.S. Attorney for the Northern District of Illinois, was a no-nonsense woman who didn't put up with the status-quo political nonsense. Julliard sought equity and justice, and that was a mission Cassandra appreciated.

Roiling with a variety of emotions, she dumped the little pad of paper and two pens into the bag before she slid out of the booth. "Well, it's getting late. I suppose I'll do the rest of my work from home."

"Okay. Drive safe. I'll see you tomorrow." Storm's face was plagued by a combination of guilt and uncertainty, but Cassandra wasn't in the mood to address the oddity.

"Yeah, you too, Storm."

Cassandra had two cases to work and a potentially dangerous boyfriend to dump. The last thing she wanted was to add an FBI agent's cryptic mind games to the mix.

She'd figure it out by herself.

She always had.

31

An invisible lead cape was draped around Amelia's shoulders as she watched Cassandra Halcott make her way out of the café. She'd *wanted* to tell the lawyer the reason for her mistrust of Joseph Larson, but at the same time, she still didn't know Cassandra well enough to discern if she'd fall back into Joseph's charms or not. If she did, then everything Amelia told her would get back to him.

Considering the photo of Brian Kolthoff and Joseph being all buddy-buddy on one of Kolthoff's yachts, Amelia didn't want to wade into that shit show without a life jacket.

She slumped down in her seat and sighed. Cassandra seemed like a tough cookie, like she'd dealt with her fair share of manipulative assholes and come away a stronger person. Hopefully, she wasn't prone to believing Joseph's gaslighting.

Hopefully, she kicks him in the balls when she dumps him.

The mental imagery brought a slight smile to Amelia's face.

As busy as the past few workdays had been, her personal life had taken a turn for the better. Zane had been discharged from the hospital twenty-four hours after he was admitted, and the doctor had ordered him to rest for a few days. Had they been in the middle of a case, Amelia was sure he'd have staunchly disobeyed the suggestion. But since they'd just wrapped up a significant investigation, he'd decided to heed the medical advice.

Rather than holing up in his apartment for half a week, he'd asked Amelia if he could stay with her. The question had made her so giddy she'd almost become lightheaded. They still hadn't discussed the official status of their relationship, but Amelia was okay with postponing the labeling process and enjoying the moment.

Her phone pinged with a new text, and she realized she'd been spacing out. Swiping to unlock the screen, her spirits lifted when she noted the sender was Zane.

Hey, when do you think you'll be getting home? Wondering if I should order us some food or something.

She tapped out a response, formulating her evening plans as she did. *I was just about to leave, actually. I'm at the Royals Café, and there's a sandwich place nearby that Steelman keeps telling me about. Herman's. It's new.*

Amelia powered down her tablet, slid the device into a cloth sleeve, and stuffed it in her handbag. After downing the remainder of her coffee, donning her coat, and tossing the paper cup, she read Zane's response.

I've heard Steelman talking about that place too. Maybe he owns stock in it or something. That sounds good, though.

Waving goodbye to the barista, Amelia shouldered open the front door to let herself out into the chilly evening. This time of year, the sun set around five o'clock, leaving her in darkness both when she went to work and when she came home.

On the walk to her car, she sorted out Zane's sandwich order and pocketed her cell. Since she'd known she and

Cassandra would be at the café for a while, she'd parked toward the back. A slight courtesy to the people who wanted to be in and out quickly.

The ruddy orange glow of a streetlamp reflected a dull glow where it shone on Amelia's filthy car. Black *seemed* like a good color to hide dirt, but in truth, the salt from the city roads stood out like a damn beacon.

A hint of white stuck out from beneath one wiper, and for a beat, Amelia thought some snow had drifted onto the windshield. As she drew nearer, however, she recognized the slip of paper for what it was.

Frowning, she glanced over at the nearest vehicles to hers. Had someone come by to put flyers on all the cars in the café parking lot?

No, none of the other cars sported anything similar.

Was she parked like an asshole?

She made note of the yellow lines on either side of her black Beemer. Nope. She was smack-dab in the middle of the space.

Dammit, don't tell me someone door dinged me and just left a note saying they're sorry.

Closing the rest of the distance, she scanned the area one more time before she lifted the wiper and snatched up the note.

Unfolding the slip of paper, she fully expected a pitiful apology about a gouge in the side of her car she had yet to see. Her palms dampened, and her pulse pounded in her ears. She scanned the parking lot for anyone looking suspicious or watching her before reading the neatly printed note.

Agent Storm,

I need to talk to you. I've been putting this off for far too long, and it's time you know the truth about what happened to Trevor. I was his confidential informant in the Gianna Passarelli case. Don't waste your time looking for my name. You won't find it.

Please understand this is very risky for me. There are fates much worse than death that await me if I'm caught. I want to meet with you. Be at this address in two weeks.

"Two weeks?"

How in the hell had this person known to find her *here*? Why hadn't he or she left the note on her car while she was parked at home?

Looking again from one light pole to the next, the answer seemed obvious.

Security cameras, or lack thereof. The café had cameras at its entrance, as well as a couple inside, but it didn't have any this far back in the parking lot.

Whoever had left that note was determined not to be discovered. They'd handwritten the message, but without having any idea *who* they were, that didn't leave her much to go on.

With one hand on her service revolver, Amelia knelt to check beneath her car for a GPS tracker, or worse.

Satisfied there were no explosives or monitoring devices affixed to her vehicle and no stalker hiding in wait, she pulled open the driver's door and slumped down into the seat.

Her motivation to pick up sandwiches for her and Zane had abruptly vanished. All she wanted now was to get home and away from whoever the hell had left the note.

With everything that had happened—the photo Alex had given her of Brian and Joseph, Michelle Timmer missing, Cassandra Halcott clearly paranoid about more than just Joseph's infidelity, and now this damn note—the time to come clean about her past was at hand.

If she didn't tell Zane about her brother, about the D'Amatos and Alex and all their baggage, she'd be fighting an uphill battle by herself. Not only did she dislike keeping information from Zane, but now, she could use his help.

Someone with his background and the CIA connections he likely still had could even the playing field.

Taking in a deep breath, she counted to five and exhaled.

She couldn't run from her past forever. The time had come to face it head-on.

For better or worse, she'd find out what happened to her brother.

The End
To be continued...

Thank you for reading.
All of the Amelia Storm Series books can be found on Amazon.

ACKNOWLEDGMENTS

How does one properly thank everyone involved in taking a dream and making it a reality? Here goes.

In addition to our families, whose unending support provided the foundation for us to find the time and energy to put these thoughts on paper, we want to thank the editors who polished our words and made them shine.

Many thanks to our publisher for risking taking on two newbies and giving us the confidence to become bona fide authors.

More than anyone, we want to thank you, our readers, for clicking on a couple of nobodies and sharing your most important asset, your time, with this book. We hope with all our hearts we made it worthwhile.

Much love,
Mary & Amy

ABOUT THE AUTHOR

Mary Stone lives among the majestic Blue Ridge Mountains of East Tennessee with her two dogs, four cats, a couple of energetic boys, and a very patient husband.

As a young girl, she would go to bed every night, wondering what type of creature might be lurking underneath. It wasn't until she was older that she learned that the creatures she needed to most fear were human.

Today, she creates vivid stories with courageous, strong heroines and dastardly villains. She invites you to enter her world of serial killers, FBI agents but never damsels in distress. Her female characters can handle themselves, going toe-to-toe with any male character, protagonist or antagonist.

Discover more about Mary Stone on her website.
www.authormarystone.com

Amy Wilson

Having spent her adult life in the heart of Atlanta, her upbringing near the Great Lakes always seems to slip into her writing. After several years as a vet tech, she has dreams of going back to school to be a veterinarian but it seems another dream of hers has come true first. Writing a novel.

Animals and books have always been her favorite things, in addition to her husband, who wanted her to have it all. He's the reason she has time to write. Their two teenage boys fill the rest of her time and help her take care of the mini zoo that now fills their home with laughter...and yes, the occasional poop.

Connect with Mary Online

- facebook.com/authormarystone
- goodreads.com/AuthorMaryStone
- bookbub.com/profile/3378576590
- pinterest.com/MaryStoneAuthor

Made in United States
North Haven, CT
24 July 2022